C

BROADWAY

A Marriage Drama

Novel by

William A. Glass

HP

Hawkeye Publishers

Hawkeye Publishers

For more information, please address Hawkeye Publishers
HawkeyePublishers.com

Library of Congress Control Number: 2021921287

Paperback: 978-1946005595
Hardcover: 978-1946005601
Ebook: 978-1946005625

This book is dedicated to my wife,
Bettina Sylvia Linden.

TABLE OF CONTENTS

Chapter One: A Dollar at a Time 1

Chapter Two: Ménage 31

Chapter Three: Out of Stock 51

Chapter Four: Whatever It Takes 81

Chapter Five: Head Over Heels 105

Chapter Six: Residual Value 113

Chapter Seven: Closest to the Pin 133

Chapter Eight: Capital Infusion 145

Chapter Nine: Detox 157

Chapter Ten: Over Hill, Over Dale 189

Chapter Eleven: Tilt 223

Chapter Twelve: The World is Not New 235

Chapter Thirteen: His and Hers 245

Chapter Fourteen: Plausible Motivation 255

Chapter Fifteen: Exit Ramp 259

CHAPTER ONE
A Dollar at a Time

"It's Friday, time to bust loose," Bill Jackson says into the payphone. He gives the address of the bar where he wants to meet, and then hits a button on the touch-tone keypad. Presto! His message is deposited into the voicemail boxes of all the Procter & Gamble salespeople in the metro New York district.

Dave Knight, a P&G key account manager, picks up Bill's message after completing a sales call on one of his New Jersey supermarkets. He's finished with his route for the day, so after filling out a report, Dave drives to Patterson and looks for the address Bill left. It turns out to be a brick storefront in a run-down neighborhood. A fading sign on the façade indicates that the building was once a five and dime. Now blackout curtains hang in the windows. The only sign of life is the cluster of cars out front.

As Dave waits for the other P&G reps, he listens to a cassette and tries not to be depressed by the view through his windshield. It's late fall, and only a few withered leaves dangle from the branches of nearby trees. They flicker uncertainly in the faint breeze, as if toying with the idea of finally giving up and letting go.

A Chevy pulls into the trash-strewn parking lot, followed by another. They're P&G fleet cars, so now Dave yanks off his tie, tucks it into a jacket pocket, and follows the other salesmen into the establishment.

After paying five bucks to a scar-faced, leather-jacketed bouncer sitting just inside the door, Dave sees that the interior of the place is as bad as he expected. A plywood bar runs along the back of the room, and every stool is taken by guys who look like they just got off from factory jobs. The walls and exposed heating and air-conditioning ducts are carelessly painted a drab black. Raucous music blares from two stadium speakers that hang from the rafters.

Since seating is limited at the bar, groups of men stand behind it holding highballs or beer bottles. Most are smoking, and embers glow in the darkened room. A spotlight cuts through the haze, shining on the reason all these gentlemen are here. She's a dark-haired beauty dancing on top of the bar, completely nude other than a garter on her thigh crammed with cash. The girl holds a scarf and uses it to briefly cover various parts of her body to temporarily frustrate the crowd.

Dave watches the dancer take the ends of the scarf in either hand, step over it, then pull the cloth back and forth between her legs. At this, howling erupts from the men. Those close enough reach up to feverishly tuck currency into the girl's garter. She pauses her gyrations to accommodate them while appearing quite bored. Then a fan at the end of the bar holds up a five-dollar bill. The dancer saunters over, turns her back, and squats with her ass practically in his face. The guy slowly inserts the money into her garter. Once he's done, the entertainer rises, twirls the scarf around her head, then tosses it to him. The man immediately attempts to smother himself with it.

"What are you drinking?" a feminine voice asks. Dave turns to see a naked girl holding a tray. She has a cute, doll-like face topped with a mop of curly brown hair. "I'll have whatever's on draft," Dave tells her.

"Make that two," Bill Jackson says, coming over to join them. He's a tall, sturdily built man with blond hair. Like Dave, he's an army veteran.

"My name's Doris," the hostess smiles. "You can look at my tits if you want."

Dave glances at the girl's chest. "I've seen worse," he deadpans. "Ouch! You're standing on my foot."

"That's not all I'll be standing on if you can't be nice," Doris threatens.

"OK, sorry," Dave laughs. He holds both hands up in mock surrender as Doris turns and heads for the bar.

"She's pretty," Bill says.

"Yeah, not bad," Dave replies. "How did you find this joint?"

"The Lever Brothers guy told me about it."

"Quite horrible, don't you think?"

"Oh, about par for the course," Bill says, with a glance at the surroundings.

Doris returns with their beers, and Bill gives her a five. "Keep it," he says when she starts to make change. Doris smiles her thanks, then disappears back into the crowd.

Now Bill and Dave swill brew and check out the scene. A dozen naked hostesses are working the room. When the first dancer goes on break, one of the other girls takes her place. This is a distinct letdown for the crowd, as the new performer is an awkward dancer whose efforts to be sexy are merely crude. She appears desperate to please, unlike the first dancer, who had evinced only contempt for her fans.

Turning away from the entertainment, Bill lights a cigarette. "How do they get away with this?" he wonders.

"Guess it's considered 'artistic expression,'" Dave replies.

"You ask me, it's a Mafia deal."

"Ya think?"

Bill blows a smoke ring then watches it float away. "So, how are you looking for quota?" he asks.

"So far, so good," Dave shrugs.

"You and Stephanie both made it again last quarter," Bill says enviously.

"Yeah, but it's the end-of-year number they look at."

"It would take a miracle for me to pull it out at this point."

Dave pokes his friend on the arm. "Oh, come on," he says.

"You deserve it with all the hours you put in," Bill declares. "But Stephanie gets by on sex appeal."

"Hey, sales is sales; you use whatever works."

Doris reappears out of the gloom. "You guys ready for another?"

"On me," Dave says, and lays some cash on her tray.

"Back in a flash."

Bill takes a final drag then drops his cigarette underfoot. "Women don't belong in business," he exhales. "They're taking jobs away from guys with families."

"That way of thinking went out with the Hula-Hoop," Dave laughs.

"But it's not right," Bill persists. "Store managers don't cooperate with me, but they let Stephanie do what she wants."

"Oh, come on," Dave protests. "What're you worried about? If women want to get into this racket, fine. As for sex, can you imagine Stephanie doing it with a store manager just to get more shelf space for Tide? If they want to fantasize and maybe give her a little extra cooperation, then what's the harm? Maybe some of my store managers fantasize about beating me at golf. That doesn't mean I'm gonna let them."

"What happened to our beers?" Bill asks, looking around for the waitress.

"Isn't that Doris at the service bar?" Dave points to where several girls are waiting.

In a few minutes, Doris comes over with the beverages. "Sorry it took so long," she says. "I ran into one of my regulars and he insisted that I give him a private dance in the VIP lounge."

"How much does it cost for a private dance?" Bill asks.

"Ten dollars for one song, fifteen for two."

"That's too much!"

"Let me know if you change your mind." Doris moves off to look for other customers.

"It's crazy," Dave says. "Imagine paying ten bucks to have some strange broad dance in your lap."

"You're right," Bill agrees. "I just came here for a few laughs like you. Hey, I've got to drain the lizard, any idea where the head is?"

"Not a clue."

"I'll be back, don't go anywhere."

"No worries."

Standing by himself, Dave taps a foot to the music and gazes around the room. He sees a roped-off area in one corner behind a sign labeled "VIP LOUNGE." Beyond the rope, men sit in armchairs while naked hostesses gyrate in their laps.

A willowy brunette sidles up and takes Dave's arm. "Would you like to spend some time in the VIP lounge with me?" she purrs.

"Thanks, but I'll pass."

"You'd be amazed at how much fun we could have."

"I believe you," Dave replies, "but ever since the heart attack, I've been trying to avoid excitement." The girl hastily moves away.

Bill hasn't returned, so Dave looks for him at the bar. Several P&G guys are there reaching out with dollar bills, trying to get their hands into the current dancer's garter. Dave smiles and shakes his head at their antics. Then he glances into the roped-off area again and sees Bill in one of the chairs, with Doris swarming over him in rhythm with the music. As the last chords of the Stones' "Sympathy for the Devil" fade, she backs away.

Moments later, Bill is back. "I thought you just came here for a few laughs," Dave says.

"That Doris is the worst prick teaser ever."

"How much did you give her?"

"Fifteen bucks."

"Ouch."

"Yeah, I know."

"Anyway, I have to go."

"So soon?"

"Yeah."

"OK, see you next week."

"You got it."

On his way home, Dave listens to a Van Morrison tape and gets back some of the optimism that was drained out of him at the strip joint. Soon he's crossing the George Washington Bridge and is amazed as always at the bright lights of the big city. He heads into Manhattan, then pulls into his parking garage.

After securing the car, Dave walks a short distance to the brownstone apartment building where he and his wife, Cindy, live. He lets himself into the turn-of-the-century building, then goes up four flights of stairs to reach the one-bedroom co-op they bought with help from her parents. Inside, he finds Cindy asleep on the sofa.

Dave makes himself dinner and eats in the kitchen. After cleaning up, he gets ready for bed, then goes into the living room, gently wakes Cindy, and leads her into the bedroom. She's quickly back asleep, so Dave picks up his current book and reads awhile before turning out the light.

In the morning, Cindy's at the kitchen table drinking coffee when Dave comes in. "Where were you last night?" she asks.

"At a titty bar in Patterson," Dave replies, "with some of the guys." He pops an English muffin into the toaster, then pours a glass of orange juice.

"Nice way for a bunch of married guys to spend an evening," Cindy observes.

"Yeah, it was rank, but you told me to be more sociable, so I'm trying."

"By sociable, I didn't mean strip clubs."

"That's what they do when there's no golf." Dave spreads margarine on the muffin. It quickly melts, then disappears into the nooks and crannies.

"How pathetic," Cindy sighs. "Now, let's go for a walk."

"Sounds good." Dave finishes breakfast while lacing on his sneakers.

Once they're outside, Cindy and Dave head up 59th Street toward Central Park. They make an attractive couple. Cindy's in her late twenties, but with her tomboy haircut and freckles, she retains the look of a college girl. Her husband is taller than average, with bright, green eyes, and a ruddy complexion. His lanky frame is topped with an unruly mop of strawberry-blonde hair.

After an energetic hike through the park, Cindy and Dave start for home. On the way, they stop at their favorite pizza place. "How are the auditions going?" Dave asks, once they've placed their order. Cindy works as the executive assistant for Sydney Glass, a Broadway producer.

"The leads were cast early on," Cindy replies. "Now we're doing all the bit parts, but it's dragging. Sydney's a hard man to satisfy."

"Yeah, you've been working some long hours."

"You too, if you call playing golf and going to strip clubs work."

"Someone's got to do it."

"Yeah, and it might as well be you, right?"

"We've got a regional sales meeting next week," Dave says. He leans back as the waiter reaches in with a pitcher of beer. "I'll be gone all of Monday but will be back Tuesday night."

"You could stay out the entire week for all I care." Cindy fills their mugs.

"That's cold!"

"Sorry, but you're getting worse."

"How?"

"You're more hyper, forgetful, and messy. The other day, I found a leaky carton of ice cream in the pantry."

"Ugh."

"It took me half an hour to clean up the mess. Of course, the ice cream was ruined."

"I'm sorry."

"You forget what you're doing right in the middle of doing it," Cindy complains. "It used to be funny but not anymore."

"I'll try to do better," Dave promises.

"Yeah, right," Cindy says. She moves her mug and the pitcher aside so the waiter can put their pizza down. Gingerly, she takes hold of a slice and drags it onto her plate. It's sizzling hot.

Cindy gets up at her regular time on Monday and leaves for work, but Dave sleeps in. He has no sales calls planned because of the regional sales meeting. It's in Philadelphia, so he has a short drive compared with those coming from some other districts.

Even after dawdling over breakfast and following speed limits on the way down, Dave gets to the meeting hotel early. But that's no problem for the always helpful Marriott staff. After a short wait, they find a freshly made-up room and give him the key.

Once inside the room, Dave turns on the TV for company, then unpacks. An hour later, the phone rings, and it's Stephanie Whitney, another key account manager. "Hey, Steph," Dave answers, then listens a moment. "OK, lunch sounds good."

At noon, Dave goes down to the lobby and finds Stephanie by the entrance to the restaurant. She's dressed in a conservative pantsuit, but with a mass of wavy blonde hair framing her cover girl face, she still looks glamorous. Stephanie's long legs slash the air as they follow the hostess to a table. "I'm going to have the soup with a side salad," she says when the waiter arrives, "oh, and an iced tea."

After Dave orders, he and Stephanie settle back to wait for their food. Both are dreading a long afternoon of meetings, and neither feels like talking. As Dave idly glances around, he just misses making eye contact with fellow P&G salespeople. That's because they quickly jerk their heads away, not wanting to get caught staring.

Promptly at one, the P&G key account managers file into a ballroom along with their district managers. After everyone is seated at tables, Nick Carroll, the regional sales manager, kicks off the meeting. "We have a lot to cover over the next two days," he tells the attendees. "This afternoon, we'll have Xerox training, followed by dinner. Tomorrow, we have a general session in the morning and district meetings all afternoon."

Now that he's set the stage, Nick allows Alex Wright, the regional sales training manager, to take over. "We're going to have a review of PSS III," Alex announces, standing next to an overhead projector at the front of the room. "Then we'll break into groups and do role-playing."

The trainer places his first transparency onto the projector and switches the machine on. The title of his presentation flashes on the screen, "XEROX Professional Selling Skills Review." Without comment, Alex removes the transparency, then puts the next one up. He has a stack of them, so the P&G reps settle back into their chairs.

"Are you going for a swim?" Bill asks Dave and Stephanie as they leave the meeting room at the end of the day.

"Sure, I'll see you down there," Dave answers.

"I have some phone calls to make, but will be down later," Stephanie promises.

Presently, the hotel's indoor pool is crowded with P&G types frolicking in the water. Some of the guys attempt to duck one another, while others engage in splash fights. Then a joust is organized. Dave sits on Bill's shoulders as they go into combat with a team from Philadelphia. The two ex-soldiers battle to pull the enemy down, but Bill and Dave get dunked instead.

Now a new pair of contestants begin to joust. This time it's New England vs Baltimore-Washington. The salesmen cheer on their favorites, but gradually it grows quiet. Stephanie has arrived. She's standing by the pool and looks stunning in a black one-piece bathing suit. A swim cap covers her hair.

Dave dog-paddles over. "Hey, you brought your suit," he says.

"Yeah, but it looks kind of rough in there," Stephanie frowns.

"The guys are just blowing off steam after all that Xerox crap. Come on in."

Stephanie looks around uncertainly, then makes up her mind. She walks to the uncrowded deep end, climbs onto the diving board, and executes a graceful jackknife. That breaks the ice, and now the men want to try it. The hooting and hollering begin again as they rush to the diving board and jostle each other, trying to cut in line.

The first few salesmen manage respectable dives, but soon they are all competing to see who can perform the most grotesque contortions while in the air. Stephanie joins in the cheering, booing, and banter during the exhibition, but doesn't get back on the board.

For his last turn, Dave does his best can opener, hoping to raise a tall column of water. But he's too scrawny, and his effort is a flop. He swims over to Stephanie. "Hey, we have to be in the lobby at seven for dinner."

"Yep, it's about time to get ready."

The guys are taking one last leap off the diving board, then grabbing towels. As activity in the pool winds down, Stephanie, Dave, and Bill leave. They ride the elevator up then go to their rooms.

After showering, Dave puts on some slacks and a button-down shirt. He forgot to bring a shoehorn and is trying to cram his foot into a loafer when Stephanie calls. "Yeah, I'm almost ready," Dave tells her. "A drink would be good."

Once he's shod, Dave grabs his jacket, goes down the hall, and raps on Stephanie's door. She pulls it open wearing a short robe. "Get what you want," she says, pointing to the minibar, "and pour me a Chablis."

Stephanie steps into the bathroom, leaving the door open, and cranks up her blow-dryer. "The ends got wet even with the cap," she yells.

"I just towel dry mine, don't even comb it." Dave rummages in the minibar, then takes Stephanie her wine.

"Looks like it," she laughs.

Sitting on the sofa, Dave empties a Jack Daniel's miniature into a glass. It doesn't look like much, so he gets another. Now he has a respectable drink.

Presently, the din in the bathroom ceases and Stephanie comes out. She puts her wine glass on a nightstand then fluffs her hair with both hands. "Don't you want ice and something to mix with that?" she asks.

"Nah, this is fine." Dave savors some straight corn whiskey.

The phone rings and Stephanie snatches up the receiver. "Where have you been?" she asks, taking a seat on the bed. As she listens, Stephanie leans back on the headboard, stretching out her tan legs. "I tried to call you shortly after five and again a few minutes ago, but no one answered." Stephanie sips her wine, frowning with concentration. "Oh, the cleaners," she says, "was my persimmon suit ready?"

While Stephanie talks, Dave tries to read Walter Cronkite's lips on the silent TV. Then Henry Kissinger appears on screen with Leonid Brezhnev. They smile for the cameras and distrustfully shake hands.

When the broadcast ends, Dave gets up to turn off the tube. Stephanie waves her empty glass, so he finds her another Chablis and more whiskey for himself. "Dave's here," Stephanie says into the phone. "We're getting lubricated before dinner."

"Hey, Karen," Dave pipes up.

"She wants to know when you're going to come over again," Stephanie says.

"Soon," Dave promises. But he's in no hurry to return to Stephanie and Karen's apartment. Last time, they allowed their cat onto the table all during dinner.

Stephanie looks at her watch. "Honey, I have to go, I love you." After a pause, she says, "No, I love you more." She bites her lip impatiently for a moment then exclaims, "That's not true, really. I love you much more. Now got to go. Bye." Stephanie puts the phone down and jumps up. "Don't look," she says, and takes off the robe.

A few minutes later, as Stephanie and Dave leave her room, Bill comes down the hall. "Ready to go down?" Dave asks.

"Yeah, it's almost time," Bill says, with a curious glance at his two colleagues.

In the lobby, the P&G crowd divides into groups, then goes outside and piles into cars for the ride to the restaurant Nick has chosen. It's an upscale steakhouse in a posh Philadelphia suburb. When they get there, Stephanie, Dave, and Bill go in together and find seats at the end of a long table with Paul Braxton, the NY Metro District Manager. Then the waiter comes around to get the drink orders. "Jack Daniel's on the rocks with a splash," Bill tells him.

"I'll have the same, only hold the rocks, hold the splash, and make it a double," Dave says, remembering a Jack Nicholson flick he saw a few years back.

Meanwhile, Stephanie has been studying the wine list. "Do you have the Raveneau by the glass?" she asks.

"Just a moment," the waiter answers. "I'll get the wine steward."

Nick, who's sitting nearby, has been watching Stephanie study the wine list. He calls over to her, "Hey, Stephanie, what have you found?"

"A '69 Raveneau," she tells him.

Nick taps a knife on his water glass to get attention, and the hubbub dies down somewhat. "Who wants red and who wants white wine with dinner?" he hollers. "First red, raise your hands. OK, now white."

The waiter reappears with the wine steward in tow. "What can you tell me about the Raveneau?" Nick asks.

"Excellent choice," the wine steward replies. "It's a full-bodied Chablis, aged in oak. We stock a more elegant vintage, but this is a racy little wine that your group would enjoy."

"OK, bring us several bottles of the Raveneau," Nick tells the steward, then pauses to look at the wine list again. "We also need a red; I see you stock a Louis Jadot Pinot Noir."

"Again, a fine choice for a gathering like this. It's a spirited, light-hearted red that wears well."

"Then keep us supplied with that as well."

Soon the wine drinkers have glass in hand, while others sip spirits. Then the head waiter brings menus. Dave's disgusted to see that this is the type of joint that charges extra for everything. He only orders a small filet mignon with a side of asparagus.

As the P&G crowd waits for the food, they work on their beverages and talk. The decibel level goes up as the alcohol goes down. "I caught the Calgon rep pocketing my reorder tags in a store last week," a salesman says. "We had it out in the parking lot."

"I had the same shit with a Lever guy a while back," another rep exclaims. "When I went into the store, he had just finished moving my Tide from eye level to the bottom shelf. Funny thing, when he came out to get into his car, all four tires were flat."

"Do you think A&P will acquire Pathmark?" Paul asks Dave.

"They need to do something," Dave replies. "Pathmark could teach A&P a lot. They know how to operate a modern supermarket. A&P is stuck in a time warp."

"It's wonderful to find someone who knows wine," Nick says, beaming at Stephanie.

"Oh, I'm sure you could teach me a thing or two about wine," she smiles.

"I'd be happy to."

Conversation tapers off as servers begin bringing dishes to the table. When his steak arrives, Dave tosses back the last of his whiskey, then reaches for a nearby bottle of Pinot Noir. He's emptying it into a wine glass when the waiter approaches holding a dish of sautéed mushrooms. "For your steak?" he asks, slowly stirring the enticements. Dave shakes his head. *What a racket*, he thinks, after the waiter moves on. Then he notices that Bill's steak is now smothered with mushrooms. *That'll add three bucks to the bill*, he muses, and gulps some wine. Compared to the whiskey, it's like drinking water.

Later, after most of the group has finished eating, the waiter makes a pitch for dessert. Some of the sales reps go for it, while others order after-dinner drinks. Once everyone has had time to consume their treat, the head waiter brings the check. Nick glances at it, then taps on his glass for attention. "Here's the deal," he announces. "We'll go around the table and give everyone a chance to guess the amount of the tab. Whoever comes closest gets to say which district will pick it up."

Dave is good at this game. He's terrible at math, but this exercise only requires an estimate. As he sips the last of his after-dinner drink, Dave considers the amount he and Cindy would pay for a nice dinner complete with wine and liquor at a high-class restaurant. Then he does some calculations, and in the end, it turns out his guess is the closest. "So, who do you want to get the check?" Nick asks him.

"You can give it to Walt," Dave announces. Walt Frazier is the District Manager for Baltimore-Washington.

Nick puts the check back into the folder and passes it to Walt. "You should have hired Knight when you had the chance," he laughs.

Walt scowls as he reaches for the company credit card he'll use to pay the tab. This night will come out of his district's entertainment budget.

As the waiter goes to run the card, the P&G crowd straggles out to the parking lot. They get back into the cars, and after everyone is accounted for, leave to go back to the Marriott. "Hey, the bar is still open," Bill exclaims when they get there.

"I'm done," Stephanie says, and quickly heads for the elevators. But Nick goes into the lobby bar accompanied by Paul and Walt. Several key account managers follow them.

"What do you think?" Bill asks.

"I hate hotel bars," Dave replies.

"Yeah, and I've had enough of those guys in any case," Bill says. "Let's go raid my minibar."

"You're on."

The minibar in Bill's room has the same assortment of candy, snacks, beer, wine, and liquor as Stephanie's. Dave gets out the Jack Daniel's and Bill tears the paper wrapping off a couple of glasses.

"I need ice with mine," Bill says. He grabs the bucket and moves toward the door.

"I'll go with you," Dave offers.

The ice machine is on a stairwell landing along with several vending machines. While Dave fills the bucket, Bill puts some coins into the soda machine. But when he pushes the button to get his mixer, nothing happens.

Bill repeatedly pokes the button, then kicks the drink machine several times. Energetically, he works the coin return and when that's unavailing, he angrily picks up a trash can and hurls it over the railing. A tremendous clanging erupts as the can bounds down the stairs to the next landing, ricochets off the wall, and keeps going. The sound echoes up and down the stairwell.

Dave cracks up at this, and soon Bill is laughing, too. "Let's get back to the room before someone comes up here to investigate," he says.

"Has it made it to the bottom yet?" Dave asks. "I think I hear it still going down." This jest provokes more laughter as they stroll up the hall to Bill's room. Once there, they drink the Jack Daniel's, then get into some Kentucky bourbon.

"So, everyone's wondering," Bill says, "what does Stephanie see in you?"

"Nothing," Dave answers.

"Oh, come on, you're obviously jumping her bones."

"Not true."

"Hey, none of my business," Bill says, holding both hands up palm outward.

With the bourbon all gone, Bill and Dave move on to vodka. Later, they sample different kinds of rum, then give gin a try. Meanwhile, Bill lines the empty miniatures up in military formation. He wants to recreate the Battle of Gettysburg.

"You can use the Old Grand-Dad to represent Lee," Dave suggests.

"Good idea."

After Pickett once again fails to carry the Union works, the battle ends. "Hey, we're almost out of booze," Bill says.

"Too bad," Dave says, quoting Lee. "Oh, too bad."

"What's Midori?"

"It's a liqueur, try it," Dave replies. "While you're at it, toss me that Kahlua."

"So, what were you doing in her room then?" Bill slurs.

"Having a drink."

"Sure!"

"Things aren't always what they seem."

"Hey, we have a meeting in a few hours."

"Might as well stay up the rest of the night then."

"OK, but we need something to talk about," Bill says. He leans back on the sofa, holding his green drink. "You could tell me your secret for making quota every time."

"Fear," Dave says.

"Your secret is fear?"

"Fear of failing, of losing my job."

"How can you be worried? Nick loves you."

"Sales is the only thing I've ever been good at. If I didn't have this, I don't know what I'd do."

"That's crazy."

"Maybe," Dave allows. "Hey, my glass is empty."

Bill goes to look in the minibar. "All that's left is Scotch," he reports.

"I hate Scotch."

"Me too," Bill says. "You want the Teachers or Ballantine?"

"Either, don't care, it's all bad. Tastes like iodine."

"We're out of ice," Bill complains. "Can't drink this shit without ice."

"I'll get it, I've got shoes on," Dave offers. He staggers to his feet, grabs the ice bucket, and goes out.

In the hall, Dave finds steering a straight course difficult. It's easier if he keeps one hand on the wall. In this manner, it takes a while to get to the exit and out onto the landing. Once there, Dave manages to fill the ice bucket. Then he remembers Bill's stunt with the trash can. He goes to the railing and looks down.

The trash can is lying on its side four stories below. "Funny, that's funny," Dave mumbles. He looks around for something he too can throw. There's nothing left on the landing except vending machines. He tries to push the soda machine. It pushes right back.

The cigarette machine looks easier to move. Dave gets behind it and shoves. The machine goes a little way toward the stairs, emitting a screech as the footrests scrape the concrete floor. "Ah-hah," Dave exults, and pushes again, resulting in more movement and another grating noise.

Soon Dave has a little rhythm going. He shoves the cigarette machine, rests a moment, gets into position, and shoves again. Suddenly, the exit door opens, and a skinny, dark-haired man dressed in polka-dot pajamas is there. Dave glances at the intruder but doesn't want to lose his timing. He again gets into his stance, puts both hands on the machine, and drives it forward, *screeeeeeeech*.

"What are you doing?" the man asks, his voice echoing in the stairwell.

"Throwing this cigarette machine down the stairs," Dave pants.

"I'm trying to sleep. My room is at the end of the hall."

More people appear in the doorway. Meanwhile, Dave has caught his breath and is ready, *screeeeeeeech*.

An irate man in a bathrobe pushes through the crowd and yells at Dave, "Are you crazy? It's almost four. Stop that racket!"

"Go fuck yourself," Dave suggests.

"What did you say?"

"I said fuck you and the horse you rode in on," Dave snaps. He gives the machine a massive shove and this time it moves a good 6 inches. His anger at the interruptions is providing extra impetus.

"I'm going to call the front desk," someone says.

"Call who you want," Dave exclaims, "just get the fuck out of here." He turns and walks toward the spectators. As they frantically back away, Dave takes hold of the door and closes it on them. Then he goes back to where the cigarette machine is now only a couple of inches from the edge. He gets into his stance and shoves the machine over the side. It cartwheels down to the landing below. Glass shatters and packages of smokes fly when it smashes into the wall.

Surveying the scene of destruction, Dave is fully satisfied. He picks up the ice bucket and carries it back to Bill's room. His buddy is out cold on the bed with four empty Scotch miniatures nearby. Dave decides to get some rest as well. He goes to his room and lies down.

It seems but a short while before Dave's brain is penetrated by the insistent buzzing of the radio alarm. He decides to ignore it, but then the phone begins ringing. Dave reaches over, picks up the handset, and drops it back onto the cradle. The ringing stops, but as he's trying to go back to sleep, Dave feels his stomach lurch. He needs to vomit.

Gradually, Dave rises into a sitting position. "Never again," he moans.

After sitting with his eyes closed awhile, Dave gets an idea. If he can make it into the bathroom, he will have the option of throwing up either into the sink or the toilet. He opens his eyes and sees a dresser with a TV. Rotating his head slowly, Dave focuses on a mirrored closet door. Beside that is the bathroom entrance. It's approximately 10 feet from where he's sitting. Dave slowly turns his head back, plotting his course. Then he closes his eyes and pushes down on the bed while slowly standing. So far, so good.

Once in the bathroom, Dave bends over the sink and lets out a burp, ready now to heave up the contents of his stomach. He gags, but aside from bile, nothing more comes. So, he opens the cold-water tap, cups both hands under the faucet, and splashes his face.

Somehow, Dave manages to spruce up, get dressed, and make it downstairs. The Marriott staff has arrayed a variety of continental breakfast items on tables outside the meeting room. Dave looks at the spread and quickly turns away. He sees Stephanie across the hallway with a plate of food in one hand and a cup of tea in the other. She crooks her little finger at him in greeting. Dave tries but cannot manage a smile.

As the district managers begin herding their salespeople into the meeting room, Bill comes down the hall. "You just made it," Dave says.

"Someone please shoot me and get it over with," Bill pleads.

"That bad?"

"Fucking Scotch."

"Yeah."

There's a binder at every place as the key account managers take their seats. On the cover is a P&G logo and the title, "Employee Benefits Guide."

Nick goes to the front of the room, and slowly it grows quiet. He places a transparency on the overhead projector and the agenda for the morning appears on screen. "As you can see, human resources is up first," Nick says, tapping the screen with a pointer. "Next comes marketing, and then we'll hear from Lyndon before lunch." Lyndon Littleton is the CEO of Procter & Gamble.

Nick sits down and Ryan Davis, Director of Benefits for P&G's human resources department, takes his place. "We have some exciting news about your employee benefits," Ryan begins, and puts his first transparency up.

As the HR exec talks, Dave feigns interest. Periodically, he glances at the closed meeting room door. At any moment, he expects a phalanx of police to burst in and arrest him for vandalizing the cigarette machine.

Time drags as Ryan drones on. Without paying much attention, Dave gathers that in the coming year, employees will be given more options to choose from for their benefits, but that none of the packages will be as generous as before. This has been the case every year since he joined the company.

Finally, Ryan comes to his last transparency and shuts the projector off. "We have time now for questions," he announces.

Dave groans as several questioners raise their hands. He needs ice water and Tylenol. However, people are unhappy with what they've seen. For half an hour, Ryan politely deflects concerns. "It's called a cafeteria plan," he keeps saying. "It's the latest thing." Finally, the questions are exhausted, and it's time for a break.

Outside the meeting room, Dave pours a glass of ice water, uses it to wash down some analgesics, then pours another glassful before moving away from the table. After a visit to the bathroom, he goes back into the meeting room and waits. He's in no mood to hobnob with the other reps around the break tables.

For the next session, Mickey Winton, Senior Brand Manager for P&G's Household Products Division, takes center stage. "If you wonder why we keep coming back to coupons, just look at these movement figures," Mickey says, placing a chart on the projector. This data is from the newspaper insert we had in all major dailies for Labor Day. As you can see, we increased retail takeaway on Tide eightfold with the coupon, but in stores that ran reduced price ads the week of the insert, we had twelve times average weekly sales, and stores that had a reduced price plus an end-aisle display saw sixteen times normal sales." The bars on Mickey's graph look like stairs. With a start, Dave again wonders when the cops are going to show up to bust him for last night.

"The good news is that we have a great sweepstakes offer featured in the insert that's coming in November," Mickey continues, "along with a fifty-cent coupon that most of the stores will double." He passes out color copies of the newspaper insert for Thanksgiving week. "The grand prize is a Hawaii vacation for two, airfare included."

Dave tries to appear interested in the marketing presentation, but his mind is elsewhere. He's starting to believe that he might escape the humiliation of being handcuffed and dragged out of the Marriott after all. *The people who saw me with the cigarette machine would have no way of knowing who I am*, he thinks.

At the next break, Dave drinks more ice water and manages to get a breakfast roll down. Then he goes back to his seat for the last presentation of the morning.

Once all the salespeople are back at their tables, Nick comes forward. "It's a great pleasure for me to turn the meeting over to Lyndon Littleton," he says.

As polite applause ripples through the room, a sharply dressed, gray-haired gentleman comes front and center. "This is a great week for me," Lyndon begins. "I'm going from one region meeting to the next and it's wonderful to get out of the office and be with you. Our sales force is the key to the company's success, and everyone in Cincinnati knows that. Now, before coming out, I thought about what I might say that would interest you and concluded that what you would most like to hear about is the stock, our acquisition strategy, and the new product pipeline. Unfortunately, our lawyers told me not to say anything about any of these topics, so now I will go sit down."

Lyndon starts to walk away as the room erupts in laughter. Then he comes back and puts a transparency on the projector. "Actually, I'm allowed to say quite a lot about each of these subjects," he explains. "As long as I stay within certain parameters. For example, I can talk about where the stock price has been, give my opinion on what factors have been responsible for recent fluctuations, and express my opinion on what conditions would be most conducive for future growth in our valuation."

As Lyndon continues, Dave thinks about what he will do during the lunch break. He has several phone calls to make, then must pack and check out. Afterward, he can try to stomach some food before the afternoon session begins.

Dave tunes back into the CEO's presentation as his last transparency appears on the screen. Then Lyndon switches off the projector and offers to answer questions. Many hands go up, but the first inquiry brings an end to the Q&A. It's posed by Tim Witherspoon, a key account manager from the Baltimore-Washington District. "When I was recruited to join P&G just out of Wharton, they told me that my MBA would eventually be useful to the marketing department," Tim tells Lyndon. "But I've been out in the stores for over two years now, and I'm wondering when I might expect to be brought into marketing?"

Lyndon is momentarily taken aback, then frostily answers, "I'm sure your district manager would be happy to discuss that with you." He looks around the room expectantly, and Walt Frazier hastily rises from his chair then rushes over to where Tim is seated. He whispers something, and as the key account manager rises from his chair, Walt takes his elbow and escorts him from the room. Simultaneously, Nick steps to the front and says, "I'm afraid that's all the time we have for questions." He turns to see if Lyndon has anything to add, but the corporate CEO only glowers at him.

Back in his room, Dave calls A&P corporate headquarters to make an appointment with the household products buyer. Next, he dials voicemail and finds several messages from store managers. After returning the calls, Dave packs his things except for the bathing suit, which is still damp. He looks for the plastic laundry bag every hotel room has, then uses it for the swimsuit, closes his suitcase, and goes downstairs.

Dave stows his luggage in the car then heads to the front desk to check out. Lunch is being served in the meeting room, so after he gets his receipt, Dave goes there and joins the other reps from his district. "What got into Tim?" Stephanie asks as they sit down to eat.

"Still waters run deep," Bill laughs.

"An MBA doesn't necessarily confer common sense," another rep opines.

"So, that's what's wrong with marketing," Stephanie laughs.

Each of the salespeople has the same box lunch consisting of a club sandwich, French fries, a Coke, and cookies. Stephanie only eats half her sandwich and none of the fries. "Aren't you going to eat those?" one of the guys asks her.

"You can have the fries," Stephanie replies, "but not the cookies."

After lunch, Paul leads his group to their assigned breakout room for a district meeting. Once everyone's seated, he uses an overhead projector to display the latest sales report showing individual progress toward quota attainment. Dave is leading the district with Stephanie close behind. Bill is ranked sixth out of eight key account managers. "Now I need to hear how each of you intends to make your numbers for the fourth quarter and the year," Paul says.

An hour later, after hearing from each member of his sales team, Paul gives them a break. Out in the hall, there's fresh coffee plus a cooler full of Dove Bars. The ice cream has a soothing effect on Dave's parched tongue. He begins to feel that life might be worth living, after all.

Back in the meeting room, Paul brings up the topic of Bounce, a radical new fabric softener that P&G introduced half a year ago. Bounce is expected to counter the threat to P&G's Downy brand that's coming from Calgon's Cling Free product. Bounce and Cling Free are dryer sheets that are more convenient to use than liquid fabric softeners. They're the first dryer sheets on the market, and both Calgon and P&G expect them to take a large share of the fabric softener category.

Paul puts up a chart with results from a Nielsen survey of laundry products in New York metro area supermarkets. "As you can see, we have a 68% share of dryer sheet fabric softeners compared with Cling Free's 32%," he declares, and uses a pointer to draw attention to the relevant numbers. "However, we only have 8% more shelf space than Cling Free in this market, and they are at parity with us when it comes to end-aisle displays." Paul hits the screen to highlight the distressing figures, and it wobbles on its rickety stand. "It's critical that we take these Nielsens to the trade and convince our accounts to reduce Cling Free's shelf space and expand ours. We must increase our display activity and get them off the end-aisles. Heads will roll if the next Nielsen doesn't show improvement in this data."

After giving each salesperson a stern glance, Paul puts up another chart. "Here's how each of our chains is doing," he says. "As you can see, Bounce is not getting enough merchandising support at Grand Union, Pathmark, Acme, or ShopRite. The only chain where we have a sufficiently dominant shelf position is A&P. We are also blowing Cling Free out of the water at A&P when it comes to displays, so it can be done."

Dave looks down and scribbles on his notepad. A&P is his account and he can feel the other salespeople glaring at him resentfully. Of course, they don't have the advantages he does. Most of them have to be home at a reasonable hour every night, but Cindy doesn't care when Dave comes in. Over the past six months, during the Bounce launch, he's been practically living in his 110 A&P stores building displays and resetting shelves. Resets must be done either early in the morning or late at night. That's because they require taking all the merchandise off the shelf in a section of the store and then putting the products back up in a new arrangement. All that work is worth it to

Dave if he can get more space for Bounce along with eye-level placement.

"We need to get people on the road," Paul says, then puts up one last transparency. "Just remember that we have two priorities for the rest of the year. Number one is quota; number two is Bounce." Paul hits the screen again with his pointer. "It's that simple," he declares.

Out in the lobby, there's a hubbub as goodbyes are said. But conversations are kept short because everyone's tired of pretending to be highly motivated. Soon Dave's behind the wheel of his Chevy heading north. On the way home, he listens to music and ponders the mystery of fate. All morning he knew that someone would be dragged out of the meeting in disgrace. It just never occurred to him that it would be Tim.

CHAPTER TWO

Ménage

It's Wednesday night and Dave's still recuperating from the sales meeting. He's at the kitchen table doing an expense report when Cindy comes in. "Smells good," she says. "What's cooking?"

"Spaghetti," Dave replies. "Sauce is almost done."

"Good, I'm starving!"

"So, how did it go today?"

"We're getting there," Cindy says. "Cast two more minor roles. Oh, I almost forgot. Mildred called while you were gone."

"What did she want?" Dave asks. Mildred Zimmermann was a friend of Dave's mother, Bobbie, who died several years ago. Now Mildred's keeping company with Dave's father.

"Mildred and the colonel will be in Washington all next week playing bridge," Cindy explains. "They want us to go down."

"Why don't they come here instead?" Dave asks. "What else have they got to do?"

"Play bridge, from the sound of it."

Dave writes a number on the report then looks up. "Well, no way," he scowls. "We've been to Texas to visit them twice, but they never come here."

"Oh, come on, we could see Susan and Phil while we're in D.C."

"I thought they lived in Richmond."

"Phil got transferred to the Washington branch of his firm."

"Oh."

"You like them," Cindy says.

"I like Susan," Dave smiles. He fills in the bottom of the expense report, then gets up and puts his business stuff away.

"So, we're going?"

"We'll have to fly. I can't take the car on a personal trip."

Cindy begins setting the table. "All right, we'll take the shuttle."

"I can make hotel reservations," Dave offers. "We'll use reward points."

"Do you want Chianti with dinner?" Cindy asks. She's already pouring herself a glass.

"Nah, I'll stick with water."

It's after seven on Friday when Cindy and Dave get to LaGuardia. They line up for the next shuttle to Washington. Most of the people in the queue are in business attire and carry briefcases. Dave's happy to be dressed casually. Over his shoulder, he has a carry-on bag. He's also toting Cindy's overnight case. She has their hangar bag with some dress-up clothes. Like Dave, Cindy's in jeans and wears running shoes in anticipation of long walks around D.C.

Eastern shuttles are first come, first served, so long lines are common during peak times. However, at this late hour, Cindy and Dave have no problem catching a flight. Once aboard, they head for the smoking section and find two aisle seats opposite each other.

After take-off, the captain comes on the intercom with a weather report for Washington where the temperature is currently 48 degrees and falling. The outlook for the following day is sunny, however, with the high close to 70. "You may unbuckle your seatbelts and move around the cabin as necessary," the captain says.

Cindy and Dave leave their seats and squeeze into one of the lavatories. Dave locks the door then pulls a joint out of his pocket. He gives it to Cindy and awkwardly lights it. They each get several tokes before putting it out in the sink. "Want to renew your membership in the mile-high club?" Dave asks, reaching his hand around Cindy's waist. "It's been over a year, and memberships expire after twelve months."

"Forget it," Cindy says, brushing Dave's hand away. "You had all the fun last time and I had none." She and Dave head back to their seats, feeling a pleasant spaciness from the grass.

The Knights don't get to their hotel until late, so they're content to order room-service rather than going out for dinner. They sleep in the following morning, then take a cab to the zoo. After getting a look at Ling-Ling and Hsing-Hsing, Cindy and Dave check out more exhibits then stroll over to the National Cathedral. They tour the massive stone structure then have lunch at a Japanese restaurant on Wisconsin Avenue. Afterward, they walk it off by window shopping.

"Hey, we need to head back," Dave says after a while.

"Bus or cab?" Cindy asks.

"Whichever comes first."

Once they're back at the hotel, Dave gets into the shower. Meanwhile, Cindy calls Susan Fauquier to make plans. Susan is one of Cindy's former college roommates. She's married to Phil Fauquier, the scion of a blue-blood Virginia family. "We're going to meet them at Clyde's," Cindy says when Dave emerges from the bathroom.

"Why not Mac's?" Dave towel-dries his hair then uses an afro pick on it.

"They wouldn't be caught dead in Mac's."

"Guess you're right."

Cindy disappears into the bathroom, so Dave gets dressed for the evening, then turns on the TV. He becomes engrossed in a college football game. After a while, he hears a blow-dryer going. "Your hair looks great," he thinks to say when Cindy comes out.

"Thanks, honey," Cindy smiles. "Now try to behave tonight. The last time we went out with them, you were rude to Phil and flirted with Susan outrageously."

"I'll try to be nice to Phil," Dave says, "but he's so lame. As for Susan, since when did you become the clingy, possessive type?"

"Oh, I don't care what you do with Susan," Cindy exclaims. She steps into a short dress then fusses to get her arms through the sleeves. "But I get tired of having to entertain Phil while you two carry on. Keeping him at bay is a full-time job."

"All right, I'll try to distract him." Dave helps Cindy with her zipper, and soon the couple is heading out the front door of the hotel.

Clyde's is an old-fashioned American pub right down to the red and white checked tablecloths, pressed tin ceiling, and uniformed waitstaff. Since there's no sign of Phil and Susan when Cindy and Dave arrive, they wait at the bar.

Presently, Dave feels a tap on his shoulder and spins around on his barstool to see Phil. He's a short, prematurely balding man, wearing a blazer over his polo shirt.

"How's it going?" Dave asks.

"They're killing me, you?"

"I'm still kicking."

Then Dave glances at Susan. She's a head taller than her husband and looks fabulous with her shoulder-length auburn hair spilling over a yellow cashmere V-neck. "Hey," she says to Dave, "what's happening?"

"Nothing, till you got here," Dave grins.

"Let's get a table," Cindy suggests. She already seems exasperated.

Soon the four of them are seated. They place their drink orders and Phil asks for a mixed platter of appetizers for everyone to share. Cindy and Susan begin catching up on news of their former classmates while Dave tries to break the ice with Phil. "Been hitting them any?" he asks.

"Not as often as I'd like," Phil says. "But something really funny happened last weekend when my uncle invited me to play at his club. He put me with a 14 handicapper while teaming himself with a 9. Still, we were up three holes on them at the turn, so they pressed the bet. By the time we got to 16, we were into them big time. Anyway, 16 is a water hole and Uncle Roger shanked his ball into the pond. Rather than taking a drop, he hit again, and bam, into the drink that went. So, my uncle threw his driver into the water, then unstrapped his bag from the cart and heaved that in as well. Afterward, he stalked off toward the parking lot."

"What a sorehead," Dave laughs.

"That's not the best part," Phil says. "After Uncle Roger left, the rest of us continued playing. We were on the tee at 17 when he came marching back then waded into the pond fully dressed. He found his bag, unzipped one of the pockets, took out his car keys and wallet, then threw the clubs back in."

"That's funny."

"Oh, yeah, we were cracking up."

"Did he pay the bet?"

"Yeah, he had to," Phil says. "My partner and I both received checks."

"I'm going to the loo," Susan says to Cindy. "Come on."

After the ladies leave, the waiter comes over. "Are you done with that?" he asks, pointing to the appetizer platter. It's barely been touched.

"Yeah, you can take it," Phil says, "but when you come back, bring us another round."

A few minutes later, Cindy and Susan return. "Everybody's getting divorced," Susan is saying as they reclaim their seats.

"I know," Cindy replies, "it's depressing."

"Now Margaret's home with two kids and no husband."

"That's the worst part, the children. They grow up fatherless."

"It's because people get married too young," Dave suggests.

"That's right," Phil agrees, "people get married then quickly get bored going to bed with the same person every night."

"We have a solution to that, though," Susan smiles, "open marriage."

"Yeah, Susan can do whatever she wants and so can I," Phil says with a lascivious grin. He downs his vodka tonic and holds the glass up to signal the waiter.

"Ready for another round?" the waiter asks.

"What we need is some shots," Phil declares, "tequila."

Soon the shots are lined up on the table and the two couples go through the ritual of downing them. Even with the lime and salt chasers, the fiery liquor makes them shudder. But that doesn't deter Phil. "One more round," he orders, "then you can bring me the check."

"Let me at least pay half," Dave offers.

"Nah, I've got this," Phil insists.

The check and the tequila arrive simultaneously. After both are taken care of, the foursome takes their leave. Out on the sidewalk, they discuss what to do next.

"Let's see who's playing at the Bayou," Susan suggests.

"I don't feel like dancing after walking all day," Cindy complains.

"We can go to Trader Vic's and have Mai Tais," Phil says.

"That sounds good," Dave agrees.

"Why don't you leave your car here and ride with us," Susan offers.

"We didn't drive," Cindy explains, "we walked over from Roslyn."

"Then let's go," Phil says, and leads the way to where his BMW is parked. Cindy and Dave get in the back.

Once the car is moving, Dave scoots forward and snakes his hand around the side of Susan's seat. She remains motionless as he gently cups her boob. Dave discerns the silky feel of a camisole under Susan's sweater, but no bra. He glances at Cindy, who seems both amused and disgusted by what he's doing.

As they enter the brightly lit commercial district of D.C., Dave reluctantly shifts back in his seat. Phil pulls up in front of the restaurant and an attendant takes the car.

The interior of Trader Vic's is a jumble of tired-looking South Pacific décor. Even though it's Saturday night, only a few tables are occupied. "Sit anywhere," the maître d' says with a sweep of his arm.

Eventually, a heavyset woman in a South Seas dress notices that one of her tables is occupied and comes over. "Four Mai Tais, please," Dave orders.

"You want a pupu platter?" she asks hopefully.

"No, thanks."

The waitress wearily collects the menus, then goes to the bar. Meanwhile, Cindy and Susan go to find the ladies' room. When they return, the Mai Tais are on the table. They're potent concoctions of rum, pineapple juice, lime juice, and two different liqueurs. "Cheers," Phil says, then eagerly slurps the intoxicating elixir.

"This is Hawaii in a glass," Dave comments after sampling his beverage. He now has a white foam mustache.

"Yeah, no need to sit on a plane for eighteen hours when you can come here anytime and drink a couple of these babies," Phil laughs.

"I still want to go sometime," Cindy sighs.

"Phil and I went to Maui a while back," Susan says.

"Lucky you!"

"It's the only place in the world you can go that's guaranteed to exceed your expectations," Phil declares.

"What about Poughkeepsie?" Dave asks. He's making a major dent in his Mai Tai.

"Oh, I heard all about that," Susan laughs.

"Not me," Phil complains.

"Oh, Dave and a friend got arrested there for hitchhiking," Cindy says, "back in the day."

"They should have called me!"

"You were still in law school."

"No matter," Dave shrugs. "The judge cut us loose the next day." He waves his empty glass at the waitress, who's sitting with some other restaurant employees. She gets the message.

Around midnight, after a few more drinks, someone turns the lights up and a massive Samoan comes out of the glare. "You got to go," he tells the haoles.

"Are you on the Redskins?" Phil asks.

"Now," the man insists.

"But we just got here," Cindy complains.

"Oh, never mind," Dave says, and throws some money on the table. "We'll go where we're wanted."

Outside, the group waits uncertainly as the tired attendant gets their car. "Now what?" Cindy wonders.

"Let's have an orgy," Phil blurts out.

"Four's too small for an orgy," Dave says. "It's only one more than a ménage."

"I'm serious," Phil insists.

Dave glances at Cindy, who gives him a negative shake of her head. He turns back to Phil. "OK, but just one rule."

"What's that?"

"No swapping."

"Oh, come on," Phil exclaims. "Then what's the point?"

Dave doesn't reply and a few moments later, the valet drives up with the BMW. "All right, it's a deal," Phil concedes. "We'll go to our place."

The Fauquiers live in an art deco apartment building on a classy stretch of Connecticut Avenue. "Good evening," the desk clerk says as the two couples roll in.

"Hey, Zac, how ya doin'?" Phil slurs.

After a ride to the sixth floor in a rickety Otis, the group heads down the hall to the Fauquiers' apartment. Once inside, they go into the living room and Phil adjusts the lights. He puts some music on, then leads Susan to the sofa. They begin foreplay while Cindy and Dave take the love seat.

In a while, Cindy and Dave take a break from making out to get rid of their clothes. They see that Susan and Phil have also shed their attire. Phil is on top of her. His little butt is going up and down like a Singer sewing machine.

The next time Dave looks over, Phil has stopped moving and Susan's eyes are closed. Cindy also seems to be conking out, so Dave pushes the cocktail table aside and eases her down onto the fur rug. He slips a cushion under Cindy's head, then lies beside her, luxuriating in the feel of shaggy sheepskin against his bare body.

Dave is drifting into unconsiousness when he feels a hand on his shoulder. He opens his eyes to see Susan kneeling next to him. "Phil's in bed totally zonked out," she whispers. "There's plenty of room in there for all of us."

"Thanks," Dave says. He wakes Cindy and they follow Susan's nude form into the bedroom. Cindy drowsily climbs into the king-size bed then scoots over to make room for Dave. Susan follows.

Within minutes, Cindy is again asleep. However, Dave is distracted by the heat of Susan's body nearby. He reaches an arm around her, and Susan immediately pushes back against him, sleepily rotating her hips. But after lightly running his hand over Susan's lithe body, Dave is incapable of more.

The sun has long been up when Dave wakes with a throbbing headache. Cindy is next to him, also awake. "My mouth tastes like the entire Ethiopian Army marched through it barefoot last night," Dave whispers.

"That's what you always say when you're hungover," Cindy hisses. Next to her, Phil is lying on his back, snoring. Susan is near Dave, breathing deeply.

"Let's get out of here," Dave suggests.

"Good plan."

Cindy and Dave cautiously exit the bed. They gently pull the blanket back up around the Fauquiers then tiptoe into the living room to find their clothes.

Once they're dressed, Cindy and Dave take the stairs down. Taxies are scarce on a quiet Sunday morning, but Dave finally flags one down. "I'm going to have a shower," Cindy says when they get to the Marriott.

"I'm next," Dave replies. "You want a couple of these?" He holds out a Tylenol bottle, and when Cindy nods, he shakes two tablets into her hand. They wash them down with water, then while Cindy's in the bathroom, Dave orders breakfast.

After they finish eating, Dave has his turn soaping off. When he comes out, Cindy's on the phone with her mother, who lives in New Jersey. "Got to go, Dave's done," she says, then listens for a minute. "No, we're not going to mass!" she snaps. "Don't start that again."

"Your mother's right," Dave says after Cindy hangs up, "a priest would love to hear your confession this morning."

"Fuck you!"

"Exactly."

While Cindy simmers, Dave gets dressed. "So, how are things in Princeton?" he asks after a while.

Cindy brightens. "They're fine. Mom told me that Dad's latest book has racked up some sales."

"What's it about?"

"Lichens."

"Tough subject."

"So, what are we going to do till it's time to meet Mildred?"

"Thought we might visit my mother's grave," Dave suggests.

"All right," Cindy agrees.

It's an easy stroll from the hotel to the main gate of Arlington National Cemetery, then a strenuous uphill climb to Bobbie's gravesite. "I was never clear about what she died of?" Cindy murmurs after they've caught their breath.

"Migraines," Dave answers.

"Your mother died of headaches?"

"The army gave her pills called APCs, for them. That's what did her in."

Cindy pauses while a jet on final approach to National roars overhead. "What was in the pills?" she asks once it's quiet.

"A combination of aspirin, phenacetin, and caffeine," Dave explains.

"Aspirin doesn't sound so bad."

"It eats away the stomach and intestinal lining." Dave looks down at the grave marker, recalling the torment Bobbie endured with ulcers.

"What does phenacetin do?" Cindy asks.

"Destroys the kidneys and causes cancer. But that didn't stop the army from dispensing millions of doses. They were still handing APCs out when I was in."

"That's crazy."

"Yes, and speaking of crazy and the army, we're supposed to meet up with Dad and Mildred in less than an hour." Dave takes Cindy's hand and leads her away from the grave.

Going downhill is a breeze, and soon Cindy and Dave are out of the cemetery. They're crossing Memorial Bridge, taking in the view, when a taxi stops. "Where ya headin'?" the driver asks with a country accent.

"The Watergate," Dave says as he and Cindy climb in.

"I'll drop y'all off there," the cabbie offers, "but won't wait. Don't want to git 'rested fer drivin' the getaway car." Cindy and

Dave laugh dutifully, guessing that the driver has told this joke many times.

When they get to the Watergate, Dave over-tips the driver since it was such a short ride. Then he and Cindy find the right building, go inside, and check in at the front desk. They take an elevator up and find the apartment number Mildred provided. Dave's father answers the door and welcomes them inside. He hugs Cindy, and ignoring her proffered cheek, kisses her on the lips.

Though long retired, Colonel David Knight is still a handsome man with craggy good looks reminiscent of Humphrey Bogart. He wears a monogrammed white shirt, gray flannel slacks, and Bally loafers on his sockless feet.

Knight releases Cindy and steps back, holding both her hands. "You look absolutely fantastic," he says. "What are you doing still hanging around with this joker?" Knight tilts his head toward Dave, acknowledging his son for the first time.

"Hi, Dad," Dave says, glancing around the apartment. There's a view of the Potomac through sliding glass doors, a well-stocked bar in the corner, and a pedestal bridge table in front of the bar. Three card players are seated around it, including Mildred. "Hi, y'all," she says, getting up. "Let me introduce you to Greg Reynolds and his wife, Linda."

"Pleased to meet you," Dave replies with a wave. "This is Cindy, and I'm Dave."

"We're from Boca Raton," Linda explains, looking up from her cards.

"We only use this condo when we come to D.C.," Greg elaborates. He and his wife appear to be in their mid-sixties. With his big head of white hair, Greg looks like a judge. Linda just looks like money.

Mildred comes over to give Cindy a peck on the cheek. She's wearing designer jeans that look to be one size too large and so appear comfortable on her petite frame. A baby-blue sweater and beige suede moccasins complete her attire. She only wears one piece of jewelry. It's a diamond solitaire worn on the ring finger of her left hand. The rock is the size of a robin's egg. "We're in the middle of a rubber," she says apologetically.

"No problem," Dave replies, "Cindy and I will enjoy the view from the balcony until you're done."

Cindy and Dave go toward the balcony, but before they get there, Knight calls out, "Hey, son, why don't you make us some of your Bloody Marys? We're running dry." He holds up a tall glass with reddish liquid in the bottom. "Oh, and you can help yourself to a cinnamon roll, they're in the kitchen."

"All right," Dave agrees. In the kitchen, he locates the ingredients he needs for the drinks and gets to work. Meanwhile, Cindy goes to the card table and collects the empty glasses. The bridge players, intent on their cards, ignore her.

"Looks like you're taking over as bartender here," Cindy whispers when she returns to the kitchen.

"Dad always hoped I might prove useful one day."

It takes a while to make the drinks, but finally Dave's finished except for the main ingredient. He goes back into the living room and grabs the vodka bottle off the bar. His father looks up and scowls. "What's taking so long?"

"The mix is over there," Dave flares, pointing to a bottle of Mr & Mrs T. "Help yourself if you're in a hurry."

Knight flushes and starts to get out of his chair, but Mildred puts a restraining hand on his arm. Turning, Dave takes the vodka into the kitchen. He pours a good four ounces into each glass to dilute the thick black liquid. After stirring the drinks, he and Cindy distribute them to the card players. Then they go out on the balcony.

It's brisk outside, but the river view is worth it. The Custis-Lee Mansion, near where they were earlier, dominates a ridge on the opposite shore. Further north is Key Bridge leading from Georgetown to Roslyn. "There's our hotel," Cindy points.

"And there's Arlington Towers right next to it," Dave says. He was living in Virginia and worked as a desk clerk at Arlington Towers Apartments when he and Cindy first met. They hold hands, take in the scenery, and watch the water rush by.

The sliding glass door opens, and Mildred steps onto the balcony holding her drink. "I'm the dummy this hand," she explains.

"Guess you get a little break then," Dave smiles.

Mildred swirls the liquid around in her half-full glass then takes a swig. "I swear, this is the best Bloody Mary I've ever tasted!"

"That's the way they make 'em at the Bucket of Blood Saloon in Nevada."

"What were you doing there?"

"Oh, that's a whole other story," Dave laughs, remembering a wild week of sales training P&G hosted at Lake Tahoe several years ago.

"Believe me, you don't want to hear it," Cindy exclaims.

"I'm so glad you two were able to come down," Mildred says abruptly. "I need to talk with you about Melissa."

"What about her?" Dave asks. Melissa is his older sister. She lives in Annapolis, Maryland with her husband and their two sons.

"She wrote your father a horrible letter," Mildred explains. "It goes on for eight pages, accusing him of ruining her childhood. The colonel is quite broken up about it."

"I guess I'm not surprised," Dave says, "they haven't spoken in years."

"Well, I don't believe your father's anything like the monster Melissa portrayed in her letter," Mildred declares. "What's gotten into her?"

"I'm not sure," Dave replies. "To me, having a bad childhood is something that must be overcome. I guess Melissa's having trouble doing that."

Mildred hesitates then changes the subject. "We're engaged to be married," she announces, holding her hand up to show off the huge diamond. She finishes her drink then gives the glass an emphatic shake that rattles the ice cubes.

"I'm very happy for you both," Dave says. This will be Mildred's third marriage. She's already buried two East Texas oilmen.

Behind them, the glass door slides open again, and Greg Reynolds comes out. "Aren't you cold?" he asks.

"It's not that bad," Mildred says.

"Well, it's the last deal. We need you now."

Mildred follows Greg back inside. As soon as the door closes, Cindy rounds on Dave. "Why didn't you tell Mildred about your father when you had the chance?" she demands.

"I did, in so many words," Dave shrugs. "But she obviously didn't want to hear it. And that's all right. I mean, why scare her off? Mildred's the only one who might keep Dad from ending up drunk in a gutter somewhere."

"Don't you ever feel like exploding the way Melissa did and telling him how you feel about what he did to you all?"

"Yes, but it's as much what he didn't do as what he did, and how do you explain that? When I try to express it, I become inarticulate, so it's better not to try."

Cindy thrusts her hands deeper into her pockets and hunches her shoulders. "I'm cold," she says. "Being out of the sun with the wind coming off the river gets to you."

"Then let's go in."

Cindy and Dave go back into the living room and sit on the sofa. As they wait for the bridge game to end, Dave picks up a recent *TIME* and flips through it. Cindy luxuriates in the warmth.

Finally, the last cards of the last hand are played and Knight totes up the score. "Looks like you owe us $287," he says.

"That's cheap," Greg comments. "If not for that last rubber, it would've been much worse." He gets his checkbook and starts scribbling.

"We've got to leave for the airport," Knight says, rising from the table. "Dave, can you help with the luggage?"

Dave follows his father into a bedroom and grabs two suitcases the colonel points out. He carries them into the living room and uses one of the bags to prop the door open. Then he takes the other one down the hall to the elevator. When he returns, Linda points to the other bedroom. "There's more in there," she says. Dave gets the Reynolds's suitcases, then he and Cindy remain out in the hallway to keep an eye on the baggage piled by the elevator.

After a while, Mildred and Linda come out of the apartment wearing coats. Their husbands follow. When the elevator arrives, Dave drags the bags on board. There's not enough room for everyone inside, so the men go down first. When they get to the lobby, the doorman comes over and grabs a couple of suitcases. "Your limo is here," he tells Greg.

Presently, the ladies emerge from the other elevator. "We're going to catch a cruise ship out of Fort Lauderdale tomorrow," Linda is telling Cindy. "It's a bridge cruise."

"We aren't taking nearly as much luggage on this trip as we took last month when we went to New York," Mildred remarks as they wait for the doorman to put the other suitcases in the limo.

"I thought the bellman at the Waldorf was going to faint when he saw all the bags we brought," Knight exclaims.

"You were at the Waldorf last month?" Dave asks. The Waldorf Astoria Hotel is only a few blocks from Cindy and Dave's apartment.

"Why, yes," Knight admits, "I meant to call you, but each day went by so fast and before long, we were leaving."

Dave has been trying but can no longer control his temper. "And I don't suppose you had time, while you were here, to visit Mom's grave?" he snaps.

"What business is that of yours?" Knights asks.

Dave turns away from his father and says to Mildred, "We have to go. I hope you enjoy the cruise."

But now Mildred just glares at Dave. She's always been jealous of Bobbie, who was more popular in high school than she was. Knight's not allowed to have pictures of his first wife in their home or to mention her name.

Dave takes Cindy's hand and they go out the door. "That was horrible," Cindy says, once they're away from the building. "He treats you like garbage."

"I should have made a couple of those Bloody Marys for us."

"That wouldn't have helped. Besides, you have to be an alcoholic to be pouring vodka down your throat this early."

"They had at least one round of drinks before we got there."

"Maybe more."

"Let's go back to the hotel, pack, then grab the van to National. We can catch an early flight."

"You're on!"

CHAPTER THREE
Out of Stock

Cindy's boss, Sydney Glass, is a rarity on Broadway. He's a successful producer-director who also happens to be black. Sydney's a kind-hearted man, so it's no surprise when he gives Cindy and the other office staff, time off for Christmas.

Dave's home for the holidays as well, so on Christmas Eve he and Cindy decorate their tree together. "Let's go ice skating," Dave suggests, once they're done.

"It'll be mobbed," Cindy says.

"So what?"

The rink at Rockefeller Center is indeed crowded, but everyone there is full of Christmas cheer and the spirit is catching. The Knights have a great time even though both have several spills on the ice. On the way home, they stop for pizza and share a pitcher of beer. When they arrive back at the apartment, the couple is in a giddy mood. "Let's get high," Cindy suggests.

As Dave rolls, Cindy lights several candles and places them around the room. Then she puts a record on the turntable and changes into a nightgown. "Good idea," Dave says, and goes to put on his pajamas. Once they're both back on the sofa, he hands Cindy the joint and lights it for her.

After a while, Dave gets up to flip the record. "I'm chilly," Cindy complains. So, Dave goes and gets the quilt off their bed. As he tucks it around her, Cindy feels his hand. "You're cold, too," she says, and rearranges the quilt so that it covers them both. Then Cindy takes her husband's hand and tucks it between her knees to warm it. One thing soon leads to another and presently they are stretched out on the sofa beneath the quilt.

Later, Cindy is breathing deeply while Dave lies beside her, dreamily reflecting on the lovely time they've had. The first line of a rhyme comes to him, and several more follow. Then Cindy stirs and comes awake. "Let's go to bed," she says.

Dave rises early and makes a Christmas card for Cindy using the verse he thought up. Later, when they open presents, Cindy furrows her brow as she reads the card:

Still cold dark nights,
Fireplace glow and Christmas lights,
Warm quilt candles stereo,
Kisses under the mistletoe,
Morning walks in Central Park,
Then ice skating after dark,
Pizza and beer in a little dive,
Then home to listen to *Frampton Comes Alive!*
This is what Christmas is all about,
For two young lovers just starting out.

"What's this, too cheap to buy a Christmas card?" Cindy asks.

"Do you like it?"

"Oh, come on."

Cindy and Dave spend the rest of the holidays knocking around the city or just kicking back in their apartment. Then all too soon, it's time to go back to work. That's not hard for Dave, as he loves his job. But Cindy's not at all happy to be stuck on the administrative side of the theater business. When Sydney hired her, he promised that if she would help him manage the office for a year or two, he would move her into production. Now, five years on, she's become indispensable to him and there's no more talk of her doing actual theater work.

As for Dave, his year starts off the way the last one ended. Thanks to a display promotion he sells to his buyer at A&P headquarters, Dave again leads the district in sales. To stay on top, he must work long hours in the stores. But early in February, Dave gets a break. His company car is due for service, and while it's in the shop, Dave's assigned to ride along with Bill.

That morning, Dave goes to the Chevrolet dealership P&G uses in New Jersey. After dropping his keys at the service desk, he goes outside to wait. Presently, Bill pulls up in his company car. "I hate Mondays," he says as Dave gets in.

"If you want to take the blue out of Monday, just work all weekend," Dave suggests. "Then it's just another day."

"Get real," Bill laughs. They leave the dealership then stop at a 7-Eleven and go inside. "I got to get my motor revved up," Bill says, taking hold of the coffee pot.

"If this stuff doesn't get you going, you're certifiably dead." Dave also fills a container with greasy black liquid.

Back in the car, the salesmen sip their hot beverages with both the heater and Don Imus turned up. Eventually, they feel sufficiently energized to tackle a retail call, so Bill drives to his first stop. "This guy's a real prick," he says as they park in front of a Grand Union Supermarket. "I've been trying to get a mandated end-aisle display, but he claims not to have space."

Inside the store, Bill and Dave go to the service desk and sign in. A balding, overweight man wearing a white shirt and blue tie hustles over. "Hello, Stan," Bill says, "this is Dave, he's working with me."

"You Procter guys think you're God's gift to the world," the store manager accuses.

"What do you mean?" Bill asks nervously.

"Isn't that your car out front?" Stan says, pointing at Bill's Chevy, which can be seen through the store's plate-glass window. "The spaces in front are reserved for customers; salesmen must park in the rear."

"Oh, sorry ... I don't know what I was thinking." Bill stammers. His hands shake and a sheen of perspiration appears on his forehead.

"Give me the keys and I'll move it," Dave offers.

Now Stan turns his glare on Dave. "All the way past that light pole." He points out the window.

"No problem," Dave smiles. "You know this is the only Grand Union I've been in that offers free coffee to the customers."

"That's because I'm the only one who does it."

"What a great idea! And I like the way you place it near the entrance, so the aroma is the first thing customers notice when they come in."

"Yeah, management loves it," Stan brags. "They're going to include it in a summary of best practices. Not only does it make customers feel at home, but it's also a way to promote our private label. Say, you're not from around here, are you?"

"No, I'm not."

"Ah-hah, I could tell from your accent. You sound like a Southerner. I find that people from the South have much nicer manners than New Yorkers." Stan gives a brief dismissive glance toward Bill.

"Thanks," Dave replies. "Now after I move the car, we're going to survey the household products section. If you don't mind, we'd like to talk with you afterward."

"That's fine." Stan returns Dave's smile. "And feel free to help yourself to the coffee. I just made a fresh pot." As the manager walks off, Dave reaches out his hand to Bill, who seems baffled. "Car key?" Dave prompts.

When Dave returns, he joins Bill in the household products section. They make notes on shelf conditions then go in search of the aisle clerk. He's in the stockroom. "Hello, Ben," Bill says.

"Hey, what's happening?"

"Looks like Lever was here."

"Yeah, him and the Clorox guy both came last week. Is it that bad?"

"They moved some Tide and Downy tags to cut down on my facings. We're supposed to have three rows of the 50 oz. Tide, for example, and those bastards cut it down to two."

"Let's go look."

In the household products aisle, Bill points out some of the depredations made by the Clorox and Lever Brothers reps. "Do you have the corporate planogram?" Ben asks.

"Right here," Bill says, and opens a binder to the Grand Union laundry products planogram. The schematic shows where each product goes on the shelf and the number of rows it should have. Each row is a facing. The placement of reorder tags is also shown. They indicate where the space for each product begins.

Ben spends several minutes looking back and forth from the planogram to the shelf, and then renders his verdict. "All right, you can change it back," he says. "But do me a favor, please don't move their tags around. I'm tired of this shit."

"You got it," Bill agrees. "And we're going to bring some product out, price it, and fully stock the shelf. That's the best way for us to keep our space."

"If you want to do my job for me, go right ahead," Ben replies.

So, Bill gets a couple of pricing guns and he and Dave get to work. An hour later, the household products section is standing tall and the two salesmen go looking for Stan. They find him up front talking to a customer. "Can you tell me why my husband was charged 89 cents for this ketchup when the ad says it's on sale?" the woman asks.

"Looks like the aisle clerk didn't put a sale price sticker on it," Stan says. "I'm sorry."

"And what if I hadn't checked the tape when he got home?" the lady replies. "We'd be out 40 cents."

"I don't blame you for being unhappy," Stan says. "So, here's what we'll do. I'm going to refund the entire amount you paid, not just the overcharge. How does that sound?"

"Great!" the woman smiles. A few minutes later, she leaves the store with ketchup in hand and coins jingling in her purse. Stan turns to find Bill and Dave waiting for him. "What do you need?" he asks.

"I want to tell you what we found in the laundry section," Bill says, and launches into an indictment of Lever Brothers and Clorox. He appears nervous and becomes more so as Stan taps his foot impatiently. So, Bill cuts to the chase. "Presidents' Day is coming," he points out, "and there's a full pallet of Tide in the stockroom for a mandatory end-aisle display."

"We only have so many ends," Stan replies scornfully, "and mine are loaded. I can't help it if corporate mandates more displays than we have room for."

"But … but … we have an insert with a 50-cent coupon in the paper that Sunday," Bill stammers, "and Tide's in your ad."

"Are you worried we're going to run out?" Stan says, raising his eyebrows. "Not with a full pallet in the back."

Bill looks to be running out of steam, so Stan turns to make his getaway. However, Dave brings him up short. "The problem is you're completely wasting one of your most heavily trafficked end-aisles," he says.

"What are you talking about?" Stan scowls.

"The holidays are over," Dave replies, "why are you displaying pumpkin pie mix, cranberry sauce, and Stove Top stuffing on an end?"

"That display was mandated by corporate," Stan replies defensively. "It wasn't my idea."

"How long has it been up?" Dave asks.

Stan pauses. "Several months now that I think about it; they sent way too much for that sale and I've been trying to get rid of it."

"So why not ship the excess back to the warehouse?"

"I've had too many other priorities. It would all have to be boxed and loaded onto a pallet."

"We can handle that," Dave offers. "What if Bill and I come back tomorrow night, after the store closes, and pack up all that holiday merchandise for you? Then we'll bring the Tide out, sticker it, and put it on that end."

"You two are gonna do all that work?"

"Oh, we'll bring some temps along to help," Dave replies. "At our expense, of course."

"OK, it's a deal," Stan says quickly.

Out in the parking lot, Bill puts his sales bag in the trunk then gets behind the wheel. "What did I tell you?" he exclaims. "Stan is a jerk."

Bill is eager to get away from the store, but the rest of his sales calls this day don't go any better. He's fine talking with cashiers and aisle clerks but loses his nerve with store managers. After their last stop, he takes Dave back to the dealership. "What a day," he moans. "I need a drink."

"Follow me," Dave says, "I know a spot just up the road."

Dave's watering hole turns out to be an Italian restaurant with a cozy lounge. Once inside, the two P&Gers sit at the bar, where a lively happy hour crowd has gathered. "I've got an A&P about a mile away," Dave explains, "that's how I found this place."

"It's nice, but I feel grungy," Bill says. "I'm going to have a long shower when I get home."

"Yeah, those stockrooms are filthy."

The bartender comes over, and Bill orders bourbon and ginger while Dave asks for a beer. The beverages quickly materialize. "Cheers," Bill toasts. He knocks back half his highball with one gulp.

Out of habit, Dave looks around the bar for any unaccompanied women. Disappointed, he reaches for his brew.

"Why are store managers such pricks?" Bill asks.

"Power corrupts," Dave replies, turning to face his buddy.

"What?"

"Somebody said that long ago."

"And?"

"It means some people can't handle having authority. It goes to their heads."

"Oh, like some of those assholes in the army?"

"Exactly."

"Fucking lifers!"

"Roger that." Dave motions to the barkeep for another round.

"I had the absolute worst platoon sergeant in 'Nam," Bill says, clutching his fresh drink.

"That bad?"

"Oh, I could tell you some shit, but you wouldn't want to hear it."

"Try me."

Bill's eyes take on a faraway look. "OK, so get this," he says, "one time, our platoon was on patrol near the Laotian border and had orders to link up with another unit for the night. It was getting late when we came to a clearing in the jungle filled with rice paddies. The lieutenant ordered us to go across, but no one wanted to. We preferred to go around, but he was afraid that would take too long, and we'd miss the rendezvous with that other platoon. So, he ordered us onto the dikes and our sergeant backed him up. Halfway across the clearing, puffs of smoke appeared in the treeline and all hell broke loose. B-40s, RPGs, and streams of green tracers came flying our way. Guys began falling, screaming, 'I'm hit, I'm hit! Medic!'"

"What about you?" Dave asks.

"I dove onto the ground and landed on the protected side of the dike," Bill says. "I was lying on my side behind the berm while bullets flew overhead. When I looked back, who did I see kneeling in the treeline we had left but our platoon sergeant and the lieutenant. The bastards sent us out and then waited to see what would happen."

"Nice."

"Yeah, I lost it. Just became completely unglued. Next thing I was on the other side of the dike, going into the paddies and grabbing guys to drag them over to the safe side. Bullets were whizzing by my head and kicking up dust at my feet while the wounded screamed as I dragged them. Explosions from the rockets going off all around. Somehow, I got everyone back. Even a couple of KIAs without realizing they were beyond help."

"It's a miracle you survived!"

"Yeah, I caught some shrapnel and was medevacked with the others. But it was nothing, just some stitches. Still, they gave me the Purple Heart at the hospital. Later, I was awarded the Silver Star."

"What happened to your platoon sergeant and the lieutenant?"

"I don't know, never saw them again. I was in the hospital a month before they got all the shrapnel out and the incisions closed. By the time I got back to my unit, it was all new guys from top to bottom."

"I'm glad you lived to tell about it."

"Me too!" Bill exclaims. They clink glasses and drink to it.

"So, what made you want to get into sales?" Dave asks.

"Honestly, I don't know. Saw an ad from Procter & Gamble about their veterans' outreach program and decided to give it a shot. I'm not sure if it's for me."

"Well, I'm happy you ended up at P&G," Dave says. "Otherwise, I never would have met you."

"Same here; it's great to talk to another vet."

"I didn't go to Vietnam, you know. I've never been in combat."

"Yeah, but at least you have an idea of what it's about," Bill says. "Hey, I've got to go, my old lady's going to kill me."

Dave looks at his watch. "Right, I need to be getting along as well."

When Dave gets home, Cindy's in bed. He makes himself a quick meal then has a shower. Afterward, he goes into the bedroom. "What are you reading?" he asks. Cindy holds the book up so he can see the cover. It features a shirtless man with a six-pack.

"Any good?"

"Fantastic."

"Well, I had a strange day."

Cindy sighs then lowers the book. "Oh?"

"Come to find out two things about my buddy Bill Jackson," Dave says. "First, he's a genuine war hero, and second, the guy's scared shitless of those nasty supermarket store managers."

"The one doesn't seem to go with the other."

"That's what's strange."

"Oh, I almost forgot, this came for you." Cindy hands Dave a small envelope.

Dave sits on the bed and opens the envelope. Inside is a wedding announcement. "Looks like Mildred and Dad tied the knot," Dave says.

"I'll send them a card," Cindy replies. She starts to go back to her book, but the phone on the nightstand rings. "Get that, will you?"

"Hello," Dave says into the phone, then, "No, that's OK, we're not doing anything." Dave listens awhile then says, "I just have my normal retail calls this week, plus several resets." He listens again, then says, "Sure, I can do that, I'll go tomorrow."

"What's going on?" Cindy asks after Dave hangs up.

"That was Paul. He said Walt Frazier, Tim Witherspoon, and several more guys from the Baltimore-Washington District got fired. Nick wants me to go and handle the Giant Food account for now.

"Poor Tim."

"Yeah, well they screwed up the Bounce launch big-time."

"Why are they sending you? Isn't there someone closer?"

"Nick knows I can find my way around D.C. Also, I'm running ahead of quota, so they don't risk much by taking me out of my territory for a week or two."

"Who's going to look after your stores?"

"Paul said he'll increase my budget for temps," Dave says. "So, I'm going to see UpTempCo tomorrow and give them a work order. Afterward, I'll drive down to Washington. That way, I can take all my stuff."

"I guess J. Willard will see more of you than I will for a while."

"It's just for a week or two. Think of all the reward points we'll rack up."

"Yeah, sure," Cindy says. "Now, I'm going to sleep. We have a long day of rehearsals tomorrow."

Cindy goes for a last visit to the bathroom. While she's in there, Dave gets her address book and writes down Susan Fauquier's number. He's on the phone, making hotel reservations, when Cindy comes back. "Use the one in the living room for that," she asks. "I'm turning out the light."

By the time Dave gets out of the shower the next morning, Cindy is gone. However, he has several phone calls to make before leaving. Once he's done, Dave packs his overnight case and sales bag. He turns off the lights, then triple-locks the door behind him on his way out.

Presently, Dave's behind the wheel of the Chevy on his way to the UpTempCo office in Morristown. He's excited about having a break in routine. To celebrate, he pops a rarely played cassette into the tape deck. Soon Dave's driving with one hand while conducting a Mozart symphony with the other.

An hour later, Dave turns into an office park comprised of two-story, glass-fronted buildings. He goes inside one to find Mindy Gore at a desk near the entrance. Her mother owns UpTempCo, and Mindy does the payroll. She's working on a stack of timesheets. "Looks like you have your hands full," Dave says.

"Always," Mindy smiles.

"Is your mom in her office?"

"Yeah, she's expecting you."

Dave goes upstairs and greets the owner's secretary, Barbara Shelton. She's an attractive older lady who used to own a beauty salon. "Can you hold on for a moment?" Barbara asks. "Michelle's on the phone."

"Sure, no problem."

As he waits, Dave looks at plaques mounted on the wall of the reception area. One reads "Northern New Jersey Chamber of Commerce 1979 Entrepreneur of the Year: MICHELLE MANSON." Another names her "Metro New York Businesswoman of the Year, 1981."

Below the plaques is a photo of Michelle and her husband, Fred. They're seated at a banquet table covered with dishes, wine glasses, and bottles. All those at the table are formally dressed, but Michelle and Fred stand out for the opulence of their attire. Not for the first time, Dave is drawn to the glamour of the entrepreneurial world. He feels vaguely ashamed to be nothing more than a mid-level corporate hack.

Barbara gets up. "You can go in now," she says, and shows Dave into Michelle's office. It's huge and dramatically furnished. In the center, a white sectional sofa circles around a glass-topped coffee table. There's a wet bar in the corner. "Barbara, please get Dave a cup of coffee," Michelle says from behind her desk.

Like Barbara, Michelle is carefully made up and nicely coiffed. She wears obviously expensive designer clothes, but the effect is ruined by an overabundance of jewelry. "Have a seat," she tells Dave.

Dave takes a chair in front of Michelle's desk and opens his briefcase. "This is the plan for the resets that we talked about earlier." He hands her a folder.

"Good," Michelle says, "I'll get Bob up here so we can go over it together." She picks up her phone and taps the keys like she's working a calculator.

Presently, Bob Stansfield, an UpTempCo field supervisor, comes in wearing a work shirt and jeans. "Hey, Dave, what's up?"

"The Empire State Building."

"That's funny, not."

Michelle passes the folder to Bob. "Here are all the details for some A&P resets that Dave needs us to do."

"Is the new planogram in here?" Bob asks with an impatient glance at the folder.

"Last page," Dave says.

Bob studies the schematic then looks up with a smile. "You got all your products at eye level."

"Yeah, plus we get more space for Bounce, and they're adding the two larger sizes."

"What's being deleted?"

"Some liquid fabric softeners that aren't selling anymore."

"So, we'll have to box that stuff up and ship it back to the warehouse."

"Right."

Now Bob studies the first page. "Is this schedule set in concrete, or can we change it?"

"It's flexible."

"Good, we have to be in Red Bank on Thursday for another client and could do that A&P then."

"Just let the manager know in advance."

"No problem, we'll get right on it."

"Thanks, Bob," Michelle says.

"I picked up the Giant account in Washington," Dave tells Michelle after Bob goes out, "and may need some temps down there. Who would you suggest?"

"Can't think of anyone offhand," Michelle says. "There aren't many temp agencies that specialize in retail the way we do."

"Yeah, wish there were more."

"I'd love to expand my territory, but I have my hands full as it is."

"You need more help!"

"I was hoping Fred would take some of the load," Michelle sighs.

"He's lucky to be alive," Dave says, "after the heart attack."

"Yes, and he won't be back to work anytime soon. That means I have to manage both the merchandising and product demonstration sides of the business."

"If anyone can do it, it's you." Dave closes his briefcase and gets up to leave.

Back in the Chevy, Dave heads for the P&G regional office in Plymouth Meeting. It's a tedious drive almost to Philadelphia on back roads. Once there, he goes inside to get the Giant files. Since Nick isn't available, the visit is brief, and Dave's quickly back on the road. He looks for the closest entrance to I-95 then drives south.

Traffic is heavy on the interstate and the scenery is grim. Dave compensates by playing one shit-kicking country music cassette after another. In no time, he's past Baltimore and approaching D.C. Before he gets to the hotel, Dave stops at a drugstore for a street map and some beer.

Once he's settled into his room at a Marriott Courtyard, Dave calls Giant headquarters for an appointment with Charlie Masters, the household products buyer. Charlie won't come to the phone, so Dave asks Lynn Easterling, his secretary, to arrange an appointment for later in the week. She agrees to try.

Next, Dave cracks open a beer. After a couple of gulps, he puts it down and calls Susan's number. He's relieved when she, not Phil, picks up. "Hey, this is Dave Knight."

"Well, hello," Susan says.

"I'm in D.C., so I thought I'd call."

"What are you doing here?"

"Business."

"Oh."

"I'm in town all week and it gets boring eating alone. Would you be able to get out one night?"

There's a pause on the other end, then, "I don't know about that."

"If nothing else, we could have a drink," Dave persists. He nervously swings the phone cord as it again grows quiet.

"Well, that might work," Susan finally says.

Dave goes for the close. "How about Friday?"

"It would have to be early," Susan insists, "say about this time."

"That's fine. Do you want to meet at Clyde's?"

"Heavens, no, that place is a fishbowl."

"What about the Toombs?" Dave suggests.

"That would be better."

"All right then, I'll see you there on Friday, around five."

"OK, see you then."

After hanging up, Dave heaves a sigh of relief. His palms are sweaty, and his heart is racing. He feels the same way he did when calling for a date in high school. Back then, girls usually said, "No."

Now Dave opens the street map and gets a Giant store list out. He's going to plot all the locations. Before starting this tedious task, he pops the top on another beer.

Three hours later, Dave's got all the Maryland stores pegged and decides that's enough work for the night. He goes to a nearby T.G.I. Friday's for a cheeseburger, then returns to the hotel and gets ready for bed.

It's still dark the next morning when Dave pulls into the parking lot at Landover Mall. Inside, he fortifies himself for the day at IHOP. While eating, he studies the map and plans his route. He wants to "blitz" the Giant stores, focusing totally on Bounce.

So, after breakfast, Dave drives to the nearest Giant. He introduces himself to the manager, then goes directly to the fabric softener section, where he makes notes on discrepancies between actual shelf conditions and the authorized planogram. Afterward, he finds the aisle clerk and gets approval to make needed changes. On the way out, he sees the manager again and suggests an end-aisle display on Bounce. Since it's not mandated, he gets turned down. So, Dave heads for the next store on his route.

Around midday, Dave stops for coffee at a 7-Eleven and uses the payphone to call Giant headquarters. "He'll see you Friday at two o'clock," Lynn says.

"Great, thanks for your help."

Over the next couple of days, Dave goes to more Giants. Then on Friday, he gets a late checkout and stays at the hotel all morning to prepare for his meeting with Charlie.

Giant headquarters is only a short drive from the Marriott. When Dave gets there, he checks in with the receptionist, Sandy Falcon. Her blonde hair and all-American good looks brighten the lobby, which is furnished with sofas and chairs clustered around low tables.

Some of the reps in the waiting area are singles like Dave. But there are also groups of sales executives, from the same company, who huddle nervously to review their presentations. It's busy, but Sandy keeps things moving as she phones the buying offices announcing visitors, then summons them when their time comes. "Where did you find the coffee?" Dave asks a saleswoman seated across from him.

"Just through that door there," she smiles.

"Thanks."

Dave picks up his sales bag, goes into the break room, and fills a Styrofoam cup with java. He looks at a box of donuts next to the coffee maker but thinks better of it. There's a bank of payphones lining the wall, so Dave settles into a chair and calls his voicemail. None of the messages require immediate attention.

As he sips his coffee, Dave eavesdrops on the phone calls going on around him. The salesman on his right is trying to explain a charge on his expense report to his boss. On the other side, a young lady holds a binder with the Colgate-Palmolive logo. She's calling in a lengthy order.

Dave wonders what everyday supermarket shoppers would think if they knew about all the behind-the-scenes activity involved in getting their favorite products onto the shelf. It feels great to be part of this arcane world!

Back in the lobby, Dave watches the time for his appointment come and go, but that's not unusual. He waits until Sandy finally calls his name. "This is my first time here," Dave tells her. "Where am I going?"

"Bank of elevators over there," Sandy says, pointing to an alcove. "Get off on the third floor, turn left, and it will be the fourth office on your right." Sandy smiles a genuinely friendly smile. She seems to thrive on the chaos.

It's not nearly as pleasant upstairs. As Dave enters Charlie's office, the buyer remains seated behind his desk. He eyes the salesman like a linebacker sizing up an opposing running back. "What happened to Tim Witherspoon?" he asks.

"Tim left P&G to pursue other opportunities." Dave settles into a chair.

"You mean Nick Carroll fired him," Charlie accuses.

"All I know is what they tell me."

"And I know Nick. He's a heartless bastard!"

"Regional managers are not noted for their empathy," Dave shrugs.

Charlie unwraps a cigar and lights it. "So, what do you want?" he asks, settling back in his chair.

"I surveyed half your stores this week and Bounce doesn't have enough space compared with how it's moving."

"You seem to have mistaken me for someone who gives a fuck."

"That's funny. Most of the buyers I know are evaluated based on out-of-stocks. Right now, 19% of your stores are out of Bounce 60s, our best-selling size."

Charlie leans forward. "What happened to the 24s?!" He drops the cigar into an ashtray and reaches for a computer printout. Hastily, he thumbs through it until he finds the right line. "Shit!"

"The 24s are an introductory size," Dave explains. "Shoppers buy them first, then decide they're never going back to liquid softeners. Next time they buy the value size."

"So, now you want me to reduce Cling Free's space and give it to you, right?" Charlie shoves the stogie back into his mouth.

"Not at all," Dave says. "Cling Free doesn't have enough facings, either." He hands Charlie a chart. "This is from the latest Nielsen for Baltimore-Washington. It shows that dryer sheets have taken a 38% share of the fabric softener category. The problem is that Giant is only giving them 20% of the space. You need to give more facings to the sheets and reduce the space you're giving liquids."

"Including Downy?"

Dave waves a hand to dispel the noxious cigar fumes wafting his way. "Yes, including Downy," he says. "You're not giving enough facings to Bounce or Cling Free because of all the space you're still giving liquids. That makes it impossible to keep enough dryer sheets on the shelf to prevent out-of-stocks."

"But Downy is your best seller!"

"You're over-faced on Downy and similar products," Dave insists. "That's why there are almost no out-of-stocks in your stores on any of the liquids." Dave hands Charlie another chart. "Look, you're only running 1.8% outs on Downy, and only 2.1% on Purex. But you have close to 20% out-of-stocks on both the Bounce 60s and the Cling Free 60s."

"OK, so what should I do?" Charlie looks at Dave expectantly as smoke wreaths his head.

"I've made a suggested planogram for your fabric softener section." Dave hands Charlie a schematic he created at the hotel using a kit supplied by marketing. "This gives both Bounce and Cling Free additional facings, reduces the space for all the liquids, and as you can see, eliminates the slower-selling brands."

Charlie examines the suggested planogram. "This looks all right," he finally says, "but I'll have to run it by my merchandise manager."

"I understand."

"If I get it approved, who's going to reset the shelves?"

"We might be able to handle the resets," Dave says. "I'll have to ask Nick for funding to hire temps. I'm sure he'll approve provided you give us authorization for an end-aisle display on Bounce, Tide, and Downy. We can build the displays while we're doing the resets."

"What's in it for me?"

"We contribute the labor for resetting the fabric softener section, allow you an 8 1/3% discount on the display merchandise, plus $3.00 per case advertising allowance. Here's a suggested order for the displays."

Charlie's eyes widen as he looks at the suggested order. "You've got to be joking," he frowns.

"We'll give you an extra thirty days to pay for it. The merchandise will all sell through before the invoice comes due."

"If all this shit sells through in sixty days, I'll suck your dick!"

Dave's taken aback. "It's … it's just … a suggestion," he stammers. "I'm not trying to force these numbers down your throat."

Now Charlie chokes, then falls into paroxysms of laughter. He clutches the cigar between his fingers and uses the other hand to steady himself as tears stream down his cheeks. Dave's face is bright red with embarrassment as he realizes what he said.

Eventually, Charlie regains his composure, and Dave tries to get back on track. "You won't see this much of a discount on these brands again anytime soon," he says. "What if I could get you an extra sixty days instead of thirty?"

"That sounds better," Charlie says, still chuckling. "We have our weekly merchandise meeting Monday. I'll bring this up then."

"Thanks," Dave says, rising to his feet. Charlie comes from behind the desk and offers his hand. "Tell Nick I want you to call on me from now on," the buyer says. "I need the comic relief."

Dave finds his way to the elevators, and once downstairs, checks out with Sandy before going across the street to his car. A light rain is falling, but his trench coat is a match for it. After stowing his sales bag in the trunk, Dave gets behind the wheel, starts the motor, and inserts a cassette. There's no easy way to get to Georgetown from Landover, so he'll have to rely on Jerry Garcia and associates to make it across D.C.'s blighted backside.

Rush hour is well underway when Dave gets into Georgetown. Miraculously, he finds a free parking space in front of a townhouse not far from the Toombs. Once inside the cellar restaurant, Dave is reassured to find the place completely unchanged from his first time there while in high school. The same World War I military recruiting posters adorn the walls, and the same mouth-watering smell of charcoal-broiled hamburgers wafts from the open kitchen.

As Dave waits to be seated, Susan comes up behind him. "Hey, there," she says. Dave turns to look directly into her hazel eyes. He'd forgotten how tall she is.

"Hi, Susan."

"Sorry I'm late."

"No worries, just got here myself."

The hostess beckons, so Dave takes Susan's hand and they follow. Once they're seated and have each ordered a drink, Susan looks across the table. "You truly are a naughty boy now, aren't you?"

"Guess so," Dave admits.

"How did you get my number?"

"Out of Cindy's address book."

Susan shakes her head disapprovingly. "Do you have any morals at all?"

"Well, I try to be upfront about things. With me, what you see is what you get."

"What I see looking into your eyes right now isn't good." Susan peers intently. "It's crazy in there!"

Dave shifts uneasily in his chair. "We may have overdone it a bit during the Sixties."

"Oh, really? I missed all that. Did you take LSD?"

"Sure."

"What did you get out of it?"

"I learned what's important in life."

"And what's that?"

"Sex, drugs, and rock 'n' roll."

Susan frowns. "I don't see that first bit in our future."

"Sorry to hear that." Dave reaches for his beer.

"Cindy's my friend," Susan insists.

"So?"

"Things I might do in front of her, I wouldn't be comfortable doing behind her back."

"You could have told me that over the phone," Dave complains.

Susan shrugs off her jacket. She's wearing a peasant blouse underneath. "Yes, but I wanted to see you," she says, "and tell you that I'm done with the swinging scene. Phil doesn't know it yet, but I'm divorcing him."

"What brought that on?" Dave asks.

"I'm tired of him trading me to guys at his firm and to strangers we meet in bars so he can bang their wives or girlfriends," Susan explains. "I hoped he'd grow out of it, but now he wants me to get my tubes tied. He says having kids would ruin our swinging lifestyle!" Susan's eyes well with tears. She reaches into her bag for a handkerchief.

Dave feels helpless as Susan quietly sobs. He tends to his beer and presently she calms.

"Sorry to unburden myself like this," she says, wiping her eyes.

"That's OK."

"Not what you expected, huh?"

"No, I thought we had some unfinished business."

"But now you understand I was mainly coming on to you before to please Phil." Susan delicately sips from her wine glass.

"Yeah, now I get it."

"It may take a while, but your ego will recover."

"I guess."

"You probably wouldn't perform any better with me now than last time, even if I was to go to some hotel with you."

"What do you mean?" Dave bristles.

"Oh, you're so shy it's pathetic," Susan laughs. "If I hadn't practically thrown myself at your feet, you'd never have had the nerve to lay a hand on me. Cindy told me she went to bed with you the first time you two met, but you wouldn't touch her. She finally had to seduce you herself."

"Cindy shouldn't be telling you stuff like that."

"Oh? What do you think we girls talk about, anyway? How to get our husbands' shirts 'whiter than white?'"

"Apparently not. Guess I better let marketing know."

"Phil's going to be home soon," Susan says, "I've got to go."

"I never could stand Phil," Dave confesses.

"My lawyer thinks we can take him to the cleaners because of the way he's abused me." Susan rises and takes her jacket off the back of the chair.

"You'll find the right guy after you dump Phil," Dave says. He gets up and helps Susan on with her jacket.

"I certainly hope so." Susan gives Dave a chaste peck on the cheek, then turns to go.

As Dave watches Susan's delightful derrière exit his life, the waiter comes over. "Ready for the check?" he asks.

"Not till I have one of those burgers."

"Just the sandwich, or do you want a platter?"

"Better make it the platter. Oh, and bring me another draft while you're at it."

After eating, Dave starts the long drive back to New York. Rush hour has died down, so the traffic leaving town isn't bad. Still, it's after ten by the time he gets home. There's no sign of Cindy in the apartment other than a note on the kitchen table. "Gone to the movies," it says.

When Dave awakes, Cindy is beside him. He eases out of bed, then pads to the front door to get the newspaper. An hour later, Cindy comes out of the bedroom. "Any coffee?" she asks.

"I'll get you a cup," Dave offers.

"Did you have breakfast already?"

"Yeah, some cereal."

"I need more than that," Cindy declares. "I'm going to make me an omelet."

"While you do that, I'll hop in the shower."

Cindy's at the sink, scrubbing a frying pan, when Dave reappears. "Let's go to the beach," he says.

"Are you crazy?"

"We walk in the park every weekend. I need some new scenery."

"It's too cold."

"The weather forecast calls for a high of 48 and sunny."

"What about the wind?"

"Dress accordingly."

On the way out of the city, Cindy tells Dave about the movie she saw. "It was very sad, the character played by Meryl Streep ends up killing herself."

"Aside from that, what was it about?" Dave asks.

"Streep plays a concentration camp survivor. She lives in Brooklyn with a crazy man who abuses her. Then she becomes friends with a writer, who lives in her building. But he finds out that she's lying about her past. Kind of confusing, I'd have to see it again to fully understand it."

"Maybe we can go watch it together next weekend."

"I'd like that."

Only a few cars are scattered about the Sandy Hook parking lot when Cindy and Dave get there. After bundling up, they stroll down a path to the beach, where a chill wind sends one white-capped wave after another crashing onto the shore. Foam races across the sand to where a cluster of seagulls waits. The birds appear to shiver as they fluff their feathers with short, jerky motions. "See, even the seagulls are cold," Cindy complains.

"We'll warm up once we start walking."

"I hope so."

The pair sets off toward North Beach with purposeful strides. Soon they're breathing heavily from the exertion of powering through the sand. "I wonder where the people in those other cars went," Cindy pants. She's gazing at the barren shoreline.

"Guess they're on the bayside," Dave says. He looks down as they walk, hoping to spot something in the flotsam along the high-water line. After a while, he finds a starfish.

"Is it alive?" Cindy asks.

"I have no idea, but I'll throw it back just in case." Dave hurls the creature into an advancing wave. Then they both turn and quickly resume walking. Neither wants to look back to see if the starfish went out with the tide or washed back up.

Cindy and Dave keep going for another mile or so then pause again. "We need to start back," Dave says.

"Want to return on the bayside?" Cindy asks. "It won't be as windy."

"Good idea."

On the way back, Cindy and Dave come across a couple and their two young children. The man is trying to get a kite into the air. It keeps going up then spinning around and diving. The crash landings necessitate repairs, and the children lose interest. But their dad is determined. Finally, he adds enough weight to the tail and the kite sails up and over the bay. "Look, look," the man implores. The children glance at the speck in the sky then go back to the sandcastle they're building.

"All that fresh air made me hungry," Dave says, when he and Cindy get back to the car.

"That's because all you ate before we left was cereal."

"Let's keep an eye out for a diner on the way home."

"Oh, all right. Maybe I can warm up in one."

The first shiny restaurant Cindy and Dave come to has a sign promising all-day pancakes. They look no farther and once settled into a booth, each orders a short stack. They sip hot chocolate while waiting for the food. "I think my feet are beginning to thaw," Cindy says after a while.

"Oh, come on, it wasn't that bad." Dave idly flips through the offerings on the tabletop jukebox.

"Not one of your better ideas," Cindy insists. "And you forgot all about Valentine's Day. It was yesterday."

"Sorry, but I have a hard time keeping track of these minor holidays."

"Minor?"

"That's right. Valentine's Day is just a scam. It was invented to sell flowers."

"Sydney took me to lunch and bought me a dozen roses."

"See what I mean? 'There's a sucker born every minute.'"

"You really can't help it, can you?"

"Help what?"

"Being an asshole," Cindy exclaims as she stands up. "Now let's go."

"What about our pancakes?"

"I've lost my appetite," Cindy snaps. She tosses some money on the table and stalks out. Dave sheepishly follows.

CHAPTER FOUR

Whatever It Takes

When's spring gonna get here? Dave wonders, gazing at the heaps of soot-blackened snow scattered around the Denny's parking lot. Shaking his head, Dave goes inside the restaurant and finds Paul sitting in a booth. Soon both men are hunched over cups of steaming java. "How's UpTempCo doing without you along on those A&P resets?" Paul asks.

"Just fine," Dave replies. "Bob and the other full-timers do a good job supervising the temps. They work alongside them, so the job gets done faster. By the way, Michelle said to tell you hi."

"How's Fred doing?"

"Not good. I looked in his office last time I was there, and it doesn't appear anyone's using it." Fred's office is on the opposite side of the upstairs reception area from Michelle's. It's about a quarter the size.

"Guess that last heart attack retired him."

"Looks like it."

"So, you're heading back to D.C.?"

"Yeah. I promised several Giant store managers that if they'd order extra cases of Bounce, I'd build displays for them. Also, I need to find a temp agency. I called Charlie on my way here. He said the Giant merchandising committee approved the planogram I gave them. Now I have to find someone to do the resets."

"That's great news!"

"It gets better. They're giving us end-aisle displays for Tide, Downy, and Bounce, and will order several truckloads. The products will be in Giant's ad and they'll keep the reduced price for six weeks."

"You know, it's a shame you never went to college," Paul exclaims.

"What do you mean?" Dave asks anxiously. He and Bill are the only ones in the district who don't have college degrees. They were exempted from the requirement because of their veteran's status.

"You'd be a shoo-in for the district manager slot in Washington if you had a degree."

"Oh, that's all right, Cindy and I are happy in New York."

"That's good, I'd hate to lose you. Besides, the key account manager position is going to become more important."

"How so?" Dave motions to a passing waiter for refills.

"KAMs won't be doing retail work in their chains anymore," Paul says as the waiter pours more coffee. "Instead, they'll be given more headquarter accounts. You can expect to pick up one or two more chains and a couple of wholesalers."

"That sounds good, but who's going to do retail?" Dave wonders. He blows on his coffee then tries a sip.

"What merchandising we do in chain stores will be handled by temps," Paul explains. "Cincinnati says it's cheaper than using full-timers."

"So, no more routine merchandising calls?"

"That's right. It just doesn't pay with the chains. Everything's done at headquarters now."

"Makes sense," Dave shrugs. "If I expand my shelf space in an A&P, I get in trouble for screwing up the corporate planogram. When I try for a display, the manager asks if it's been authorized by headquarters."

"Exactly."

"So, temp agencies will be doing all the resets and putting up mandated displays, huh?"

"Yep."

"That means Michelle is sitting pretty."

"I'd say." Paul looks at his watch. "Hey, I've got to go."

After the meeting, Dave gets back in the Chevy. On the way to Washington, he mulls the changes taking place in the consumer products business. Recently, several manufacturers have been swallowed up by larger firms, including P&G. Meanwhile, small supermarket chains and independents are being acquired by mega-chains. It's clear that fewer salespeople will be needed in the coming years, especially if the retail work is outsourced. As Dave nears the outskirts of Washington, a stark truth dawns on him: his job is an endangered species.

Dave checks into the same Marriott Courtyard he used during his last trip to Washington then goes to the T.G.I. Friday's where he had dinner before. He recalls that during a P&G sales training session, the instructor described the fundamental theory of marketing by comparing consumers to cattle. "If you can get them to go down a path once," the instructor said, "they'll keep taking that same path over and over again." Dave laughs as he considers how well this describes himself. *Guess I'll have breakfast at the IHOP tomorrow*, he thinks.

For some reason, the wake-up call Dave requested isn't made the following morning. However, his travel alarm comes through. So, by eight-thirty, Dave has showered, shaved, and is on the phone making appointments with temp agencies. Afterward, he stops by Landover Mall for a late breakfast, then goes to the first Giant on his list and puts up a Bounce display. It takes him the rest of the morning to pack out, price, and put up thirty cases. After lunch, he handles three more stores. By the time he's finished, rush hour is over.

The next day is more of the same until three o'clock, when Dave goes to a meeting at the Workpower office in Lanham. He identifies himself to the receptionist, and after a short wait, is shown into the office of Alan Lowery, the branch manager.

"Procter & Gamble, huh," Alan says, holding Dave's card.

"Yes, we need help with resets."

"What's a reset?"

"Don't you do retail work?"

"I'm sure we have."

"Then your temps can read a planogram?"

"Sorry, but I'm not sure what that is." Alan nervously cracks his knuckles.

"That's OK," Dave says, getting up. "Clearly merchandising is not in your wheelhouse. I need people with retail experience. That's what I told the receptionist when I made the appointment. She said, 'No problem.'"

"That's because, with a little training, our workers can do anything."

"We don't have time to train inexperienced people, but thanks anyway."

Dave fits meetings with other temp agencies into his schedule over the next few days, but none have experience with retail work. On Friday, he goes to the last Giant on his list then after several hours spent building a display, he gets on the highway back to New York. While driving, Dave has an idea and stops at a rest area to call UpTempCo. He makes an appointment with Michelle for Monday, then dials his voicemail and finds several messages. He spends another hour in the phone booth returning calls.

When Dave gets back to Manhattan, Cindy's in bed watching TV. Her replies to Dave's conversational gambits are mostly monosyllabic. When he broaches the idea of going to a showing of *Sophie's Choice* the next day, her response is, "See it yourself."

But Dave's too anxious about the Giant deal to want to do much. He spends the weekend perched in front of the TV, ostensibly watching basketball but really fretting about how to get the Giant resets done. It's a relief when Monday morning comes and he can get back to work. On his way to the parking garage, Dave stops at a deli for coffee and a bagel. Then he drives to Morristown.

"What would you think about doing a big job for me in Washington?" Dave asks Michelle as he takes a seat in front of her desk.

"How big?"

"Reset the fabric softener section and build end-aisle displays in ninety Giant stores. Each will take three people all day, so figure twenty-four billable hours per store, maybe more."

As Michelle taps her calculator, the diamonds on her plump fingers sparkle. "That would make for a nice billing," she says, "but I don't have any people there."

"You could hire some, plus send Bob and the guys."

"And have them stay in motels the whole time?"

"Here's a financial projection I worked up." Dave hands Michelle a worksheet. "It would be profitable even with the travel expense."

Michelle studies the figures then says, "I'd like to expand my territory, but after going to all the trouble to hire people in Washington, the whole thing would be a waste if I'm not going to do any more work there."

"If we pull this off, I'm certain Nick would be impressed. He'd make sure the new district manager he hires for Washington keeps using you."

"Hey, Barbara," Michelle calls, "get Brenda and Bob up here if you would."

Presently, Bob Stansfield and Brenda Wagner, Staffing Manager for UpTempCo, are standing next to Michelle's desk. "Dave has a big job for us in Washington," Michelle tells them. "It's going to require twenty-four work hours per store for ninety stores."

"I don't have anyone in Washington," Brenda points out.

"Who cares?" Bob says. "Warren, Stan, and me could do it ourselves." Warren Langford and Stan Ibrahimović are UpTempCo's other full-time field supervisors.

"It would go faster if you had some help, and faster means less travel expense," Michelle says. "Brenda, can you run some ads in Washington?"

"Sure, if that's what you want, and I can post the jobs with state employment offices."

"All right then, we'll do it," Michelle declares.

That afternoon, Dave calls the P&G shipping department in Cincinnati to make sure the promotional order for Giant has been delivered to Landover. Afterward, he calls Charlie and reminds him to push the promotional merchandise for the displays out to the stores. "I'll take care of it," Charlie says. "Now, you do your part."

"We'll have crews in the stores the week after next," Dave promises.

"I'll send a bulletin so the managers will expect you."

"Great."

Even with three reset teams working eight or more hours a day, it still takes a month to get all the Giants done. Dave shuttles between stores, pitching in to help where needed. Meanwhile, Bob, Warren, and Stan each supervise a crew. They know that making each store manager happy is the key. In the end, they succeed, and the word that filters up from the stores to Giant headquarters is all good.

Michelle is pleased as well. After the last store is done, she invites Dave to lunch. They meet at Winding Creek Country Club on a sunny, early spring afternoon. "Let's eat on the terrace," Michelle suggests. "It's too nice to sit in the stuffy dining room."

Outside, the waiter seats Michelle and Dave, then takes their order. A foursome is teeing off on the first hole, and Dave watches the golfers enviously. He's played the course a few times with Fred and knows how nice it is. Then the drinks arrive. "Cheers," Michelle says, before sipping her wine.

"I wonder what the poor people are doing right now," Dave jokes. He savors some imported brew.

"They're probably at work in the middle of the week," Michelle replies, "like me. Of course, those golfers are working, too. They do business out on the course even if it looks like they're goofing off."

"Right," Dave says dubiously. He never discusses business when playing with customers.

"You guys did great in Washington," Michelle says, "and I've picked up more work there. I wanted to have you to lunch to show my appreciation."

"Thanks. This is a step up from the places where I normally eat."

"You goin' to the salad bar?" Michelle asks, rising from her chair.

"I'll pass."

While Michelle's gone, Dave glances at customers seated at nearby tables. Most appear to be businesspeople. The rhythmic thud of tennis balls coming from somewhere nearby punctuates their conversations.

The waiter stops by and drops off a bowl of soup for Michelle, along with Dave's pasta. "Care for another?" he asks.

"Sure." Dave finishes what's left of his beverage.

"Me too," Michelle says as she squeezes back into her chair. She has a big plate of salad doused with creamy white dressing.

"Back in a flash," the waiter smiles. He takes Michelle's empty wine glass.

"This is all I'm having," Michelle brags. "Need to drop a few pounds."

"Good for you," Dave smiles.

Michelle transfixes a cherry tomato and forks it into her mouth. "The guys tell me you're a demon for work," she says between chews.

"Had to be just to keep up with them."

"Not what I heard," Michelle smiles. "Bob says you always wanted to do one more."

"No point in going back to the motel," Dave shrugs, "nothing to do there."

"And it was your idea to have applicants come directly to the stores, fill out their W-9s, and get right to work."

"It was the best way to find out if they were any good. We let the bad ones go after a couple of hours. The others worked every day for a month earning good money. Now Brenda has them in her card file."

"No reason we couldn't do that in Philly and maybe even Boston," Michelle says. "But the merchandising end is getting too big for me. I've got to stay on top of my product demonstrations business."

"How many demos do you have running each weekend?"

"Anywhere from four hundred to six hundred."

"Wow."

"Yeah, so you see how important that is to UpTempCo."

The waiter reappears and collects their empty plates. "We have tiramisu today," he announces.

"Oh, goody," Michelle exclaims.

"Just coffee for me," Dave says.

"Oh, come on, live a little."

"If I get too full, I'll fall asleep on the way back."

"Don't want that," Michelle concedes. "Anyway, what I was going to say is that while demos are UpTempCo's bread and butter, merchandising's where the growth is. So, I've decided to split that part of the business off and bring someone in to run it. That's what I want to speak with you about."

"I appreciate you thinking of me," Dave says, "but I'm fine where I am."

"What are you making with Procter?" Michelle asks.

"Close to thirty."

"We could pay forty and give you equity."

"Equity?"

"Part ownership," Michelle explains. "In return for a modest investment." She leans back in her chair as the waiter sets her dessert down.

"I don't have much money saved," Dave confesses.

"Then you can buy the stock a little at a time."

"You've given this some thought."

"Yes, and I discussed it with my lawyer and accountant. They helped me come up with this offer. If you don't take it, I'll run ads and interview people until I find the right person. But I'd rather have a known quantity like you. Who better to talk Nick into giving us Philly and Boston?"

"I'm flattered, but I have to talk this over with my wife."

"Don't you think she'd like to come here on weekends? Oh, I forgot to mention, a club membership is included in the offer."

"I would need a car. Mine is from P&G."

"I get a Cadillac from the firm and so does Fred. We'll do the same for you."

"That's generous. You've given me a lot to consider."

"Good, then I suggest you think about it over the weekend." Michelle scrapes the dessert plate with her fork then licks it. "Maybe you can let me know something Monday?"

"Sure."

During the drive back, Dave has a hard time suppressing his excitement. No matter what other thoughts come to mind, the vision of himself on the first tee at Winding Creek keeps intruding. He bursts into the apartment, wanting to tell Cindy about it, but she's in a bad mood. He decides to wait and talk to her over the weekend.

That Saturday, Cindy and Dave go for their regular walk in Central Park then stop on the way home for beer and pizza. "I'm going nowhere with P&G," Dave complains, sloshing some suds into their mugs.

"What do you mean?" Cindy asks. "They've given you several more accounts and no more retail work. For once, you're getting home at a reasonable hour."

"Yeah, but now I spend most of my time at the district office processing orders, tracking shipments, and handling ad claims. I'm not a salesman anymore, just a clerk."

"So, what else is there?"

"Michelle wants me to go to work for UpTempCo. I'd be a part-owner."

"Part-owner?"

"They'll give me a salary increase, company car, and I can buy stock in the firm."

"You'd leave P&G to work for a temp agency? You must be out of your mind!"

"Without a college degree, I've gone as far as I can with Procter."

"So, enroll at City, and go to night school. You can do it. You're not completely stupid."

Cindy is raising her voice, and an older couple at a nearby table keeps looking at them. "I haven't decided anything yet," Dave says soothingly. "It's just an idea. Let's drop it."

"Hell, yeah, drop it," Cindy exclaims. "You have a perfectly good job, don't mess with it."

On Monday, Dave calls UpTempCo from his cubicle at the district office. Michelle is tied up, so he leaves a message. A little later, she calls back and Dave tells her about Cindy's reaction. Still, Michelle won't throw in the towel. "You two need to meet up with me and Fred at the club next weekend," she says. "We can give Cindy a nice meal and answer her concerns."

"I'll see if she'll come," Dave promises.

After the call, Dave glances at the stack of advertising allowance claims in his box then takes one out. Before he can get started on it, Bill stops by. "Going to lunch?" he asks.

"Sure," Dave replies, "let's get out of here."

It's a sunny day, so Bill and Dave walk to the pub where they often eat. It's a dimly lit establishment with a pool table and several pinball machines. The two salesmen sit at the bar and each orders a draft to have while they wait for their cheeseburgers. "Guess no one will know we're drinking," Dave says.

"Not unless Paul comes in." Bill darts a glance toward the entrance then swills some brew.

"I hate the new rule against drinking at lunch."

"Yeah, what business is it of theirs?"

"Apparently, Cinci's got nothing more important to worry about."

"Guess not."

A server in a white apron comes out of the kitchen with their burgers. "Need anything else?"

"Just ketchup and mustard," Bill says.

"I've got it." The bartender reaches for the condiments.

"Hey, talk about malfeasance. Did you hear about Rick?" Bill asks.

"What about him?" Dave shakes the ketchup, but nothing comes out.

"Got caught cheating on his expenses."

"No shit."

"Yeah, now he's out of a job," Bill laughs. "Here, give me that." The ex-paratrooper delivers a series of blows to the bottom of the ketchup bottle and several dollops plop onto his French fries. "That's how you do it," he explains.

"So, who's going to handle the non-food accounts?" Dave asks. He douses his burger with the now free-flowing red stuff.

"They're dividing them among the rest of us."

"Oh no!"

"So, I guess drinking at lunch isn't the worst crime you can commit."

"Then we might as well have another."

"Why not?"

It's good that Paul is away, because Bill and Dave are over an hour late getting back to the office. Neither is in the mood to do any paperwork, so after a while, Bill leaves ostensibly to do store checks. Shortly thereafter, Dave follows suit. They reconvene a short while later at a municipal golf course.

That evening, when Dave gets home, Cindy is waiting. "When I came in, the lights were all blazing," she complains. "I guess you think we're rich."

"Sorry," Dave mumbles.

"I've told you a million times, if you're going to leave after me, you need to make sure the lights are all off."

"All right."

"And look here," Cindy continues. She goes to the coffee maker and opens the lid. "What's wrong with this picture?"

"Uh-oh," Dave replies. He takes the damp filter with the used grounds out of the machine and drops it into the trash. Then he rinses the holder and places it in the dishwasher.

"Let's face it, you're a pig," Cindy says. "I have to tell you everything."

"I'll try to do better," Dave promises.

The tenseness goes out of Cindy's body now that she's blown off steam. Hoping to continue the trend, Dave gets out a bag of dope and starts rolling. Cindy puts a record on the stereo then joins Dave on the sofa. They pass a joint back and forth. When the record runs out, Dave tries his luck. "Michelle invited us out to her country club for lunch Sunday."

Cindy frowns. "I thought we agreed you were going to forget that job."

"We did, but Michelle thinks she can convince us otherwise."

"Well, no way!"

"Oh, come on, what can it hurt to hear her out? If nothing else, we'll have a pleasant ride out to the country and a free meal."

"I'll think about it," Cindy mutters. "Now, I'm going to bed."

Curiosity gets the better of Cindy that weekend, and she agrees to meet Michelle. "All you do is talk about her," Cindy says. "Guess I need to see for myself."

So, Dave calls Michelle and it's all set. But rather than a peaceful drive out to the country on Sunday, Cindy and Dave find themselves backed up behind one traffic light after another. "What's with all these people?" Cindy complains.

"Guess they work in the city," Dave says. "Weekends are the only time they can run errands."

Finally, Cindy and Dave reach Morristown and turn onto the long, treelined driveway that leads to the Winding Creek clubhouse. "Looks like they modeled it on Tara," Cindy says, pointing at the two-story white clubhouse. Dave parks, then he and Cindy take a cart path around to the terrace. Michelle and Fred are already seated at one of the wrought-iron tables. "Don't get up," Dave exclaims as Fred struggles to rise.

Michelle's husband is a tall, distinguished-looking man, attired in a tasteful sport coat. The top of his head is bald and richly tanned. White hair grows thick on the sides. Like his wife, Fred wears too much jewelry, including several rings, a heavy gold chain, and a Rolex. Dave has known Fred for a long time and is shocked by his gaunt appearance.

After Dave makes the introductions, he and Cindy grab chairs across from their hosts. Immediately, a young waitress comes to the table. "Haven't you spent your minimum yet this month?" she asks Michelle jokingly.

"Oh, mercy, Wendy, a long time ago," Michelle laughs. "We just keep coming back for more."

"You want me to get your drinks while you look at the menu?"

"Sure, I'll have a glass of Chardonnay, whatever's open, what about you?" Michelle asks Cindy.

"That sounds fine."

"I'll just have a Perrier," Fred says, and now Dave, who was looking forward to a beer, decides to keep his friend company. "Me too," he tells Wendy.

"The special today is grilled salmon with asparagus and rice pilaf," she says. "I'll be right back."

Michelle turns to Cindy. "I'm so proud of Fred," she brags, "he ain't had a drink since the heart attack."

"That's what Dave needs," Cindy says brightly.

"A heart attack?"

"Whatever it takes."

Wendy returns with a laden tray. She places full wine glasses in front of the ladies, then gives each of the guys a glass of ice, slice of lime, and an open bottle of Perrier. While she takes the food orders, Dave fills his glass from the green bottle. He's disappointed to see that the water isn't bubbling. *It's flat*, he thinks, *must have been open for a while*.

Nevertheless, Dave drops the lime into his drink and takes a swallow. To his credit, he keeps from coughing as the straight vodka burns the back of his throat. He looks over at Fred, who's grinning at him knowingly. "Nothing like a nice cool glass of sparkling water," Fred says with a wink.

"Absolutely," Dave agrees weakly.

A trip to the salad bar is included with the meal, and now Michelle rises, beckoning Cindy to join her. "You stay there," she tells Fred, "I'll fetch your salad for you."

Once the ladies are out of earshot, Fred laughs. "You shoulda seen your face."

"What gives?"

"I have everyone here trained so when I order Perrier, what I really get is vodka," Fred explains. "The bartender dumps the water out and refills the bottle with Stoli. Michelle is none the wiser."

"Don't you think you ought to actually quit?" Dave asks. "Way I hear it, you have 'one foot in the grave and the other on a roller skate.'"

"All the more reason to drink," Fred says cheerfully.

Dave quits preaching and goes to make his salad. When he gets back to the table, he sees that Wendy has been by and the others have already started on the main course. Michelle is talking to Cindy between bites of fish. "I've been after Dave to come work for me," she says.

"That's what I hear," Cindy replies. She too ordered the special.

"He can have my job as vice president," Fred declares, "and take my office."

"That's right, Dave can have Fred's old office," Michelle echoes, "and he'll get a company car, just like P&G. We'll even pay for a membership here."

"Dave has a solid future at Procter & Gamble," Cindy replies. "They have a great retirement plan and he'll be fully vested after four more years."

"Procter is a great company," Michelle agrees, "but he ain't never gonna get rich working there. I'm an entrepreneur and we don't worry about some old retirement plan. We think about where to invest all the money we're making. Dave's a great salesman. He could do very well with me."

"Entrepreneurs often go bankrupt," Cindy argues. "We'll never go broke as long as Dave has a job at P&G."

As Cindy and Michelle battle it out, Fred and Dave polish off their meals and "Perrier." Presently, Fred's head is drooping.

"You all right, honey?" Michelle wonders.

"I'm fine, just fine," Fred mumbles. "Time for my nap."

"Anyone want dessert?" Michelle asks.

"No, thanks," Cindy hastily replies.

Michelle catches Wendy's eye, and requests a golf cart for her husband. When it arrives, driven by one of the staff, Dave helps Fred into the conveyance. Then he, Cindy, and Michelle follow the cart until they get to where Michelle's caddy is parked.

"Well, I hope you both will at least think about it," Michelle says after Fred's been buckled in. "We'd love to have you join the UpTempCo family."

"I'll call you," Dave promises.

"Thanks for lunch," Cindy says politely.

But after Michelle and Fred drive off, Cindy blows her stack. "I can't believe I let you talk me into coming here," she hisses, getting into the Chevy. "What a bitch!"

Dave settles behind the wheel and starts the motor. "It wasn't that bad," he protests as they exit the parking lot.

"What? And where were you while she's telling me what's best for my husband? I mean, some example she sets, hauling Fred out of his sickbed to try and influence you. She knows you're pals. Or drinking buddies more like it."

"Maybe Fred wanted to come to lunch."

"Bullshit! She brought him here for you. He was coached on what to say and what a pathetic pitch he made. You take his job? Vice president? From what you told me, all Fred ever did was go out and work resets with Bob and them. Oh, and of course, drink and play golf with you and the other clients. And Michelle, what a sleazebag. Wearing St. John for lunch! She's a lowlife from the backwoods trying to act like high society."

Slowly, the torrent of words tapers off and it grows quiet in the car. Cindy stares fixedly out of the window with jaw clenched and arms crossed. Once they're home, she goes about the rest of the evening as if Dave isn't there.

The start of the week finds Dave back at the P&G district office in his cubicle. Mondays never bothered him when he was out in the stores, but now, it's different. And having to call UpTempCo to turn down Michelle's offer doesn't make this Monday any better. Finally, he picks up the phone and dials. "Sorry Michelle," he says, "but Cindy wants me to stay put. You'll have to run an ad to fill the position."

After hanging up, Dave gazes morosely at his inbox. It's filled with ad claims from small supermarket chains that buy from B.F. Green, a wholesaler now on his list of accounts. Dave opens an envelope from an eleven-store chain with an invoice for $365.00 in ad money. He gets a claim form and starts filling it out.

Dave's still grinding away that afternoon when his intercom buzzes. "I need to see you," Paul says. Dave's happy to leave the paperwork and go down the hall to his boss's corner office.

"I'm assigning you another of Rick's non-food accounts," Paul says, handing Dave a thin file marked "Pyramid Vending." Inside the folder is a multi-page contract. Dave quickly thumbs through it. Most of the agreement is a list of New York and New Jersey street addresses.

"They buy miniature sizes of Tide and Downy for vending machines," Paul explains. "Those addresses are for laundromats where their machines are installed. We pay them a display allowance of $3.00 per location every month as long as they give us two slots for Tide and one for Downy in each one."

"So, what am I supposed to do?"

"The contract is past due for renewal, but their purchases have been declining for years. You need to spot-check five percent of these locations for verification."

"There must be a thousand locations!"

"Only 800," Paul says. "If all forty places you check meet the terms of the agreement, you can sign the contract and mail it to them. If not, you'll have to go to their office in the Bronx and find out what the problem is. If they've lost some locations, then you must revise the agreement and only credit them with the current number of machines."

Dave shrugs, takes the file, and goes back to his cubicle. He gets out a street map and starts plotting addresses. After a time, Dave hears the cleaning crew arrive and later, he senses the bustle as they clean around him. The workers are long gone by the time he finishes with the map. On the way home, all Dave can think about is the cold beer waiting for him in the fridge.

After dawdling over breakfast the next morning, Dave goes to the first address on his list. It's a boarded-up tenement with no sign of a laundromat. The next place is a seedy-looking bar, and that's how it goes until he gets to the tenth location and finds an actual laundry. He goes inside, and sure enough, there's a vending machine with both Tide and Downy for sale. A sticker with the Pyramid logo is on the side.

There's nowhere nearby to have lunch, so Dave keeps going until rush hour begins. At that point, he calls it quits for the day and heads home.

The following morning, Dave goes to the remainder of the Pyramid addresses he plotted. In the end, only twelve of the forty locations were bona fide. So, Dave drives to Pyramid's main office in the Bronx. It turns out to be a decrepit brick factory building in a neighborhood that looks almost as bad as some of the bombed-out cities Dave saw while growing up in Germany.

Broken glass crunches under the Chevy's tires as Dave parallel parks between two stripped cars. He goes up a well-worn flight of concrete steps to the entrance and pushes the button on an intercom. Moments later, a male voice answers, "Yeah?"

"I'm with Procter & Gamble, here about your vending contract."

"What?"

"Procter & Gamble."

"Hang on."

After a wait, the intercom crackles to life again. "Step up to the peephole."

Dave does as instructed, and presently the rusted green door opens a crack. A heavyset man with well-muscled arms, brawny shoulders, and an often-broken nose looks Dave up and down. "Where's Rick?" he asks.

"Gone."

"Oh, yeah? Well, what do you want?"

"It's about your contract."

The man steps aside. After Dave enters, he slams three deadbolts home. They proceed across a deeply grooved cement factory floor into a wide-open space. Above them, skylights that may once have allowed some illumination in are now covered with a thick layer of grime. In the gloom, vending machines are scattered about along with a variety of jukeboxes, pinball machines, and other coin-activated devices. Most are in various stages of disrepair, with their innards showing and parts lying nearby on the filthy floor. Dave follows his guide through the clutter to where a pair of double doors lead out of the work area and down a dark hallway. "The office is this way," the man explains.

The fake wood paneling in the hall is peeling and the offices on either side are empty. They pass a rusty water fountain filled with cigarette butts then come to a dusty reception area with broken fifties-style furniture. Dave's guide knocks on a door. "Come," someone says, and they enter a brightly lit, nicely furnished executive office.

The gold carpet in the office is clean and so is everything else. Sitting behind the desk is a dapper fellow with dark curly hair and an equally dark mustache. "I'm Vito Pastorino," he says, getting up, "this is Eddie." He nods to the doorman.

"I'm Dave Knight from Procter & Gamble."

"Pleased to meetcha, take a chair."

"Thanks."

"Where's Rick?" Vito asks once both men are seated.

"He no longer works for us."

"Stole too much off his expense account, huh?"

"He left the company to pursue other opportunities."

"Yeah, he left on his own, right? And monkeys might fly out of my butt!" Vito laughs. "So, what's this about our contract?"

"I'm required to spot-check five percent of your claimed locations for verification. So, over the last couple of days, I went to 40 of the addresses you gave us. Only 12 of them had your machines."

Vito looks at Eddie and says, "Go see what Candy is doing."

Eddie goes out and Vito turns back to Dave. "Care for a drink?"

"Thanks, but I'm good."

Presently, Eddie returns, followed by a statuesque blonde. She's wearing a slinky silver lame V-neck over a pair of black pedal pushers. Incongruously, a high school athletic jacket completes the ensemble. A megaphone is embroidered on the letter. "Dave, this is Candy," Vito says.

"Nice to meet you," Dave smiles. "We didn't have cheerleaders like you where I went to high school. Otherwise, I might have gone out for football."

"Candy, why don't you take my friend upstairs and show him around?" Vito suggests.

"Uh, sorry, I've got to run," Dave says hastily.

"So soon?" Vito asks.

"I'll send a new agreement giving you credit for 400 locations."

"Well, you know, my uh, supervisor, he ain't gonna like this."

"Tell him it could be worse." Dave gets to his feet. "We'll still be overpaying you."

"Good point," Vito allows. "You know, it's all chicken feed anyway."

"Exactly."

Vito glances at Candy and seems surprised she's still there. "You can scoot," he tells her.

"See you next time maybe," Candy pouts, then sashays out.

"I can't believe you drove all over five fuckin' boroughs looking for them addresses," Vito laughs. "Rick used to just drop by now and then for a date with Candy and leave it at that."

"She's a lovely girl," Dave comments.

"Yeah, not bad, but check out this baby." Vito leads Dave to a vintage Coca-Cola machine behind his desk. "I'll show you how it works," he says, and opens a desk drawer. Dave glances down and sees a clutter of loose change, pens, paper clips, and a well-oiled .38 snub nose. Vito reaches past the gun, takes a nickel, and deposits it into the vending machine. He pulls the handle, and after an enticing rumble, an 8oz Coke clatters down the chute then tentatively pokes its head out of the opening. Vito inserts it into the opener, then hands the drink to Dave. "For your ride back," he smiles.

"That's nice of you."

"Fugetaboutit."

CHAPTER FIVE
Head Over Heels

Dave's in his cubicle at the Procter & Gamble district office on a Friday afternoon when his phone rings. "Hey, boy, you need to get over here," Fred says by way of greeting. "I got something to show you."

"What's that?" Dave says quietly. He doesn't want the other salespeople to hear him on a personal call.

"Our new vice president, you got to see him hit a golf ball."

"You aren't back playing, are you?"

"Nah, I just ride around with the guys and maybe roll a few putts. But I'm doing much better. Doc says I might can swing a club before the snow flies."

"So, tell me about this VP."

"He used to be the manager at Winding Creek, name of Mike Boehner. Why don't you come play a round with us tomorrow?"

"I would, but I promised Cindy I'd go shopping."

"What about Sunday?"

"It would have to be early. I can't leave her all day."

"First tee time is seven."

"All right, I'll be there."

"See ya then, buddy boy!"

Shopping isn't high on Dave's list, but on Saturday he good-naturedly trails Cindy from store to store toting her purchases. The ordeal reminds him of childhood Sunday mornings, when sitting in church he would pray for the service to be over. This day, his prayers for the shopping to end don't come true until late afternoon.

That evening, Dave lays the groundwork for his golf outing. "Fred and I have an early tee time," he says. "I'll be back by one, and we can go for our walk then."

"Suit yourself," Cindy shrugs. "Don't rush home on account of me."

So, the next morning, before dawn, Dave slips out of bed and quietly gets into some golf togs. Soon he's heading for Morristown with little traffic to impede him. It's cold in the car, but Dave doesn't want to turn the heater on and admit summer is gone.

When he gets to Winding Creek, Dave leaves his clubs at the bag drop then goes to park. A few minutes later, Fred pulls into a handicapped spot and he and another man get out of the Cadillac. "Dave, meet Mike Boehner," Fred says

Dave shakes hands with the middle-aged, craggy-faced ex-manager of Winding Creek. With his prominent beer belly, Mike doesn't look athletic. But a little later, when they tee off, he smashes a towering drive 260 yards straight down the fairway. It's a thing of beauty, and fortunately the sun has risen far enough for them to see it.

Three hours later, after seventeen more impeccable tee shots by Mike, the three men return to the clubhouse. Fred adds up their scores, then gives a low whistle. "Only two over," he says to Mike.

"Why did you quit your job here to go with UpTempCo?" Dave asks as he's changing out of his golf shoes.

"I love Winding Creek, but the job was killing me," Mike answers. "I spent every waking hour here. Only went home to sleep."

"Yeah, when you're a manager, there's no limit on the number of hours they can work you," Fred exclaims.

"Michelle promised if I bring in some customers, she'll let me into the company as part-owner," Mike says.

"Have you ever been in sales?" Dave asks.

"No, but after working here so long, I know every rich guy in New Jersey. They're always after me to play golf, and that's where the deals are done, on the course."

"Hey, I've got to go," Dave says with a glance at his watch.

On his way back to the city, Dave replays the round in his head. He barely broke 90. *Too many 3-putts*, he thinks. *I need to practice, but when?*

It's a little after one, and the apartment is empty when Dave gets home. After changing into jeans and a sweatshirt, he lies on the sofa to watch TV. The next thing Dave knows, Cindy is rattling her key in the door. Hastily, he gets up from his nap and lets her in. "Got tired of waiting for you and went to the park by myself," she says. "It was beautiful with the leaves turning."

"The trees at Winding Creek are full of color as well."

"I stopped for pizza on the way back, so I won't need anything for supper tonight," Cindy says. "You can make something for yourself."

"No problem," Dave agrees. He switches the channel to a football game that's about to start. It's the Dallas Cowboys and Philadelphia Eagles. He's not a fan of either but watches anyway.

Once the game is over, Dave makes himself a baked bean and hotdog casserole. He takes his time eating while perusing the paper. Afterward, he goes into the bedroom. "What have you got going this week?" Cindy asks, looking up from her book.

"More non-food accounts," Dave replies. "I have Duane Reade in the morning."

"If you're going to be in town, why don't we have lunch?"

"Sure, that would be great." Dave's slightly baffled. They haven't gone to lunch in years.

"How about sushi?" Cindy asks. "We could meet at Shogun."

"Sounds good."

Midway through the next morning, Dave leaves the apartment and takes a cab to the corporate office for Duane Reade. It's a drug chain that does incredible business. The stores are concentrated in Manhattan and have big display windows to catch the attention of pedestrians. That's the key to the account—having your product displayed in the window at a discount price. They mostly feature health and beauty aids, but Dave does his best to get a Tide promotion. He strikes out.

After the sales call, Dave takes a cab to the Shogun restaurant and gets into line for a table. By the time Cindy arrives, he's seated sipping a Sapporo. When the waiter comes, Cindy gets one as well. They place an order for an assortment of the house specialty.

It doesn't take long for the sushi to arrive, and soon Cindy and Dave are wielding chopsticks. Both are hungry; nevertheless, they duly consider each selection, making sure to leave one of each thing for the other. Even so, it doesn't take long to polish off most of the morsels. "You want that?" Dave asks, indicating the last piece of sashimi.

"No, you can have it," Cindy says, then watches distastefully as Dave slathers wasabi on the delicacy. "Why do you use so much?" she asks.

"To kill the taste," Dave replies. "Otherwise, you think I'd be sitting here eating a mess of raw fish?"

"You are such a hick. Don't know how I missed that in the beginning."

"Oh, come on. I'm joking."

"And that's another part of the problem, your sick sense of humor."

"What do you mean? What problem?"

Cindy takes a deep breath then blurts out, "I don't love you anymore."

"Oh? Well, that's normal after ten years," Dave shrugs. "No one stays head over heels in love forever."

"I know that," Cindy exclaims. "Most people are content to settle into a rut like us. But I'm too young to spend the rest of my life this way. I've been thinking about it for a long time, and now I want you to move out. My parents put up the down payment for the apartment, so it's only right I should have it."

Dave is suddenly trembling. It feels like every bad emotion he's ever had is coming back and filling him with doom. He looks around at the mundane surroundings. The dirty dishes and half-full glasses on an un-bussed table. A wadded-up napkin on the floor. *This can't be happening*, he thinks.

"Would you care for anything else?" the waiter asks. Cindy shakes her head, so he scribbles on his pad then drops the check on the table.

"You can stay there the rest of the week," Dave hears Cindy say through the roaring in his ears. "Sydney gave me some time off, and Mom is coming to pick me up after work. I'll stay with her and Dad in the meantime."

"You can't just suddenly do this," Dave pleads. "It's not right. What about marriage counseling? What about some kind of warning?"

"I've been warning you for years," Cindy snaps, "and show me the marriage counselor who's going to make you stop sprinkling pee on the bathroom floor when you shake your dick off. Show me the marriage counselor who will remind you to shave and not go around looking like a bum all weekend."

As tears roll down Dave's cheeks, nearby customers look on with prurient interest, ears cocked to hear the next line in the drama. "I chose a restaurant so you couldn't make a scene," Cindy hisses. "But there you sit, making a spectacle of yourself!" She picks up the check, glances at it, and lays several bills on the table. Then she grabs her purse and hurriedly departs.

Now that it's over, Dave begins to enjoy the maudlin self-pity that washes over him. It makes him nostalgic for his childhood, and he wants to wallow in it. But Dave can't help cheering up. There's something about being at rock bottom that appeals to him. He wipes his eyes with a paper napkin, then uses it to loudly blow his nose. Other customers glare, but Dave doesn't care. The waiter is also angry. He wants the table.

Dave has been sitting so long it feels like his vertebrae have settled, one upon the other, and are now all stuck together. Creakily, he hauls himself erect and makes his way to the door. Once there, he looks back to where he and Cindy were sitting.

The table has already been bussed, and the hostess is seating another couple. It's as if the whole scene never happened.

Over the next several days, Dave alternates time in the office with apartment hunting. Finding a place in New York on his salary is a challenge. But on Thursday, he stumbles upon a studio apartment for rent on the same block as his parking garage. The last tenant vacated without giving notice, thus forfeiting the deposit. So, the landlord is happy to take a down payment from Dave and double his money. It's a small room with a nook for the kitchenette. The tiny bathroom has a shower but no tub. It'll be a tight fit, but Dave would rather live this way in Manhattan than get a bigger place in New Jersey.

That evening, Dave calls Bill for help with the move. They work in their cubicles until mid-afternoon the next day, then leave the office to pick up a rental van. It only takes them two trips to transport the furniture Dave got a long time ago from his grandfather's house. Bill helps fit the antique sofa along one wall of Dave's new place. The glass-fronted bookcase goes next to the bathroom and the marble-topped dresser on the opposite side. There's no room remaining for a bed, so they go to an Army & Navy store and buy a cot.

It's long after rush hour by the time the two salesmen turn in the truck. They return to the apartment and relax for a while, with a beer. Then Bill heads home. He leaves Dave with his books, records, some family photos, and the familiar furniture to comfort him. When bedtime rolls around, Dave gets into the army cot, and it brings back memories of his time in the service. He drifts off to sleep with visions of the treeless mountains of Korea floating in his head.

On Monday, when Dave gets to work, Paul is waiting. "Heard all about it," he says. "I wasn't sure if you would be in or not."

"There are too many fish in the sea to care if you lose one," Dave says nonchalantly. But he's not fooling anyone.

CHAPTER SIX
Residual Value

It takes a few months, but eventually Dave gets used to living alone. He often shared housekeeping duties with Cindy, so it's not hard now to do them for himself. During the winter, he spends his free time either walking around the city or relaxing in his apartment. By March, Dave's ready for golf season and begins keeping clubs in his trunk. Often, he stops at a municipal golf course after work and walks as many holes as possible before it gets too dark.

One Friday afternoon just before Easter, Fred calls Dave at the office and invites him to play Winding Creek again. "It's supposed to be nice tomorrow—sunshine and just a light breeze."

"I'm in," Dave exclaims, thinking about the rolling fairways and manicured greens at the country club. He sets two alarms that night but wakes early the following morning before either one goes off. Hastily, Dave dresses then grabs an apple for breakfast on his way out.

Fred has their cart pulled up next to the first tee when Dave gets there. "I thought you said it was going to be nice," Dave complains as clouds of condensation form around his words.

"If you think this is cold, try the Southern Tier in February," Fred smiles. "My father used to get me up at four every morning to muck out the barn. That permanently cured me of farming."

"I believe you."

Fred tees up a Titleist, takes a few practice swings, then whacks the ball. With his weak swing, it only carries a hundred yards or so. Dave's drive isn't much better, but as the round progresses, he finds his groove. Meanwhile, Fred hits a few more drives which he picks up instead of playing out the hole. Sometimes he drops a ball on the green and tries a putt.

After the round, Fred and Dave go into the clubhouse and sit at a table. When Wendy comes over, Dave asks for a draft and Fred orders his usual. "Sure you don't want to join me in a Perrier?" he grins.

"That last one almost put me on my ass," Dave laughs. "I'll stick with beer."

"You're a wuss."

"Ha-ha."

"Speaking of wussies, Mike hasn't done jack shit since he took the VP job."

"I was afraid of that," Dave says. "You hired a guy with no sales experience."

"Michelle is convinced that big contracts get signed on the golf course. She thought Mike would be closing deals right and left out there."

"He may know a lot of rich stockbrokers and car dealers, but what would they need UpTempCo for?"

"The other day, I looked in my old office and Mike was just sitting there."

Fred pauses while Wendy sets their drinks on the table. "Anything else?" she asks.

"No, thanks," Fred says. After Wendy leaves, he continues, "Mike had his feet up and was just staring at the ceiling."

Dave sips brew through the foam. "Poor guy's in over his head."

"Well, Michelle says that the offer she made you is still on the table. You'd get a big bump in pay, plus equity."

"The problem with that deal is it's only a base salary," Dave says. "Salespeople need an incentive. It's not natural to make the same pay whether you do well or not."

"What do you get at P&G?" Fred asks.

"My salary, of course, plus we set sales goals. By hitting all my targets, I can make an extra thousand per quarter."

"Suppose we give you the salary increase Michelle offered plus a $2,000 per quarter bonus?"

Dave chokes on his beer then coughs. "That's eight grand a year," he sputters.

"No shit Sherlock."

"In addition to the base?"

"Yes."

"That's crazy!"

"Michelle told me to do whatever's necessary to get you on board. I'm not one to fuck around."

"What hoops would I need to jump through to get the quarterly bonus?"

"Satisfactory performance, that's it. As long as Michelle's happy with you, the money will be there."

"That's fair," Dave says. "What about the stock?"

"You can buy 5% of the shares each year for five years. At that point, you'll own a quarter of the firm."

Dave's excited but tries to slow things down. "I'll need to see financial statements before investing anything."

Fred slides a folder across the table. "Michelle said you'd want them."

Several stapled-together papers are inside the folder. UPTEMPCO, LLC is at the top of the cover sheet in bold letters, with the accounting firm's name underneath. There's a notation that these are compiled financial statements.

First, Dave looks at the top line on the income statement and sees that UpTempCo brought in $5,150,000 the previous year. The bottom line shows earnings before interest and taxes of $276,180. "How much does Michelle want for 25% of the stock?" Dave asks.

"She said to make it an even one-hundred grand," Fred says. "You only need to put 10% down. The rest can be handled with payments withheld from your salary."

Dave does some math in his head and concludes that this would be a great bargain. He knows that companies are valued based on a multiple of earnings. Even using a conservative multiple, Michelle is way undervaluing her company. *And this is my chance to prove Cindy wrong*, he thinks.

Fred drums his fingers on the tabletop impatiently. "Well, what do you say?" he asks.

"I'm inclined to do this," Dave replies.

Fred holds his hand up and Wendy rushes over. "Now?" she asks.

"Now!" Fred replies.

Wendy disappears as Dave continues to page through the report. On the balance sheet, the figure for accounts receivable is as large as the one for revenue. Dave wonders if that's normal. "Hey, guys," Michelle says, sweeping into the room, "Wendy says you have something to tell me."

"Dave says he's in," Fred announces.

Michelle squeals then rushes around the table to hug Dave, who gets up just in time to defend himself. As he's being pressed against Michelle's ample bosom, Dave hears squeaking wheels and the rattle of ice cubes. Turning, he sees Wendy pushing a cart laden with a silver ice bucket. The neck of a Dom Pérignon bottle is poking out of it.

Soon Dave and the Mansons are toasting each other. For the occasion, Michelle turns a blind eye to Fred's enthusiastic approach to the wine. Presently, he's at the bar entertaining some friends with a joke. Meanwhile, Dave sips his bubbly and tries to determine why Dom Pérignon costs so much compared with other champagne. Another bottle is brought out and, after a while, he no longer cares.

Wine hangovers are the worst, so Dave can only limp through what's left of the weekend. On Monday, he gets to the office early and writes his resignation letter. It's waiting when Paul stops by Dave's cubicle and asks, "What's happening?"

"I'm resigning," Dave answers, and hands Paul the letter.

"Why's everybody bailing on me?" Paul asks. He looks at Dave's letter disgustedly. "You're the third KAM to quit this year."

"The job has become a massive grind—paperwork, paperwork, paperwork."

"Yeah, I get that all the time." Paul pulls up a chair and sits.

"And look at the Nielsens." Dave reaches for a binder and hands it to his boss. "My A&Ps look like shit since I stopped working the stores."

Paul flips through the pages of the Nielsen report. "It's not my doing," he says. "It's Cinci. They say it's now up to store operations to maintain planograms."

"Store operations is a joke," Dave declares.

"Well, that's too bad, 'cause we're done doing their work for them." Paul hands the binder back to Dave. "But that's enough about us, what are you going to do?"

"VP at UpTempCo."

"I'm happy for you," Paul says, "but best keep an eye on them two. Michelle and Fred got their start in multilevel marketing and have forgotten more about selling than either of us will ever know. Several years ago, Michelle went to work for a temp agency, got tight with their biggest client, then started UpTempCo, taking the client with her."

"Which client was that?" Dave asks, guessing the answer.

"Me," Paul laughs. "She used to be quite a dish."

"I may need your help with Nick," Dave says. "We want to expand into Philly and Boston the same way as Washington."

"I'll see what I can do," Paul agrees. He gets up and pushes the chair back against the wall. "Are you getting a company car?"

"Yep."

"Well, forget it then. I was going to say you could buy out the lease on yours."

"They promised me a Cadillac," Dave says. "But come to think of it, I'd rather have the Chevy than one of those boats. Let me see if they'll buy it for me."

"Tell Michelle she can have it for the residual value," Paul offers. He sticks his hand out. "Sorry to lose you."

"Yeah, it's been a slice," Dave smiles. The two men shake, then Paul goes out.

Over the next two weeks, Dave works long hours catching up on the paperwork in his tray. Bill is going to take some of his accounts and Stephanie the rest. He doesn't want to leave them holding the bag.

When his last day rolls around, Dave's inbox is empty. Paul takes him and the other sales reps out to eat. Thanks to P&G's new policy against drinking at lunch, the outing is a bore. Afterward, Dave goes home and immediately cracks open a beer to celebrate. "Onward and upward!" he toasts.

Dave's commute to Morristown goes smoothly the next morning. There are few backups since he's going out of the city while most traffic is coming in. He's happy to still be driving the Chevy complete with the aftermarket tape deck he had installed when the car was new. To celebrate, Dave cranks up an Allman Brothers cassette and rolls all the windows down to create a convertible effect.

When Dave gets to the UpTempCo office, Mindy is perched at her desk up front. It's the perfect spot for her to keep an eye on the comings and goings of the staff. As the boss's daughter, Mindy feels that's her prerogative. "So, you're one of us now," she greets Dave.

"That's right," Dave replies. "I even went out and got me an UpTempCo tattoo."

"No kidding, where?"

"Where the sun don't shine, and the moon don't glow."

"You're full of shit."

"That could be, now what's all this?" Dave indicates the stacks of paperwork on Mindy's desk.

"Store reports," Mindy says, and hands one to Dave. "Temps have to mail them in after each job." Dave glances at the form and sees that it's for a Sara Lee demo promotion. He puts it back onto the pile.

"They come to me first," Mindy continues. "I check to make sure that each was signed and stamped by a store manager. Then I add the hours to the temp's timesheet. Twice a month, I pull the sheets and do payroll."

"You said these come to you first, who gets them next?"

"Delores. Come on, I'll introduce you."

Dave follows Mindy into one of the offices along the back wall. It's occupied by a gray-haired woman with a harried expression. There's no place to sit in the office because store reports are stacked everywhere.

"Hey, Delores, how's your back?" Mindy asks.

"Oh, about the same," Delores grimaces.

"This here is Dave Knight, our new vice president."

"I heard you were coming."

"Yeah, Michelle was bragging on you all last week," Mindy tells Dave.

"She said you're gonna bring in a lot more business," Delores says.

"Looks like you've got all you can handle," Dave observes. "What do you do with these store reports?"

"I need them for invoicing," Delores explains. "Right now, I'm working on an invoice for a demo promotion we did two weeks ago. It was 680 stores sampling sausages for Hillshire Farms. I can't send the invoice until we have all the signed and stamped store reports."

"Do you send them with the invoice?" Dave asks. "I don't recall getting the individual store reports when my invoices for reset jobs came."

"No, we keep the reports on file here," Delores says. "In case the client wants to check on us. We also need them for the annual bank audit."

"And I thought there was a lot of paperwork at my last job," Dave exclaims.

"Well, your desk is clean now anyway," Mindy says. "It was delivered Friday. You should go and check it out."

Upstairs, Dave discovers he will be sharing Fred's old office with Mike Boehner. The desk Dave will use is a mahogany job with brass fittings. The shiny surface is bare except for the telephone, a set of office keys, and a box of business cards. Dave hastily opens his briefcase and gets out his appointment calendar and address book. Now the desktop looks busier.

Barbara comes in with a sack of office supplies. "Hi, Dave," she says. "Michelle needs you when you have a moment."

"Tell her I'll be right in."

Dave grabs his calendar and a legal pad then goes across the way to see his new boss. "How's everything looking?" Michelle asks.

"Just fine, I have everything I need."

"Good, well here's what we have coming up, so make sure you write these dates down. First off, Principal Bank has its golf outing on May 28 at Shady Grove Country Club. On June 10, you have an outing with the Northern New Jersey Chamber of Commerce at Little Turtle. After that, there's the United Way tournament on the 22nd at Devils Bluff." Michelle continues giving Dave golf dates until his calendar is sprinkled with them. "That's it," she finally says. "I expect you to make plenty of contacts at these events."

"I'm sure," Dave answers. "Anything else?"

"That's it for now."

An hour later, Dave is on the phone with store operations at Pathmark when Mike comes in. The former country club manager spends the morning seated at his desk, doodling on a pad. Then he gets up and stretches. "Want to go to the club for lunch?" he asks.

"No, thanks, you go ahead."

It's a relief to have the office to himself, and Dave gets back on the phone. When Mike returns three hours later, he smells like a brewery. "Went to the practice tee after eating and hit a few," he explains. Dave smiles but says nothing. His calendar for June is filling up, and he's made appointments going into July and August as well.

"I'll be in the warehouse," Mike says after a while.

The next time Dave looks up, it's after five and the office has cleared out. He stays another hour to let the rush hour traffic die down then leaves for the city. Once home, he changes into workout clothes and goes for a jog. As he dodges pedestrians on the city streets, Dave mulls over his first day at UpTempCo. He has a lot to learn about being an entrepreneur.

Mindy's at her customary spot when Dave gets to the office the following morning. "Where's Bob and the other supervisors?" he asks her.

"In the warehouse, if they haven't left," Mindy replies. "Go down the hall and through the double doors."

The warehouse is a high-ceilinged open space that takes up the back half of the building. It's decorated with promotional posters from various consumer products companies. A life-size blow-up of the Pillsbury Doughboy hangs from the ceiling next to a cut-out of Joe Camel. Pallets loaded with cardboard boxes take up the middle of the concrete floor. More boxes are stacked on metal shelves that line the walls. A workstation with a Pitney Bowes postage meter is centrally located.

"Hey, guys," Dave says as he approaches the counter.

"Oh, look who's here," Bob replies. He's putting a postage sticker on a package.

"Sure you ain't lost?" Warren asks. "Executive suite is upstairs."

"Yeah, nice of you to come down and visit us working stiffs," Stan laughs.

"I wasn't sure you guys would still be here," Dave says.

"Normally we wouldn't, but there are no merchandising jobs for us to do, so we're inside today," Bob explains. "We're helping Bryan get out some demo kits. Have you met him?"

"No."

"That's Bryan Sanders," Bob says, pointing to a man on a forklift.

"Come meet the new VP," Warren hollers.

"Hope he's a better salesman than the last VP they brought in here!" Bryan climbs off the forklift.

"Mike's a good guy," Bob says, "but he hasn't brought in any jobs."

"Spends half the day hanging out in here watching me work," Bryan complains.

"What do you do mostly?" Dave asks.

"I receive bulk shipments of demo kits from ActMedia, Sunflower, and the other national marketing companies for each event. Then we split the shipments up and send a kit to each temp assigned to the promotion. Every kit has instructions along with signs, aprons, tablecloths, cups, napkins, and so on. The demonstrators have their own card tables and cooking appliances."

"We always have plenty of demo work," Bob explains, "but hardly any merchandising jobs lately."

"Well, I'm here to fix that," Dave says, "and you can help. When you're in a store and see a company sales rep, be sure to introduce yourself."

"That's what we always do," Stan says.

"Great, then keep it up. And try to get a business card for me."

Once he's finished in the warehouse, Dave goes upstairs and finds several messages from people he phoned the previous day. At once, he begins returning calls. A little later, during a lull, Barbara transfers an inbound call.

"Hey, this is Ron Wilson from Clorox, Charlie Masters suggested I contact you."

"Hi, Ron. I spoke to Charlie earlier. He said you might call."

"Yes, well Giant approved a new planogram for the laundry aids section. They want us to hire temps to help with the resets."

"We'll be happy to help," Dave replies. He gets all the details from Ron and promises to call back with a quote. Then he goes out to where Barbara is sitting.

"Have you got a copy of a recent proposal that was sent to a client?"

"We don't do proposals. We just give them our rates," Barbara says. She hands Dave an UpTempCo rate card.

Dave goes back to his desk, gets his calculator, and works up a proposal for Clorox from scratch. Then he calls Ron back with the figures. "Let me check with my district manager," Ron says.

While he waits to hear back, Dave rummages in his P&G files and finds an old ad contract. He uses it as a template to create an agreement for the Clorox job and has it finished when Ron calls back with the go-ahead. "Great, we'll mail you a contract today," Dave tells him. He gives the draft to Barbara to type then goes downstairs to see Brenda.

"Hi, Dave," Brenda says. "How do you like it so far?"

"As long as the only paperwork I do is proposals and contracts, it'll be fine," Dave replies. "And speaking of that, we just got a reset job in Washington. I'll get you a copy of the agreement as soon as it's ready, but I wanted to give you a heads-up. Do you think we can use the same guys we hired for the Giant project last year?"

"We'll contact them and see," Brenda says, getting up from her desk. "Come on, I'll show you the call center."

Dave follows Brenda into the room next door, which is filled with cubicles occupied by temps who are working the phones. "They're staffing a round of demos that just came in from Sunflower Marketing," Brenda explains. She leads Dave to one of the stations, and they wait for the elderly lady seated there to finish a call. When she hangs up, Brenda says, "Shirley, this is Dave Knight, our new vice president."

"Hi, welcome to UpTempCo!"

"Shirley does the staffing for our merchandising jobs when we have them," Brenda explains, "otherwise she helps with demos."

"Did you staff the Giant resets last year?" Dave asks.

"Yes, I did."

"We just got another reset job for the same stores," Dave says, "this time for Clorox."

"Great, we should be able to use many of the same temps as last time."

"I'm going to run an ad this weekend just in case," Brenda promises.

"That'll help," Shirley says.

When Dave gets back upstairs, Barbara is waiting. "Where did you learn to write?" she asks.

"I know, it's pretty bad."

"That's putting it mildly," Barbara says, pointing to a word she has underlined. "Now, what's this supposed to be?"

Dave sees that Barbara has underlined quite a bit of the proposal. He sits with her and together they decipher his writing. "I'm sure I'll get the hang of it after a while," Barbara says doubtfully.

Late that afternoon, Dave's at his desk, now littered with store lists, yellow sticky notes, business cards, and open files. He hears Michelle out in the hall whooping. Then she comes in waving the Clorox contract. "This is your first UpTempCo deal," she exclaims, "we got to celebrate."

Mike jumps up from his desk and comes around to shake Dave's hand. "Great job," he says, then turns to Michelle. "You should see this man work. I'm learning a lot just by watching him."

"Let's all go out for a drink," Michelle suggests, "I'm buying!"

"You guys go on without me," Dave says, "I have to write up a proposal for Benckiser."

"Oh, come on," Michelle pouts.

"Sorry," Dave says, "If I don't do it now, it'll take up half the morning tomorrow."

Dave's in the office until almost nine. Then he goes out to the Chevy and gets a gym bag from the trunk. After changing into running togs, he stretches, does some calisthenics, then jogs laps around the now-deserted office complex. The cool air is refreshing, and as he runs, Dave feels the tenseness go out of him. On the way home, he pops in an old Simon & Garfunkel tape. It's still one of his favorites.

By Friday, Dave has secured commitments for three more reset projects. One is for P&G, and Michelle is elated. "We're going to the club," she says at the end of the day.

"Me too," Dave replies. "I need to play some and get ready for the outing next week."

"Come have a drink with us when you're finished."

"OK, thanks."

The first tee at Winding Creek is free when Dave gets there. "Take any cart you want," Lane Ely, the club pro, tells him.

"I'm just going to take a few clubs and walk."

"Suit yourself," Lane shrugs.

It's almost dark by the time Dave finishes nine holes. After changing out of his golf shoes, he goes inside to the bar room. "Hey, boy, get over here," Fred calls. He and Michelle are at a long table crowded with UpTempCo employees. Dave pulls up a chair, and when the waiter comes, orders a beer. "He means Perrier," Fred says, holding up his bottle.

"No Perrier," Dave insists, "a cold draft will do just fine."

While he waits for his beverage, Dave darts glances at those seated around the table. They've all had a few drinks judging by the animation. Everyone seems to be talking at once, but Michelle's voice is the loudest. From time to time, she punctuates her comments with a braying laugh.

The waiter slides a foaming mug in front of Dave, who drinks thirstily. Barbara is seated next to him, steadily working on a glass of wine. "Meet my husband, Albert," she says.

"Hello, Albert," Dave smiles.

"Dave's the hotshot salesman Michelle hired," Barbara explains. "He's a go-getter."

"So, you're the guy who's working my wife half to death nowadays," Albert scowls.

"Oh, it's OK, honey," Barbara says hastily, "makes the day go by faster."

Brenda is seated down the table a way, and now she introduces Dave to her husband, Robert. "I used to work at UpTempCo with Fred," Robert says. "We went out on resets together. Finally, I had to quit and get a real job. Just wasn't making enough money."

"What are you doing now?" Dave asks.

"Selling water filters. I signed up a new distributor today in Trenton."

"Congratulations."

At the far end of the table, Mindy is sitting with a guy Dave assumes to be her husband. They're talking with Bob and the woman he's with. Then the waiter comes, and everyone orders another drink except Dave. He begs off, pleading the long drive back to Manhattan.

Soon Dave's in the Chevy, putting distance between himself and the depressing party at the club. *Hope she doesn't charge the tab to the firm*, he thinks.

The idea of driving to Morristown doesn't appeal to Dave the following morning, so he spends a pleasant day in the city. But on Sunday afternoon, Dave arouses from his lethargy, goes to the office, and tackles the disorder on his desk. Afterward, he walks the back nine at Winding Creek. The dining room is closed by the time he putts out at 18, so Dave grabs something to eat at a diner on the way home.

First thing on Monday, Dave fires up the Chevy and drives down to the P&G regional office near Philadelphia. On the way, he passes a hellish series of refineries and chemical plants. Even with the windows rolled up, the stench is overpowering. *Why do people live here?* he wonders for the eightieth time.

The scenery improves once Dave exists the interstate. Soon, he's passing through an area where tidy Pennsylvania Dutch farms are giving way to suburban sprawl. Another hour of driving brings him to a nicely landscaped office park. Dave finds a space for the Chevy in front of P&G's building and goes inside.

Nick greets Dave warmly when he gets upstairs. During a friendly meeting, the regional manager agrees to recommend UpTempCo to his district managers in Washington, Boston, and Philadelphia. Afterward, they go out to lunch at a place in Plymouth Meeting. It's a sober affair, in keeping with P&G policy, so they don't dwell over lunch. By mid-afternoon, Dave is on his way back north. The traffic is heavy but that doesn't keep some drivers from weaving in and out looking for an advantage. Dave goes straight home and is happy to make it there in one piece. He foregoes his customary exercise routine and heads straight for the refrigerator.

But the trip to Plymouth Meeting turns out to be well worth it. The next day, Dave gets a call from a P&G key account manager in Philadelphia requesting a quote for a reset project in Acme Supermarkets. Acme operates 280 stores in the Mid-Atlantic, and a lot of hours are going to be required. After working up the proposal, Dave is happy to see that it totals a whopping $56,000. It's accepted the following morning.

Dave has no more meetings scheduled until the end of the week, so he decides to get on the phone and see how things are going with the Clorox job. Over the next couple of days, he calls Giant stores on the laundry aids reset schedule. Happily, an UpTempCo merchandiser is there to represent Clorox at every store he checks.

On Friday afternoon, Dave gets ready for his last appointment of the week. Once his briefcase is packed, he goes downstairs. Brenda is there talking with Mindy. "Great job in Washington," Dave says.

"Thanks," Brenda smiles. "Now get us more work there."

"Will do."

Dave has the door open to go out when Mindy speaks up, "And where might you be going on a sunny Friday afternoon?"

"Don't fuckin' worry about it," Dave replies with a grin.

Mindy's expression freezes for a moment, then she nervously smiles. "Ah, well, OK then, see you next week."

The lobby at A&P headquarters is practically deserted when Dave gets there. Most salespeople are spending Friday afternoon either catching up on paperwork or chasing that little white ball. So, it's not long before he's called in for his meeting with the VP of merchandising. "My problem is getting manufacturers to do their part on resets and store remodels," Ed McDowell complains. "They promise to have someone there, then nobody shows."

"Yeah, I've been on a lot of resets where that happened," Dave replies.

"It's getting worse because so many companies have cut their sales force," Ed says. "My idea is to tell vendors they must be represented, or we'll have UpTempCo send a merchandiser at their expense. When you bill us for the hours, we'll deduct that amount from the next invoice we receive from that supplier then use the accrued funds to pay you."

"Sounds like a plan," Dave replies. "I'll write up an open-ended agreement guaranteeing our rates for the year."

After the meeting, Dave thinks about going straight home but decides to return to the office and write the A&P contract instead. When he gets back to Morristown, it's after five, but cars are still parked in front of the UpTempCo office.

Dave lets himself in and starts to go upstairs, but he hears chatter coming from down the hall and decides to investigate. The noise is coming from the conference room, so he goes inside and finds Michelle, Brenda, Mindy, Barbara, Delores, and several staffing managers seated around the conference table. They're filling out store report forms. A basket full of assorted pens and pencils is in the middle of the table. Stacks of blank forms are positioned at strategic spots. Ink pads and a variety of store stamps are scattered about.

"Hello, ladies," Dave says, "working late, I see." He goes to the table and picks up a form that Delores has just completed.

"Thought you'd be over at the practice tee," Michelle exclaims. "Don't you guys have the United Way outing tomorrow?"

"I need to write a contract," Dave says, examining the form. It's a store report for a Keebler demo. Delores has put in a date, the name of the event, beginning inventory of cookies, ending inventory, number of packages sold, number of packages used as samples, and number of coupons given out. At the bottom, Delores scrawled a name for the store manager and used one of the store stamps.

Someone is knocking on the office door, and when Dave goes to open it, he finds a pizza delivery man holding a stack of boxes. Michelle comes up behind him. "How much?" she asks.

"Total is $67.50."

Michelle pulls a roll of hundreds out of her bag and peels one off. "Keep it," she says.

"Great, thanks!" the driver smiles.

Dave carries the stack of boxes into the conference room. "Break time, pizza's here," Michelle announces.

As the ladies help themselves, Dave approaches Michelle with the forged demo report. "What gives?" he asks.

"The temps we use for demos are often too stupid to complete a simple form and mail it back," Michelle explains. "And we can't invoice the job until we get them. So rather than calling each demonstrator repeatedly, we sometimes do the forms ourselves."

"Can't you just refuse to pay them?"

"If we do that, they'll quit, and you know it ain't easy to find people to work for minimum wage."

"Got it," Dave says. He grabs a slice of pizza and a Coke then goes upstairs to work on the A&P agreement. When he leaves two hours later, the paperwork party in the conference room is still going strong.

CHAPTER SEVEN
Closest to the Pin

There's more than a hint of fall in the air on a Friday evening as Dave drives the short distance from work to Winding Creek. The men's locker room is full when he gets there, and the auction for the club's annual Calcutta golf tournament is about to begin. Michelle signed Dave, Fred, and Mike up and paid the hefty $500 entry fee for each. She still believes that golf is the key to business. Dave has not tried to dissuade her.

Most of the golfers in the clubhouse are guzzling beer, so Dave grabs a cold one from one of the coolers and finds a chair. A few minutes later, Lane Ely begins putting teams together by randomly drawing names of golfers out of fishbowls. He has four of them labeled A, B, C, and D.

Over the next couple of hours, Lane assembles teams and auctions them off to gamblers who will win big if a team they buy finishes in the top five of the tournament.

Each team is comprised of a scratch golfer (A), a low handicapper (B), medium handicapper (C), and a duffer (D). Dave ends up as the D golfer for team 16 and is joined by Dennis Crawley as the C player, Frank Brantley as the B, and Matt Philbeck as the A. They gather at the front of the room to be sold, and Lane starts the bidding.

There isn't much interest from the gamblers in team 16, since Matt and Dennis aren't members and no one knows them. As for Frank and Dave, both are new to the club, and their playing ability is also unproven. Finally, a gambler makes the minimum bid of $600. When no other hands are raised, team 16 gathers to confer. "We can't let that guy buy us for only $600," Dennis exclaims.

"I'll go as high as $800 and no more," Matt says. So, Dennis raises his hand to bid, and that does it. Each member of team 16 will have to kick in $200, but now they own themselves. That means if they win any prize money the next day, they'll get to keep it.

After the auction, a boombox is cranked up, and raunchy rhythm and blues music fills the locker room. Two girls, brought in for the occasion, prance around in bikinis, and the atmosphere degenerates. The guys are tired, drunk, and some are riddled with anxiety over the amount of money they wagered. One of them yells, "Hey, take off your top for Chrissake." Other voices join in as Dave heads for the exit.

There are still a few openings at the practice tee when Dave gets to Winding Creek in the morning. He claims one and gets a pitching wedge out of his bag. After hitting several shots with every club in his set, he gives up his spot and goes to find the other members team 16.

As the start time approaches, the golfers gather around Lane to hear the tournament rules. It's four-player best ball full handicap, meaning that for each hole, the best score achieved by any of the four team members is what counts, subtracting any strokes that player is given for his handicap. Lane finishes the briefing by emphasizing the basic requirements of good sportsmanship. Then the teams go to their holes for the shotgun start.

While waiting to tee off, Dave sizes up the other players. Dennis is a big guy who tries to act confident but talks too much. Frank, on the other hand, is a diminutive, darkly handsome man with the calm demeanor of a surgeon. Both are attired in sharp country club golf outfits, unlike Matt. The A golfer's no-name golf shirt is frayed at the collar, his khaki slacks have a torn pocket, and his golf shoes look like they've been up and down the Appalachian Trail. With his longish sun-bleached blond hair, crinkly blue eyes, and attractive but careworn features, he looks like a forty-year-old boy.

Hole 16 is a par 4 dogleg right. When the clubhouse horn sounds to signal the start, Dave, as the D golfer, goes first. The others hope he will put one out there and take some pressure off. In this, Dave fails miserably, hitting a worm-burner a scant 100 yards up the fairway. "You moved your back foot," Dennis complains, then similarly disappoints the team when after a promising start, his ball makes a sharp right turn into the woods.

Matt looks down at the ground a moment as if hoping to find a rusty razor blade lying there. But he cheers up moments later when after a couple of impressive-looking practice swings, Frank smacks a three-wood straight out to a landing area that will give him a good look at the green. This means Matt is free to try and cut the corner, which he does in a workmanlike manner, blasting a towering drive 280 yards over the trees.

For his next shot, Dave tries to hit over the trees like Matt. Although he makes good contact, the ball hits the outstretched arms of a large oak. "Might as well pick up," Frank advises.

Dennis has been wandering in the woods but is unable to find his drive. That means Frank is away. After studying the yardage, he hits a nice five-iron to the front of the green. The shot turns out to be unnecessary, however, because Matt's ball ended up on the apron. He makes birdie after a tidy up and down.

Soon the euphoria of the opening birdie wears off as the team can do no better than par the next few holes. Then Frank, who has shown himself to be a true low handicapper, birdies 4 to put the team 2-under.

Dave has yet to hit a decent drive. After another poor effort on 5, Dennis growls, "I'm gonna step on that back foot of yours if I have to, so you quit moving it." Again, the team makes a disappointing par and appears to be back in a rut.

Hole 6 is a long par 5 with two water hazards. The first is a pond in the middle of the fairway about 160 yards out. The second is the course's namesake waterway that flows in front of the green. The key is to clear the pond with the first shot, then either go for the green or lay up in front of the creek. But Dave hacks a low bouncing drive that doesn't even make it to the pond. It takes him two more shots to get within a 6-iron of the pin. When that shot lands on the back of the green, he's looking at a putt of over 50 feet just for par.

By now, Dennis is out of the hole, but Matt and Frank are both on the green in regulation. Neither has a realistic birdie putt, so there's an outside possibility Dave's score might be needed. His putt is downhill all the way and once Dave gets it rolling, the ball—seemingly on rails—goes straight into the hole. It's his fifth stroke, but with handicap this is a birdie. The team is now 3-under.

A dispiriting string of pars follows, but Matt finally manages another birdie on 13. This breathes new life into the team as they come to Winding Creek's signature hole. It's a 130-yard par 3 with an island green accessed by a bridge. Matt leads the way with a towering shot that looks good but takes a bad hop and goes off the side into the drink. Dave's up next and launches an eight-iron directly at the pin. "Be the right club," Matt prays, and it is. The ball drops in front of the hole then settles inches away.

After the foursome crosses the bridge, Matt watches over Dave like a mother hen as he taps in. Including handicap, Dave's score goes onto the card as an ace. Even better, 14 is the closest-to-the-pin hole. Dave now has a lock on that lucrative prize.

As if inspired, Matt hits a powerful drive deep into the recommended landing area on their last hole then stakes a sand wedge to give himself a makeable birdie putt. The team ends the day a respectable 7-under. Everyone has contributed except Dennis. As they walk off the 15th green, Matt wears the bemused expression of a man who has survived a bad car wreck with nary a scratch.

Back at the clubhouse, Matt gives his team's scorecard to Lane then wearily pulls a cold one out of an ice chest. It's a tense wait until the last group comes in, and the results are posted. The best score is 12-under and that foursome receives a bundle of cash. It turns out 7-under is good for fifth place, so team 16 wins back their entry fees plus the bet they made on themselves.

Matt collects the winnings amid all the whooping and hollering from excited gamblers. He gives each team member his share, then counts six crisp Benjamins into Dave's hand. "Closest to the pin," Matt smiles. Then the A player is gone.

The Calcutta is the last outing of the golf season. Soon the Winding Creek course closes for the winter. With his bank account bulging, Dave decides to take up skiing and splurges on some clothing and equipment. Over the holidays, he heads to Vermont and hits the bunny slope.

When Dave arrives back at the UpTempCo office after New Year's, Mindy's not at her desk to greet him. A babble of excited voices is coming from the conference room, so Dave goes inside. He finds a crowd of employees sorting piles of cash. Several bags full of the green stuff are scattered around the table. "Look at all the money I won in Las Vegas," Michelle crows when she spots Dave standing in the doorway.

"That's amazing," Dave says, "you beat the odds."

"She has a foolproof method for winning jackpots," Barbara exclaims.

"Yeah, I only play at the Stardust," Michelle says, "in the VIP room. I tip the hostesses, and they tell me which slot machines are due to pay off."

Mindy and Delores are counting out bills and putting paper wrappers around each stack. "We have to get all this ready for the bank," Mindy says.

"So, what did you do for the holidays," Michelle asks Dave.

"Went skiing over Christmas then met up with some P&G buddies on New Year's. I was at home in bed by midnight, though."

"Not us," Barbara pipes up. "I went to the VIP slot room with Michelle. They gave us all the champagne we wanted. Good stuff, too."

"Not bad," Michelle sniffs. "But it wasn't Dom Pérignon."

"I ain't complaining," Barbara declares. "The entire trip didn't cost Albert or me a dime."

"The Stardust comped everything," Michelle explains, "even paid our airfare."

"Sounds like you've been there before," Dave says.

"That's right," Fred agrees, "they know us by now and always roll out the red carpet when we come for a stay."

"I watched her play for several hours on New Year's but didn't see her win any," Barbara says, reaching into a bag for more currency. "Then the champagne made me tired, so I went to bed."

"Should have stuck around. I hit the jackpot right after you left," Michelle boasts.

"Well, congratulations," Dave says. Then he goes upstairs to his office. On the way, he tries to dispel the notion that something is amiss. *Slot machines are programmed to take money, not give it*, he thinks.

That afternoon, Dave's at his desk, writing a contract for a new client, when Michelle comes in. "P&G still ain't paid the invoice for the Acme job," she complains. "It's $56,000."

"Is it already due?" Dave asks.

Michelle shows Dave the invoice. "It was due December 18."

"That's only ten days from date of issuance. Nobody pays that fast."

"Well, we need the money," Michelle insists. "So, here's what I'll do. If that check is here by the fifteenth, you get a hundred dollars."

As Michelle goes out, Dave reaches for the phone. He calls Cincinnati and after some small talk, a friend in P&G's accounts payable department agrees to move the UpTempCo invoice to the top of her pile. This is not the first time Michelle has asked Dave to do collections and he doesn't mind. It's a quick way to earn a C-note.

The next morning, when Dave gets to the office, Mindy beckons him to her desk. "The bank's here," she says quietly.

"Oh?"

"They come once a year for an audit."

"What for?"

"It has something to do with accounts receivable. Michelle is in the conference room with them now. She asked me to send you back."

The scene in the conference room is a lot different from yesterday. There are no bags of cash on the table, just ledger books, binders, and stacks of store reports. Two nerdy-looking young men wearing three-piece suits are going over the paperwork with Delores. "Where are the invoices for January?" one of them asks.

"Right here," Delores says, reaching for a binder.

"And I need to see the store reports for each job."

"No problem," Delores says. "We have them in chronological order."

"Wonderful, wish all our clients were this organized."

Michelle is in a corner talking with a tall, darkly handsome man in a black pinstriped suit. The UpTempCo owner catches Dave's eye and beckons him over. "This is Rich Little, our loan officer from Garden State National Bank," she says. "Rich, this is Dave Knight, Executive Vice President."

"I think I saw you at Winding Creek last fall," Rich says, "at the Calcutta."

"Oh, that's why you look familiar. Didn't your team come in second?"

"We got lucky," Rich says modestly. "It was a fun day. Winding Creek's a nice track."

"Why don't you two play there some time," Michelle suggests. "Dave's a member. He can host you."

"That would be great!"

"I'll call you," Dave promises, "as soon as the snow melts."

"Dave used to work for Procter & Gamble," Michelle brags.

"So, what do you think of the entrepreneurial world?" Rich asks.

"Wild and woolly doesn't begin to describe it," Dave laughs. "And that reminds me, I've got to go."

"Where to?"

"Boston, we're doing a project for my former employer in all the Stop & Shop stores."

"I didn't know you were covering New England."

"There's always a first time," Dave says. "Brenda's been running ads there, so we have a number of temps lined up to help. Me, Mike, Bob, Warren, and Stan are each going to get a crew together then work the stores."

"Better you than me," Rich laughs.

It's the middle of the month by the time Dave is finished with Stop & Shop. He's back in the office, sorting through a stack of phone messages, when Michelle comes in. She peels a $100 bill off her roll and casually tosses it onto his desk. "I don't know how you do it," she says. "P&G's check came in yesterday."

After his boss leaves, Dave glances around with a feeling that something isn't right. Then he realizes Mike's desk is gone. The former country club manager is now supervising reset crews full time.

Dave picks up one of the messages and calls James Mallard, who operates a national merchandising company called Retail Action. They get projects from small consumer product companies then farm the work out to agencies like UpTempCo. "Michelle tells me I have to talk to you now," James says when Dave gets him on the phone.

"Yes, she and I have divided up the work," Dave replies. "I run the merchandising side, and she does the demos."

"What would it cost to cut in three new products at A&P for Luzianne? They're coming with a line of teabags."

"How many stores?"

"A total of 135, and it will take two hours each."

"At least," Dave exclaims. "We'll have to reset the tea section."

"It's only 8 linear feet," James says. "I did a test store. Got it done in two hours easy."

"What about drive time?"

"I can't get money from Luzianne for that."

"OK, I'll call you back."

An hour later, Dave calls and gives James a quote. "You've got to be joking," James says and slams down the phone.

A few minutes later, Michelle comes in. "What did you say to make James so mad?"

"I gave him a proposal based on the hourly rate that P&G and my other clients pay."

"That's about 50% more than he normally pays," Michelle laughs. "I always cut the national companies a deal because they have to make money, too. You know James is just the middleman. He can't price jobs through the roof to his clients."

"If we cut the rate in half, it's a loss out the door."

"Yes, but it will give our temps something to do between jobs," Michelle says, "and I want the bank to see we're busy."

"All right, I'll rework the figures and call him back."

"Oh, that reminds me," Michelle says. "I have a meeting with Garden State on Monday, and I want you to come."

"Why?"

"We passed the audit, so now is a good time to ask the bank to increase our credit line. You can help by telling them about all the new business you're bringing in."

"Whatever you say."

CHAPTER EIGHT
Capital Infusion

Dave is idling away Sunday afternoon in his apartment when the phone rings. He picks up and hears the Texas drawl of his father's second wife. "Hi, Mildred," he says, "it's nice to hear from you."

"I just realized that we haven't spoken since Christmas," Mildred replies.

"Yep, it's been a while."

"Cindy called us over Christmas as well."

"That's nice."

"You two should get back together."

"Not much chance of that."

"Sorry to hear it," Mildred says. "But that's not why I called. It's your father."

"What about him?"

"His drinking," Mildred explains. "Two weeks ago, he was on the sofa in the living room at two o'clock in the afternoon and just fell over, out cold. This morning, I found him in the pantry chugging vodka straight out of the bottle."

"OK, I'll call him."

"Don't tell him I put you up to it."

"No worries, Mildred."

A little later, Dave calls back. "Why, hello, Dave," Mildred loudly answers. "What a nice surprise to hear from you." Then she cuts the act and gets the colonel.

"Hi, son," he rasps, "how are things at Procter & Gamble?"

"I'm not there anymore. I told you." Anticipating a long call, Dave gets up and paces to the limit of the extension cord.

"Oh, you got fired, right?" Knight chuckles.

"No, I quit."

"Whatever for?"

"Another job."

"That was stupid!"

"Could be," Dave says, "time will tell. Now, what are you up to?"

"Nothing much."

"Do you remember us talking about AA?"

"For you?"

"No, for you!"

"Ha-ha."

Dave goes to the coffee pot for a warm-up. "If you keep drinking, you're gonna blow everything," he says.

"Did Mildred call you again?" Knight asks.

"No," Dave lies. He settles back on the sofa with his coffee. "I'm just checking to see if you went to a meeting as you promised."

"Yeah, I went, and I've never seen such a bunch of losers."

"Then quit cold turkey."

"Why?" the colonel asks. "What's wrong with a little drink now and then? Everyone drinks."

"Not everyone guzzles straight vodka for breakfast," Dave retorts.

"So, Mildred did call you!"

"She's worried she married an alcoholic."

"Well, I'm not an alcoholic," Knight declares. "I'm the happiest guy in the world."

"Maybe the reason you're happy is that you're drunk all the time," Dave snaps.

There's a clattering sound as Knight angrily seeks to replace the phone in its cradle, then a click and silence. Dave doesn't try to call back.

When his alarm goes off the next morning, Dave leaps out of bed, glad that the tedious weekend is over. Impatiently, he gets ready for work, and soon he's on the way to Morristown.

No sooner does Dave get settled behind his desk then Michelle comes in. "We need more demo business," she says. "I heard Grand Union plans to grant an exclusive. Can you try to make a deal with them?"

"Sure."

It takes several calls to find out who's in charge of demos at Grand Union, but Dave eventually discovers that Grant Becker, Vice President of Store Operations, is the man to see. Dave talks to Grant's secretary and makes an appointment.

After he hangs up, Dave goes downstairs to meet with Brenda about A&P. She's become the point person for the account and is doing a great job getting their resets staffed. "I just saw the report for last month," Dave tells her. "We reduced no-shows by almost 20%."

"That's because I'm double-staffing problem stores," Brenda says.

"Great idea!"

Dave turns to see Michelle coming down the stairs carrying her purse. "Let's go," she says. "We'll need half an hour to get to the bank."

"Oh, that's right," Dave exclaims. "Hang on a minute." He races up the stairs, grabs his suit jacket and a notepad, then runs back down.

Michelle insists on driving, so Dave looks out the window and relaxes on the way to Newark. When they get there, Michelle leaves her car with an attendant and they enter the skyscraper that Garden State calls home.

After a lengthy elevator ride, punctuated with numerous stops, Michelle and Dave reach the top floor and are ushered into a luxuriously appointed conference room. A rotund, balding gentleman is seated at the table but gets up when Michelle walks in. He good-naturedly succumbs to her overly affectionate greeting. "This is Don Howell," Michelle says when she's done hugging, "my accountant."

"Pleased to meet you, I'm Dave Knight."

Soon the three of them are joined by the auditors who visited UpTempCo the first week of January. A few minutes later, Rich Little comes in. With deft footwork, the handsome loan officer avoids a clinch with his client. "You look like you've been in the sun," Michelle says once they're all seated around the table.

"Just got back from a weekend modeling assignment in Nevis," Rich says. He goes on to describe the little-known island and his photoshoot. Dave can't help but wonder what the guy's doing working at a bank.

The small talk is harshly interrupted when the door bangs open, and a trio of impeccably attired gentlemen strides into the room. "I'm Wolfgang Lander," the leader of the group announces with a German accent, "Senior Vice President for Credit." He hustles over and shakes hands with Michelle, Dave, and Donald, then curtly introduces his colleagues as David Clayton and Collin Bessie.

David is a white-haired elderly man with piercing blue eyes lighting up an otherwise gray face. Collin has the no-nonsense look of a high school assistant principal. His dark hair is combed straight back, and though he's middle-aged, Collin looks like he could drop down and knock out fifty push-ups with no trouble. He glares at the visitors as if he suspects them of stealing. Then Collin glances around the conference room to make sure all the lamps and ashtrays are still there.

After the introductions are complete, Wolfgang strides to the head of the table and sits without unbuttoning his suit jacket. He rests his forearms on the table and shoots out French cuffs to reveal clunky gold links embossed with his initials. "I understand that you've tapped out your credit line and want us to bump it up again," he says to Michelle.

"I thought this would be a good time to ask for an increase," Michelle replies. "We just had an audit and came through with flying colors."

"That audit had nothing to do with the creditworthiness of your firm or the veracity of your financial statements," Wolfgang says. "We have a lien on your receivables, and the audit was simply to make sure your internal paperwork fits together and that the invoices you issued last year were legitimate."

"I think the statements for last year look quite good," Donald ventures.

"Yes, and the Hindenburg looked good just before it got to Lakehurst in 1937," Wolfgang replies. "Meaning that when I look at these reports, I see a bad accident waiting to happen."

"What ... what do you mean?" Michelle stammers.

"Your accounts receivable is out of control," Wolfgang declares. "You have no cash on hand and no liquid assets. In short, you are insolvent."

"I won't be talked to this way," Michelle retorts. "If you're not careful, I'll take my business elsewhere."

"Don't be ridiculous," Wolfgang says. "No other bank would have you."

Now Michelle starts bawling, and it's not a pretty sight. The men shift uneasily in their seats except for Wolfgang, who remains impassive. He appears to have seen this movie before. Impatiently, he waits for Michelle to recover, but she just meekly sobs. Don looks at his watch. He'd like to be someplace else right now.

Finally, Wolfgang walks around the table, taking a blindingly white handkerchief out of his suit pocket. He hands it to Michelle, then looks on disgustedly while she wipes her eyes then blows her nose with a honking sound. Michelle folds the handkerchief into a square and offers it back to the banker. Wolfgang backs away, raising both hands. "Please keep it," he begs.

"I am not insolvent," Michelle whimpers. "You cannot say that I'm insolvent."

"Madam, there is no doubt about it," Wolfgang insists.

Michelle buries her face in trembling hands. "How can we do business like this?" Wolfgang exclaims. He looks to his colleagues for suggestions, but they seem equally discomfited.

"We'll have a ten-minute break," the VP for Credit announces. "Afterward, we must return and see what can be done."

Wolfgang and his sidekicks depart. A few minutes later, Michelle goes to find a restroom.

"That was a shock," Dave says once he and Don are alone.

"And how," Don agrees. "I updated the financials for December but haven't seen the January bank statement yet. Apparently, she used up the cash reserve and exhausted the credit line in the meantime."

"Ugh," Dave comments.

Neither man has anything to add. After a few moments of silence, Dave takes a quarter out of his pocket, tees it up on the table, and flicks it to start the coin spinning.

"Haven't seen anyone do that since high school," Don says.

"Kind of thing we used to do in detention."

"Oh, really?"

"Didn't you ever have to go?" The quarter wobbles, so Dave gets it going again.

"No, I was a little goody two shoes," Don sighs.

"Detention was a hoot."

"I believe you."

Michelle comes back in with her eyes freshly made up. "You need to say something," she tells Dave.

"All right." Dave slips the quarter back into his pocket.

The door slams open again, and Wolfgang enters with his cohort. "Your mistake was bringing this to my attention," he tells Michelle upon regaining his chair.

"I certainly didn't mean to do that," Michelle says with a wan smile.

"Anything over five million comes to me for approval," Wolfgang explains. "If you had asked for a smaller extension, the same fool that approved the previous increases might have waved this one through." Wolfgang glares at Rich Little.

"Now that we've heard the bad news, I'd like to share some good news about UpTempCo," Dave interjects. "We're getting more direct business, and that's improving margin and cash flow."

"How so?" Wolfgang asks.

"Up till now, we've been a subcontractor to national marketing firms and had to discount our rates and wait to be paid. Recently our growth has come from jobs I get directly from manufacturers. On those, we charge full price and get paid faster."

"We've seen the sales increase," Wolfgang says. "But the cash flow hasn't improved, and accounts receivable continues to grow."

"That's why we need to increase the credit line," Dave explains. "Sales are exploding, but there's a lag between the time we must pay the independent contractors and when we get paid by the client. That creates a cash crunch."

"Maybe Mrs. Manson hasn't told you," Wolfgang replies, "but the way it's supposed to work is that when you finish a job and issue the invoice, we get the receivable for collateral. At that point, you're allowed to draw the invoice amount from your credit line to use for payroll. When remittance for the job is received from the client, you're supposed to use that money to pay down the line. That's what's not happening. So, if we increase your facility again, we'll need a lockbox to make sure all payments come to the bank."

"Over my dead body!" Michelle snaps. "I'd rather go bankrupt."

"What's your problem with a lockbox?" Collin asks suspiciously.

"Then the bank would be running the company, not me."

"That would be an improvement. You've run it into the ground."

"Look, we're just trying to salvage this," Wolfgang interrupts. "So that each of us gets what we need. You want to leave this meeting with a going concern. We want to have a performing loan."

"I agree with that," Michelle says with a gleam in her eye. "We're in the same boat."

Wolfgang looks at Don. "Mr. Howell, what about doing an audited statement?"

"It's too late for that," Don says. "We've been doing compilations for years. My firm won't sign off on an audit at this point."

"I just wonder what idiot agreed to compiled statements to begin with," Wolfgang muses, looking around the room. He taps on the table with his fountain pen then says, "At least we can do an accounts receivable verification."

"No way," Michelle protests. "I'm not going to have the bank calling my customers and asking about money matters. They'd think we're in trouble and begin using other agencies. If you call a single customer, I'll sue Garden State for tortious interference."

Michelle glares at Wolfgang, and now he looks down.

The room grows quiet while the banker doodles on his pad pensively. "You require a capital infusion," he finally says. "We will extend your line to six million, but at your burn rate this will not last long. It's mandatory that you bring some outside investors in."

"All right," Michelle agrees.

Wolfgang tears a blank page from his pad, carefully prints a name and phone number, then brings the paper to Michelle. "Call Mr. Franklin. He can help you."

Michelle glances at the paper, then tucks it into her purse. "I want us to meet here again in three months, so you can report your progress," Wolfgang says. He stalks out, and the other bankers hastily follow.

"Whew, let's get out of here," Michelle says, rising from her chair.

When they get downstairs, Michelle, Don, and Dave huddle in a corner of the lobby. "We've got him over a barrel," Michelle gloats. "If Wolfgang pulls the plug now, Garden State has to write off five big ones."

"Yes, but he won't pump money into the company indefinitely," Dave worries.

"That's where you come in." Michelle reaches into her purse then hands Dave the note Wolfgang gave her. "Call this guy and get us some investors. Now, I've got to find a toilet."

As Michelle hurries off, Dave turns to Don. "What's the difference between compiled and audited statements?"

"Compiled is when the accountant prepares statements based solely on the client's figures," Don explains. "Audited means that the accountant has examined the client's books and supporting documents, and certifies the statement's veracity."

"So, your firm in no way stands behind UpTempCo's financial statements?"

"Correct."

Dave frowns as he digests this information. "Do you think the receivables are legit?" he asks.

"Your guess is as good as mine," Don whispers as Michelle comes toward them, jauntily swinging her purse. The UpTempCo owner has regained her customary swagger.

CHAPTER NINE

Detox

At Grand Union headquarters, Dave expects Grant Becker to be a hard-ass, and he's not disappointed. "They stuck me with this demo shit," the VP of Store Operations says, "and I'm not happy about it."

"Then let us handle it for you," Dave smiles.

"You and every other temp agency," Grant says. He picks up a fistful of brochures and waves them at Dave. "What makes you different?"

"Retail is our specialty," Dave explains. "Demos and merchandising, that's it."

"So, you're gonna send some reset guys to fry bratwurst in my stores?"

Dave shakes his head. "No way," he says. "UpTempCo has two separate divisions, one for merchandising and the other for demos. We don't send product demonstrators out on store remodels, and we don't send reset crews to perform demos. We don't have to. Our demo supervisors have card files full of temps who are equipped with crock pots, electric skillets, toaster ovens, card tables, and so on. We staff an average of 600 demos each weekend. Those companies sending you brochures have never staffed a demo before."

"Let's see your rates."

"I've got everything right here," Dave says. "But first, let's discuss our capabilities." He takes a binder from his briefcase and hands it to Grant. "Please turn to the first tab. It has a map of the metro area with green triangles to indicate your stores."

"What are the red circles?" Grant asks.

"Those are the locations of current UpTempCo product demonstrators. As you can see, we have all your stores covered."

"Anyone can draw circles on a map!"

"Turn the page, and you'll see a printout of our demonstrators with addresses."

Grant flips through the next few pages. "OK, so you have the stores covered," he concedes.

"Now turn to the second tab," Dave asks. "It has our selection process and the standard interview we use for hiring new demonstrators. Once hired, every demonstrator is brought in for the training program shown under the third tab."

"What does this mean?" Grant asks, pointing to the training curriculum. "Sounds kind of kinky."

Dave looks where Grant is pointing. "Oh, role-playing," he says, "that's when one of the new hires plays the part of a demonstrator, and the other is a shopper walking past. It's part of the sales training. We want our demonstrators to sell, not just give away free food."

"Very impressive."

"The next tab has an example of the report we'll have on your desk first thing every Monday with a breakdown of the previous weekend's demo results rolled up by store, district, and chain."

Grant studies the report. "What's all this going to cost me?" he asks.

"Our pricing is under the last tab," Dave replies. "We can do it for $96.00 per demo day."

"What? Twelve bucks an hour? Apex does it for eleven, Workpower is only ten-fifty. Everybody knows Workpower, whoever heard of UpTempCo?"

"Apex and Workpower mainly provide temps for factory jobs," Dave says. "Is that the sort of people you want handling food in your stores?"

"OK, I'll think about it." Grants stands to indicate the meeting is over.

After checking out with the Grand Union receptionist, Dave heads back to Morristown. It's a bright early spring day, so instead of going to the office, he drives to Winding Creek and spends the rest of the afternoon playing golf.

The next morning, Dave pulls into the office parking lot and is getting out of the Chevy when a silver Mercedes 450 SL convertible parks next to him. Dave darts an admiring glance at the car and is shocked to see Michelle behind the wheel. "Isn't it a beauty?" she asks after extricating herself from the low-slung machine.

"Yeah, maybe a little out of my price range."

"It's leased using my personal money; this is not from the company."

"That's good," Dave says. "Now, don't forget, we have a meeting this morning with the guy Wolfgang recommended."

"It's on my calendar."

An hour later, Barbara brings a visitor to Dave's door. "This is Ralph Franklin," she announces as the man ducks into the office. Dave rises to shake hands and finds himself admiring Ralph's tiepin. "Ever play any roundball?" he asks.

"Ha-ha, Rutgers."

"I figured." Dave steps back and sees that aside from being tall and gangly, Ralph's a bit on the homely side. He's not totally unattractive, but his ears stick out like handles and that, plus a gap between his front teeth, gives him a goofy look. "Let's go across the way so I can introduce you to the owner," Dave suggests.

Michelle remains seated as the two men walk in. "This is Ralph Franklin," Dave says, "meet Michelle Manson."

"Hi, Mrs. Manson."

"Thanks for coming."

"My pleasure."

"Barbara, please get us some coffee," Michelle asks as the men settle into chairs.

Once everyone has a steaming mug, Ralph kicks off the meeting, "Wolfgang told me you require a capital infusion. I have some investors who may be interested."

"I'd love to meet them," Michelle smiles.

"First, I have to get a handle on the business." Ralph tries a sip of java, but it's too hot.

"OK, so what do you need from me?"

"Permission to go around the office and interview the employees."

Michelle pours cream into her cup and stirs. "What for?" she asks.

"May I?" Ralph holds out his hand for the creamer. "I need to learn all about your firm to determine which of my investors would be suitable."

"Wolfgang said our financials would scare off other banks."

Ralph smiles. "I work with venture capitalists," he says. "They see things banks don't."

"Like what?"

"Cash flows."

"Right now, there ain't none," Michelle sighs.

"I beg to differ," Ralph says. "You have cash flow, it's just going in the wrong direction. My job is to see if we can fix that."

"How're you gonna do that?"

"One of my tricks, once I get to know a business, is to do a reconstituted cash flow projection."

"Sounds like voodoo," Dave exclaims.

Ralph turns to Dave. "You're a funny guy," he chuckles. "I'm going to enjoy working with you."

"Then why don't you interview him first?" Michelle asks.

"You got time right now?"

"Sure," Dave replies.

"It was nice meeting you," Ralph says to Michelle. He takes his mug and follows Dave out.

Once he and Ralph are back across the hall, Dave has a question. "Seriously, what's a reconstituted cash flow projection?"

"It's a pro forma financial statement that takes out all unnecessary spending." Ralph gets a notebook out of his briefcase and sits across from Dave. "I met with Don Howell last week and went over UpTempCo's financials going back several years. There's a lot of waste, and it's been getting worse."

"Like what?"

"Fred's salary and car, for instance."

"Fred's still drawing a salary?"

"Same as you plus he gets the same quarterly bonus payout, a car, and the company pays for his benefits, including life insurance."

"The life insurance can't be cheap."

"It's four figures."

"Every month?"

Ralph nods his head.

"Ouch."

"There's more, and I'm confident that when we show investors what UpTempCo's financials would look like without all the unnecessary spending, they'll be interested."

"So, how are these investors going to curtail the extravagance with Michelle in charge?"

"Let's get started, shall we?" Ralph replies. "How would you describe your job?"

The interview with Ralph takes a big bite out of Dave's day. So, he's still grinding away in the office after everyone else has left. He wanted to go to Winding Creek and play a few holes, but now it's dark out. There's a rap on his door, and Bob comes in with Warren.

"We were just bringing the truck back after a Pathmark reset," Bob says, "and saw your light."

"How's it going?"

"Great, we've been raking in the overtime," Warren smiles.

"Guess some extra money doesn't hurt."

"Damn straight!"

"Why don't you grab a seat?"

"Nah, I've got to get home."

"Me too," Bob says. "But we ran into a guy you should talk to." He hands Dave a card. "Earl is the owner of Falcon Candy Company. Pathmark is their biggest customer."

"Up till now anyway," Warren says. "Earl told us Pathmark is threatening to throw them out."

"They want him to lower his margin, huh?" Dave asks.

"That's not it," Bob explains. "The problem is that right now, a Pathmark aisle clerk does the candy inventory, writes the replenishment order, and phones it to Falcon. All they do is deliver the goods. Pathmark does the restocking."

"I think I see where this is going," Dave says.

"Yeah, another vendor came in and offered to do everything for just 5% more. Now, Falcon has to go full-service or lose the business."

"I'll call him tomorrow and make an appointment."

The next morning, Dave goes to Winding Creek and spends an hour at the practice tee before going to work. He's in his office later when Michelle sticks her head in the door. "Fred needs to earn his keep around here," she says. "He can't do resets in his condition. Maybe you can take him on some sales calls?"

"Sure, I just made an appointment that would be good."

After Michelle goes out, Dave calls Fred. "You been hitting 'em any?" he asks.

"Yeah, played nine holes Wednesday."

"It's supposed to go up near seventy tomorrow."

"Not bad for April."

"Let's play. It's Saturday."

"OK."

"Oh, and I almost forgot, want to go on a sales call with me?"

"Hell, yeah."

"I'll give you all the details tomorrow."

"Sounds good."

The earliest tee time Dave can get is eleven o'clock. He gets to the course early to hit balls and find's Fred already there. They warm up together then tee off at the appointed time.

After the first few holes, both men shed a layer of clothing. "The sun feels good on my face," Fred says as they sit in the cart, waiting for the foursome ahead of them to hit their second shots.

"It's nice out of the wind," Dave agrees. Finally, the group in front gets back in their carts and heads toward the green. Fred slides off the seat and gets his professional-grade driver. "Put one out there," Dave says by way of encouragement.

The course is jammed with weekend golfers and it's slow-going all the way around. Neither Fred nor Dave care. It's great to be outdoors after the long, gray winter.

Back at the clubhouse, Fred totes up the score. "You almost broke 80," he says.

"Would have but for that 3-putt on the back," Dave mopes.

"Want to join me for a Perrier?"

"Nah, I'm going to stop by the office and attack my inbox awhile. But I'll see you Wednesday. The appointment with Falcon Candy is set for two. We can meet at the office beforehand."

"Can't wait."

At the office, Dave makes a pot of coffee then dives into his paperwork. It's late by the time he finishes, so he goes straight home. The remainder of the weekend is spent reading, walking, and watching TV.

On Monday, Ralph Franklin is sitting with Mindy when Dave comes in. "Must be nice to come and go as you please," she says. "The rest of us have to be here at eight-thirty or else."

"That just proves one thing," Dave replies.

"What's that?"

"Your life sucks."

Ralph suppresses a guffaw as Dave heads upstairs. Over the next couple of days, the financial consultant meets with more employees, including the warehouse crew. On Wednesday, he's in the lobby when Fred arrives to meet up with Dave. "I'm interviewing all the UpTempCo employees," Ralph tells Fred. "When would be a good time for us to talk?"

"How about breakfast tomorrow?" Fred suggests. "At the Blue Jay."

"What time?"

"I'm usually there when they open at seven."

"Sounds good."

Fred and Dave leave for their appointment with Falcon Candy. On the way, Dave cranks up the volume on a Waylon Jennings cassette. "How can you listen to that country shit?" Fred complains.

"Sometimes I forget you're a Yankee," Dave laughs. "Take that as a compliment."

Fred folds his arms and sulks all the way to Newark. Meanwhile, Dave focuses on the traffic. He's stopped at a light in a depressed part of the city, when a bearded man raps on the window. Dave makes sure the door is locked then lowers the glass an inch or two. "Listen, bud," the man says, "I ain't gonna lie to you about being hungry or nothin'. What I need bad right now is a tall boy, and a dollar would do it for me."

Dave gets his wallet and passes a bill to the derelict. "That's the best line I've heard lately," he says as the man shambles off.

"Bullshit, you should keep your hard-earned money for yourself," Fred scowls.

The light changes and Dave steers the Chevy onto another blighted block. "There's a world of power in the truth, Fred," he says. "You should try it sometime."

"Ha-ha," Fred replies mirthlessly.

"What's got into you this morning?"

"Fuckin' baseball's kicking my ass."

"What are you talking about? There is no baseball."

"Preseason," Fred explains.

"You're betting on preseason baseball?" Dave is incredulous.

"There's nothing else this time of year. Basketball's over."

"You need help!"

"After yesterday I quit, I swear to God," Fred exclaims. "I mean, the Tigers are leading 3–0 then give up a grand slam to Buddy Bell in the bottom of the ninth. Tell me, how do the Tigers lose to the Indians? How?"

Dave is driving past a line of red-brick warehouses. Some are surrounded by chain-link fences topped with razor wire. Others have cinder block walls with shards of broken glass embedded on top. He finds the street number he's looking for and pulls to the curb.

After stowing all valuables in the trunk, Dave follows Fred over to a wrought iron gate. They use the intercom to identify themselves and are buzzed through to a courtyard leading to the front door.

Inside, an attractive middle-aged receptionist greets the two visitors. She ushers them into a conference room, where the Falcon owners are seated. Eric Falcon is a dapper young African American sporting a pencil-thin mustache. His father Earl is a white-haired, distinguished-looking gentleman on the north side of sixty.

Once introductions are taken care of, Dave asks about the business. It turns out Earl started Falcon Candy thirty years ago upon returning from World War II. "I flew fighters over Germany," he says.

"I read about the Tuskegee airmen," Dave replies, "never expected to meet one."

"Well, now you have," Earl smiles.

"I've been working in the business since I got out of college," Eric explains. "Dad is gradually turning the day-to-day running of the company over to me as his retirement approaches."

"But there may not be much of a business if we can't find a way to service Pathmark," Earl chimes in.

"We can help you there," Dave says. "UpTempCo specializes in retail merchandising. Our workers are adept at inventorying, ordering, and packing out merchandise." As Dave launches into his spiel, he's disconcerted to see that Eric is ignoring him. The young man seems to be more interested in Fred. "Do you have a question for Mr. Manson?" Dave asks him.

"Well, yes, I do," Eric replies. "How big is that diamond?" he's pointing at the ring on Fred's pinkie.

"Four carats, want to see it?" Fred is already twisting the ring off.

After the young man finishes handling the ring, Fred politely asks to see Eric's gold pendant. "It's the Egyptian symbol for love," Eric explains. He pulls the chain over his head and hands it over.

As Fred holds the necklace, the light catches the diamond-encrusted bezel of his Rolex. "Now that's a nice watch!" Earl exclaims. Fred is happy to unsnap it and hand the thing over for inspection.

Dave waits patiently as this show-and-tell session drags on. He's wearing an old Seiko with a smelly leather band. After briefly considering handing this item over for consideration, Dave thinks better of it.

"You must be the man," Eric says to Fred.

"That's right, I own UpTempCo, this fellow just works for me," Fred says grandly. "Go ahead with what you were saying now, boy," he tells Dave.

Dave stifles a laugh then plays along. "As I was saying, our experienced merchandisers will have no problem inventorying and ordering the candy. Once the order is delivered, they'll come back, price each item, and put everything up. Here is the cost projection I worked up for you." Dave hands copies of the pricing page of his presentation to the Falcons. They gasp.

"We can't afford this," Earl declares.

"No way," his son dittos.

"I understand your concern with the figures," Dave replies, "but this is less than a third of what it would cost you to have full-time salaried salesmen do the job. Can you share with me the total amount of your billings to Pathmark last year?"

"Close to three mil," Earl says.

"Well, if Pathmark is willing to pay a 5% upcharge for full-service, that'll cover most of our cost."

"But not all," Earl complains.

Eric studies Dave's cost projection then looks up. "Dad, if we hire full-time salesmen to do this, we'll go broke; 5% is not enough to cover salary and benefits, plus we'd have the travel expense. This way, we keep Pathmark happy, and it only costs a portion of the profit."

"I guess we don't have much choice," Earl sighs. "How soon can you get us a contract to review?" he asks Dave.

"I'll write one up tonight and send it over tomorrow," Dave promises.

Fred glances at his watch. "I'm glad we have this settled," he says. "I have a tee time over at the country club at two."

"We truly appreciate you coming today," Earl says.

"When I heard Dave had an appointment with Falcon Candy, I insisted on coming," Fred explains. "I wasn't going to let him handle something this important on his own."

At that, Dave gets up to signify the meeting is over. "Sorry, but I have to get Mr. Manson to the golf course," he says, "then write up your contract."

Once Fred and Dave are back in the car, the older man has a suggestion. "You need to take me every time."

"I'm not sure I could handle your bullshit that often."

Fred laughs. "Just remember what I always say, buddy boy. You can never lay it on too thick!"

It's a drag returning to the office after a sales call, but there's a stack of messages waiting, so Dave has no choice. He's at his desk, preparing to call A&P, when Michelle comes in. "That Ralph is a mover and shaker," she says. "He took me to lunch today with a potential investor."

"Tell me about it."

"The guy's name is Lindsey Grisham. He owns Pace Courier."

"How did it go?"

"He sees a lot of synergies between our two companies."

"That sounds promising."

"I have a conference call with Lindsey and his board of directors tomorrow."

"Great, let me know how it goes."

Dave finds himself working late again that night because he wants to have a draft of the Falcon contract sitting on Barbara's desk when she comes in the next morning. It's past nine when he gets back to Manhattan and cracks open a beer. Shortly afterward, the phone rings. "Where have you been?" Mildred asks. "I've been trying to reach you all evening."

"I had to work late," Dave says, then swills some brew. *This is not going to be good*, he thinks.

"You won't believe what your father did today," Mildred exclaims.

"Tell me."

"Said he was going to the store for cigarettes, then took a wrong turn and started driving the wrong way up the new bypass."

"Anyone could make that mistake."

"Sheriff Wilson said he wouldn't stop. Just kept driving into the oncoming traffic. People were going off the road right and left. It's a miracle no one was killed."

"So, he's OK?"

"The sheriff took him to get blood drawn. Said it was more alcohol than blood. Never saw such a high reading."

"Guess he needs to sleep it off."

"Yes, well Bucky has him over at his house," Mildred says. Bucky Zimmermann is Mildred's brother whom Dave has met during previous visits to Palestine. He's as much white trash as his sister is a lady.

"Why's Dad with Bucky?" Dave asks.

"I can't deal with him anymore," Mildred declares. "Bucky will keep him off the booze till we can get him out of here."

"What do you mean?"

"Sheriff Wilson hasn't charged your father as a favor to me, but the Palestine police want him gone. Either you or Melissa will have to take him."

"I don't think Melissa's a possibility."

"That leaves you. I'll tell Bucky to put him on a flight to New York."

"Have you told Dad?"

"Yes, I told him that if he gets some help, dries out, whatever, then I'll take him back."

"Really?"

"No, but that's what I told him, and he agreed to go. Bucky will call you with the flight information."

"OK, but tell him to make it Newark, that would be easier for me than LaGuardia."

After hanging up, Dave needs a fresh beer. It comes in handy a little later when Bucky calls. "So, how's things in Jew York?" the redneck asks.

"NEW York is fine," Dave replies. "How are you?"

"Just got back from vacation," Bucky answers. "Me and the Mrs. stayed right on the beach in Corpus. Man, it was great. Walk outside the room onto the sand, look to the right, look to the left, all you see is white people." Bucky waits expectantly, but Dave allows the silence to drag out.

"Not like around here," Bucky persists. "Damn niggers everywhere, act like they own the place." Still, Dave has no comment, so after a long moment Bucky continues, "Well, I guess you're used to that up north there. Probably like it.

Anyways, your father will be arriving at Newark tomorrow evenin' at six-thirty on American."

"Got it," Dave says, and hangs up. He goes to the fridge and finds he's out of beer. Wearily, Dave laces his shoes then grabs a jacket for the trip to the corner.

At the office the next day, Dave works to clear up loose ends so he can leave for the airport on time. He has called Grant Becker several times to follow up on the proposal he gave Grand Union, but the VP hasn't called back. Dave ponders what to do next, then inspiration strikes. He picks up the phone and dials. "Cathy Downing, please," he tells the Grand Union receptionist.

Cathy is Grant's secretary, and Dave has gotten to know her by calling so often. "This is Dave Knight, how's everything?" he asks when she comes on the line.

"Almost Friday, so things are looking up."

"I know what you mean. It's been a long week."

"And how."

"Are you doing anything special this weekend?"

"Little League has started up, and my son Reid is the pitcher for his team; they have two games Saturday."

"That's exciting."

"It's a preseason tournament. If they win Saturday, they'll play for the championship on Sunday."

"I'll keep my fingers crossed for you."

"Thanks."

"Can you check Grant's calendar for me? I'd like an appointment one day next week if he has an opening."

"Let me look," Cathy says. There's a pause, then she asks, "Can you come in at eight on Wednesday?"

"Sure, that's perfect."

"OK, we'll see you then."

After hanging up, Dave writes the appointment with Grand Union on his calendar then sits back in his chair with relief.

"Those bastards!" Michelle shrieks, throwing her office door open. Dave jumps up and goes into the hallway, where Michelle is pitching a fit. "What a bunch of assholes," she hollers. "The nerve!"

"What's going on?"

"Oh, they think they're smart, but I'm smarter."

"Who?"

"Lindsey Grisham and his partners."

"Calm down and tell me about it." Dave takes Michelle's arm and leads her to a chair in his office.

"On the conference call just now with the Pace Courier board, they were all so sweet," Michelle says heatedly. "Very complimentary about UpTempCo. Said they want to put money in and be part of the family. That I would be in charge, would still make all the decisions, and so on. At the end, we agreed to a meeting next week and said goodbye. Then, for whatever reason, I didn't hang up. Next thing, I heard Lindsey say, 'She's gone, we can talk,' and one of the other guys said, 'What an airhead,' another one piped up, 'Dizzy broad, no wonder her company's on the ropes.' Then Lindsey spoke again, 'Yeah, but it has real potential once we get rid of her. We'll just wait till UpTempCo goes belly up then pick up the pieces for nothing.'"

"Sounds like a flock of vultures looking over some roadkill," Dave observes.

Michelle slams her hand down on Dave's desk. "Well, I'm not roadkill," she snaps, "I've got a lot of life left in me!"

"So, what's next?"

"Ralph's bringing this multimillionaire over next Wednesday, can you be here?"

"I've got a meeting with Grand Union that morning."

"Ralph and the investor won't get here till five or so."

"Then, no problem," Dave agrees.

Michelle gets up. "Don't tell Ralph what I said about Lindsey and those jerks," she asks. "I'm just going to string them along now that I know their game."

After work, Dave heads for the airport and gets there with time to spare. He's inside the terminal watching passengers emerge from the American Airlines gate area when a decrepit man diverts from the crowd and hobbles toward him. The old-timer's sport coat is flecked with ash, and the white shirt underneath is ventilated with innumerable burn holes. Dave steps back, fearing he will be asked for money. As he looks at the derelict's jaundiced face, a feeling of horror overtakes him. "Hello, son," his father says.

"You look like a hundred miles of bad road," Dave replies.

"And a pleasant good day to you as well."

"Let's go get your bags."

On the way down the concourse, father and son pass a crowded bar. "Let's stop, I need a drink," the colonel says.

"That's the last thing you need," Dave snorts.

"You're wrong, son," Knight pleads. "My doctor says if I quit drinking cold turkey, I could die. He said I need to detox first."

"Then you can have a beer when we get home."

"Or two?" Knight asks.

"That's possible," Dave agrees, thinking, *After today, I'm going to need more than one myself.*

The next morning, as Dave cooks breakfast, he recalls all the times, on cold school mornings, when his father made French toast for the Knight children. Now he's happy to return the favor, but the colonel shows little appetite. He sips coffee while idly rearranging the food on his plate, taking only an occasional bite.

"I have a couple of calls to make," Dave says, after washing the dishes, "then we can leave."

"Where are we going?" Knight asks.

"To a VA hospital."

"What for?"

"Detox."

"I just got here, can't that wait?"

"I thought you wanted to get back with Mildred."

"I do."

"She told me you can't return to Texas until you've been through rehab. That starts with detox."

"OK, then."

It's past ten by the time Dave and his father get to a VA hospital in New Jersey. Knight shows his military ID at the front desk and is given a number. They look for a place to sit, but the waiting room is full. Then a number is called, and two people get up. The Knights take their chairs. "What time did you get here?" Dave asks the man next to him.

"Seven, that's when they open, but there was already a line to get in."

"Have you been here before?"

"Yeah."

"So, how does it work?"

"You take a number. Then they call you up to see what you need. If it's something simple like a prescription refill or getting blood drawn, you can often get it done right away. Otherwise, you have to go to another ward and wait some more."

"Got it," Dave says, and opens his newspaper. He also has a paperback, confident that the slow pace of bureaucracy will leave plenty of time for reading.

Knight's number is finally called shortly before noon. After a brief consultation with a patient representative, he and Dave are told to go to the psych ward on the fifth floor. "Alcoholism is under mental health," the man tells them.

When they get upstairs, Knight receives a lengthy questionnaire to fill out. All the substance abuse counselors are at lunch, and several patients are ahead of them, so it's past two when a tired psychologist wearing a plaid sport coat finally calls the Knights into his office. "Based on the information you provided, detoxification is called for," the counselor says. "However, we only have twelve beds here, and they are all booked until September."

178 | WILLIAM A. GLASS

"What other suggestions do you have?" Dave demands. "At the rate he's going, my father won't be alive by September."

"I can put Colonel Knight on a waiting list and let you know if a bed comes open before then," the counselor shrugs. "You could also try Lyons. They might have something."

"Thanks," Dave says, getting up.

"Do you want me to put him on the list for September?"

"Sure, I'll call and cancel if we find something sooner."

Dave and his father go out to the parking lot. "What next?" Knight asks.

"Lyons is the other VA near here," Dave says, "maybe you can get in there."

It's late afternoon by the time the Knights get to Lyons, and only a few patients are in the waiting room. After a short wait, they're referred to the mental health unit and find that the story there is the same as they ran into earlier—not enough beds. The colonel's name is added to the waiting list.

"I've got to have a drink," Knight says, once he and Dave are on their way home.

Dave looks ahead at bumper-to-bumper traffic as far as the eye can see. "All right," he says. "We can stop somewhere until rush hour is over." He keeps his eyes peeled for a likely spot, and a little while later, pulls into the parking lot of a T.G.I. Friday's.

Inside, a raucous crowd is enjoying happy hour. Rather than join the mob at the bar, Dave steers his father over to the hostess stand. As they wait for a table, he looks at the eclectic collection of antique decorative items crammed onto the walls and into corners of the place. He wonders if the stuff is fake.

Finally, they're seated, and Dave orders two schooners of draft beer. His father grasps his in both hands and takes a copious gulp. "I'm running out of ideas on where to take you," Dave sighs.

"Beats me," Knight says. "I've never been to a VA before. Used to go to Mildred's doctor in Palestine."

"And pay cash?"

"No, I used this." Knight digs out his wallet and hands Dave a card.

"What's CHAMPUS?" Dave asks, looking at the card.

"A health care program for retired military."

"Why didn't you tell me?"

"You didn't ask."

"We'll try it Monday at a regular hospital."

"Should work," Knight shrugs.

Dave watches his father chug more beer. "You want something to eat?" he asks.

"Might as well."

The waiter comes by, and Dave orders cheeseburgers and more brew. When the sandwiches come, Knight nibbles on his then chews on a few French fries. He waits until Dave finishes eating, then lights a cigarette.

As the two men relax with their beer in the dimly lit bar, waiters walk by in white- and red-striped uniforms carrying platters of food and drink. Busboys hustle to clear off tables. "You see these people?" the colonel asks, pointing at one of the restaurant employees. "They're like sticks of furniture to me."

Knight grins at Dave from across the table, then drags on his cigarette without noticing how long the ash has grown. It falls, and he hurriedly attempts to brush the tiny embers away before they further aerate his clothes. Knight nods toward a black man busily clearing off a nearby table. "I mean, these people are nothing to me, absolutely nothing."

"Like enlisted men in the army?" Dave needles.

"Exactly," Knight nods. "People like them have their uses but should just do their jobs, then disappear back into the woodwork."

"I thought that kind of thinking went out with the 18th century."

"What's so great about this century? There's no discipline, respect, or order. Oh, I know you don't care. You've walked away from your heritage and everything our family name stands for. We fought alongside Robert the Bruce, for Chrissake."

"No one cares what someone in your family did a thousand years ago. They want to know what you're doing now."

"And now you're nothing but a cheap salesman for a no-name company," Knight sneers. "I wrote you off a long time ago."

Dave finishes his beer then puts some money on the table. "Ironic, isn't it?" he says, getting to his feet. "'Cause now I'm all you've got."

The radio alarm comes on early the following morning, and Dave hastens to turn it off. Then he checks to make sure his father is still asleep on the sofa. Satisfied, Dave gets ready to go meet Fred and Rich Little at Winding Creek. Michelle arranged the outing weeks ago.

When Dave gets to the club, the staff already has his bag strapped to a golf cart. He drives it over to the practice tee and begins hitting approach shots with his pitching wedge. He plans to work his way from the short irons through the longer irons and then finish with his driver.

Half an hour later, Fred and Rich pull up in a golf cart. "I'm done," Dave tells them, "you can have my spot." He relaxes and watches the others hit a few. Rich booms his shots while Fred's are anemic.

After a while, the starter comes over. "You've got five minutes, Mr. Manson," he says.

"Got it," Fred replies. He and Rich gather the clubs they've been using, and the three golfers head for the first hole.

While they wait for the group ahead of them to clear the fairway, Fred tees up a ball and takes some practice swings. "We need to make this interesting," he says.

"What do you suggest?" Rich smiles.

"What about Bingo Bango Bongo?" Fred asks. "Say a dollar a point?"

"That'll work."

After the round, the threesome goes to the terrace for refreshments. Fred totes up the score, and it turns out Rich is the big winner. Fred and Dave cheerfully pay up. "This has been fun," Rich comments as he pockets his winnings. "Thanks for inviting me."

"It was all Michelle's idea," Fred explains. "She wants us to stay on good terms with the bank."

"We're solid as far as I'm concerned," Rich says. "But I don't count for much. Wolfgang is the guy you need to please, and he's not happy."

"What's bugging him?" Fred asks.

"He says the accounts receivable is still growing even though Dave promised to bring in better-paying customers."

"That's bullshit," Dave exclaims. "My customers pay."

"That's not what I hear," Rich says, taking a sip of gin and tonic. He runs a hand through his wavy hair.

"OK, so you're telling me that A&P, P&G, Clorox, and Pillsbury aren't paying their invoices?"

"That's right."

"I don't believe it."

"Then talk to Michelle," Rich says. "She knows what's going on. In the meantime, Wolfgang is threatening to cut her off."

Wendy comes by and asks if they want another round. "I have to be going," Rich says.

"Me too," Dave echoes.

"I'm meeting Michelle here for lunch," Fred says, "so I'll stick around."

Rich and Dave walk up the cart path to the parking lot together. Rich sets his bag down next to his car. "Thanks again for having me out," he says.

"Invest the money you took off us wisely," Dave jokes.

As he turns to go, Rich says, "Hey, I just thought of something I have in the car that would interest you."

"What's that?"

"UpTempCo's accounts receivable listing."

"Let's see it."

"Michelle said to keep it confidential."

"I won't tell if you don't."

"It's a deal," Rich says, then reaches into his car for a slim briefcase. He takes a folder out and hands it to Dave.

Inside the folder is an eight-page document entitled, "UpTempCo Accounts Receivable Detail." There are several columns on each page for invoice date, client name, invoice amount, and days past due. The invoices are listed in order by date, and the first three pages are billings to the national marketing companies that are Michelle's customers.

On the fourth page of the report, Dave sees an invoice for Clorox. It was the first job he sold and should have been paid months ago. Further down, he sees two big P&G invoices. Both are listed as over 120 days past due. "This one has definitely been paid," Dave exclaims, pointing to one for $56,000. "I collected it myself."

"Are you sure?"

"Yes, Michelle gave me a $100 bonus for getting it paid early."

Dave reads through the rest of the report and points to several more invoices from his customers that he collected on Michelle's orders. "I can guarantee you that these invoices have been paid as well."

"Interesting," Rich comments as Dave gives him back the folder.

On the way home, Dave worries about his employment situation. It sounds like UpTempCo is out of money again, and Michelle is playing games with the bank. He wonders where all the money is going, then shrugs it off.

At a discount liquor store, Dave gets a bottle of vodka to help his father through the weekend. When he gets to the apartment, Knight's on the sofa watching TV.

"Have you had anything to eat?" Dave asks.

"Just some toast and cereal."

"I see you got the Mr. Coffee going."

"Yep, first thing this morning; there's enough left for you."

"Thanks, I'll have a cup while I make lunch."

Dave turns the oven on preheat then pours a coffee and sits next to his father. "Who's playing?"

"Minnesota and Cleveland."

"I'll take the Indians," Dave says, and immediately regrets his choice when Joe Charboneau, the Tribe's one legitimate prospect, whiffs to end the inning. "How many chicken pot pies do you want?" he asks, getting up.

"One should do it," Knight replies.

"I'll make you a peanut butter sandwich to go with it."

"Great combination."

After lunch, Dave stretches out on his cot. "Can you turn the volume down a tad?" he asks.

"No problem."

Later, rays from the setting sun slant through the one window in Dave's apartment. He opens his eyes to see the colonel conked out on the sofa. Soon the old man stirs and comes awake.

"Let's go for a walk," Dave suggests.

"I'm in no condition to walk anywhere," Knight complains.

Dave goes to the cabinet where he stashed the vodka. "You can have a shot now and another one when we come back," he says, showing his dad the bottle. "We'll just go around the block."

"I can manage that," Knight says, licking his lips.

Traffic is light in Manhattan this early on a Saturday night, and few people are on the sidewalk. Still, progress is slow because Knight is devoid of energy. He walks hesitantly, like a wind-up toy that is close to winding down. Halfway around, Dave considers calling a cab. Then his father rallies as if inspired by the bottle of Smirnoff that's waiting. They press on and make it back to Dave's building.

"Now what?" the colonel asks once they're back inside the apartment. He holds his drink like a drowning man clutching a lifesaver.

"*Jaws* is going to be on ABC at nine," Dave says.

"Again?"

"The other channels are showing reruns as well."

"I see you have a chess set," Knight says. "Want to play a game?"

"Sure."

Dave unfolds the wooden chess board on the coffee table. Sitting on the floor, he arranges the pieces while his father gets ice out of the fridge and pours himself another drink. "Get me a beer, please," Dave asks.

Knight brings the beverages back to the table, and the game begins. After a period during which both players develop their positions, the colonel leaves a rook exposed, and Dave gains the advantage. His father responds by moving a knight, so Dave uses his queen to counter it. He's shocked when the old man quickly moves the knight so that it threatens both Dave's king and queen. It's the dreaded fork move!

"Check," the colonel says, taking a swig of his drink. He sits back on the sofa with a self-satisfied air.

Despair rises in Dave's chest. *How did this happen?* he wonders. Mentally, Dave recreates the situation on the board as it was before the last move. He identifies the space his father's knight was on, then counts the number of squares it just moved. Two squares down—that's OK. Then he counts two squares over to the knight's current position, and that's not OK. His father moved the knight one space more than allowed. Dave goes through the analysis again to double-check himself, then looks across the table. "Do you cheat at bridge, too?" he asks.

Far from being chagrined at getting caught, the colonel throws his head back and laughs. "What do you mean cheat?" he snorts. "That was my world-famous knight's plutonian shore move."

Grinning mightily, Knight pulls a wrinkled pack of Chesterfields from his pocket and extracts one of the remaining fags with yellowed fingers. He picks up his chrome Zippo and tamps the cigarette on it several times with a vigorous, practiced motion. Dave has seen his father holding the lighter, with the crossed flags of the Signal Corps embossed on it, all his life. He hates it, and right now, he hates his father.

"Did you think I was going to let you beat me?" Knight sneers. He leans forward and, with a backhand motion, sweeps the chess pieces onto the floor.

At first, Dave is stunned. Then he realizes that his father just resigned the match. For the first time, Dave has beaten him at chess.

Knight rises and goes to the refrigerator. As he fixes another drink, the kitchen light illuminates his emaciated frame, unkempt hair, and the white stubble on his cheeks. Like most of his clothes, the expensive silk dressing gown Knight wears is peppered with burn holes.

Despondently, Dave picks up the chess pieces, then puts the board away. He plods across the small apartment to the bathroom. "It's late, Dad," he says, "I'm going to get ready for bed."

Later, Dave is lying on his cot in the dark with his father across the room on the sofa. "Didn't Poe get kicked out of West Point?" he murmurs.

"I'm leaving everything to Mildred," Knight responds. "I don't owe any of you children anything."

CHAPTER TEN
Over Hill, Over Dale

Dave rises early on Monday, fires up Mr. Coffee, and once the hot beverage is ready, wakes his dad. "I'm going to the corner to get some bagels, be right back."

When Dave returns with their breakfast, he finds his father dressed and ready for the day. They eat, then leave the apartment. Once outside, Dave waves his arm until a cab pulls over. "St. Vincent's," he tells the driver.

St. Vincent's is a Catholic charity hospital with a lobby that has all the ambiance of a prison visitor's waiting room. The Knights enter it cautiously, as if expecting to be frisked. "My father's retired army, and is covered by CHAMPUS," Dave tells the nun at the admitting desk.

"I'll need to see the card and his military ID."

Knight hands over the requested items. After a glance, the woman renders her verdict, "CHAMPUS is good here just like any other kind of medical insurance."

"That's great because he needs treatment for alcoholism," Dave declares.

"First, he'll have to be evaluated." The nun gives Knight a clipboard with several forms. "Bring this back once you've filled them out."

Less than an hour later, the Knights are called to the front desk and given directions to the substance abuse clinic. Despite a couple of false turns, they eventually push through a set of double doors into the right place.

The clinic's reception area is comfortably furnished with a couch and several overstuffed chairs. Soothing watercolors decorate the walls. At the far end, a nun in a black habit beckons them. "Colonel Knight," she smiles, "I see you found us."

"Nothing to it," Knight replies with a grin.

"I'm Sister Sandy," the nun says. "Please make yourselves at home. Dr. Carmichael will be right with you."

Twenty minutes later, a middle-aged brunette wearing a maroon jacket over a black skirt comes out of a side door. "I'm Dr. Carmichael," she says, extending her hand.

Once introductions are complete, the Knights follow Dr. Carmichael back to her office. After everyone's seated, she gets down to business. "Colonel Knight, I've looked over the questionnaire you filled out and want to follow up on a couple of things if that's all right."

"Sure."

"You say drinking is not a problem for you?"

"That's correct. I don't drink any more than anyone else."

"What crap!" Dave exclaims. "He got run out of Palestine, Texas, for driving with a blood alcohol level five times the legal limit."

The psychiatrist glances at Dave then redirects her attention to his father. "If alcohol isn't a problem, please tell me what brings you here?"

"He made me come." Knight points at Dave.

"Oh, come on," Dave protests. "Tell her what your doctor in Texas said about why you shouldn't stop drinking cold turkey."

"Like I said, everybody I know drinks," Knight shrugs. "You get to be my age and are accustomed to it. Sure, Dr. Smathers said I would need to phase out if I wanted to stop. He said it would be dangerous to up and quit."

"He said you'd get delirium tremens," Dave interjects.

"Smathers didn't really say that, I just told you that," Knight says.

"Why did you tell your son something that's not true?" Dr. Carmichael inquires.

Knight starts to say something, then thinks better of it.

"Did you say that so he would give you something to drink?"

Still, Knight is mute.

"So, how did you happen to be talking about quitting drinking with Dr. Smathers if alcohol is not a problem?" Dr. Carmichael raises her eyebrows.

"My wife complained about my drinking," Knight admits.

"Yeah, she complained," Dave blurts out. "So, he talked to Dr. Smathers to placate her, and the doctor told him to get treatment but no, he kept drinking, so finally she threw him out. Now he's sleeping on my couch!"

Dr. Carmichael looks at Dave. "I understand this is not easy for you," she says soothingly. "Family members often need as much help as alcoholics. Today, though, we must focus on your dad."

"You're right," Dave says, sitting back in his chair. "Sorry."

"So, what do you want to do?" Dr. Carmichael asks Knight.

"My wife wants me to quit drinking."

"That's not what I asked."

"Right, well then, it's me. I want to stop drinking. I want to go home."

"You should know that detoxification is just the first step," Dr. Carmichael says. "Afterward, I recommend a residential treatment program. We have a place in the Catskills called Abbey Farms. You'll be there three months and afterward will need to attend AA meetings. In the beginning, you'll need AA every day. After a few years, you may be able to scale back. I tell you this because you need to know what you're getting into. If you're not serious, then I don't need you taking up a bed here that we could use for someone who is."

"I'm serious," Knight insists. "Mildred won't take me back unless I quit. I have to stop."

"OK then," Dr. Carmichael says, getting up, "we'll admit you." The psychiatrist leads the way back out to the reception area. "Sister Sandy will assist you with the admissions process," she says. "I have a meeting to attend."

In lieu of handshakes, Dr. Carmichael half waves before turning to go. Meanwhile, Sister Sandy comes around her desk and hands Knight a clipboard. "Please sit and fill these forms out," she tells Knight. "Did you bring your things?"

"What things?"

"Clothes, toiletries, and so on."

"No."

"Perhaps your son could fetch an overnight bag while we do the paperwork?" Sister Sandy glances at Dave.

"No problem," Dave says. "I'll be back in an hour."

"Don't forget my slippers," Knight asks.

"All right."

By the time Dave gets back to St. Vincent's, his father has been admitted, and an attendant is waiting to take him upstairs. "Good luck," Dave says, and kisses his father's bristly cheek the way he did as a little boy.

"Thanks, son," Knight says, and suddenly his eyes are brimming. "I'm sorry about all this."

"Just get better, that's the main thing."

Dave makes it over to the UpTempCo office late that afternoon to be greeted by a quizzical look from Mindy. By now, the bosses' daughter knows better than to ask where he's been.

Upstairs, Dave sees an envelope from Falcon Candy on his desk. He eagerly opens it to find the signed contract inside. Then he starts listening to voicemails. They're mainly from store managers complaining about no-shows. He starts to return the oldest call, then glances at the Falcon contract again. An idea hits him, so he phones Fred.

"You ready to go on another sales call?"

"Anytime, buddy boy."

"Meet me at Grand Union headquarters in Elmwood Park on Wednesday at 7:45."

"You got it."

Dave grinds away the rest of the day, and most of Tuesday returning calls and fighting fires. Then Wednesday morning, he pulls into the Grand Union parking lot to find Fred standing next to his black Sedan DeVille smoking a cigarette.

"Where you been, boy?" Fred asks. "I've been waiting."

"Looks like I created a monster," Dave jokes, "a sales monster."

"You set 'em up, I knock 'em down."

After signing in at the reception desk, Fred and Dave find a place to sit then make plans for the upcoming meeting. A little past eight, Cathy Downing comes into the lobby and looks around. Dave waves to her, and she beckons. "Come on, Fred," Dave says, "that's our cue."

"How did Reid do this weekend?" Dave asks Cathy as they walk up the hallway.

"He pitched three no-hit innings in the first game on Saturday and came in for two innings of relief in the second game. They won both games and advanced to the final on Sunday. Reid started and only gave up three hits the first five innings, but they got a single and a home run off him in the sixth, so his team lost."

"Sounds like his arm got tired."

"Exactly."

Cathy shows them into Grant's office, then goes back to her desk. When the VP looks up and sees Dave, he scowls. "What do you want?" he asks.

"To follow up on my proposal."

"Who's Daddy Warbucks?"

"This is Fred Manson," Dave replies, "he owns UpTempCo."

"Get him a straw hat, and he'd fit right in with the pimps downtown."

Dave guides Fred over to the chairs in front of Grant's desk. They sit before he can object. "Did you come up with a better price for me?" the VP asks.

"As I said previously, the rate we charge is governed by the minimum wage law," Dave explains. "Our provision for profit is very low. That's why all the temp agencies have pretty much the same hourly rate."

"If you can't lower my cost, then there's nothing for us to discuss."

"I understand you're busy, but I want to make sure you know why UpTempCo would be the best bet for Grand Union's demo program." Dave takes a presentation out of his briefcase and slides one of the pages across the desk. "Every Monday morning, you'll get a report like this, with the demo results rolled up by store, district, and chain."

Grant glances at the paper then tosses it back. "You already gave me this."

"Did I explain how we staff the stores? Our managers overlay acetates showing the location of each demonstrator with a map showing your store locations."

"Yeah, you showed me those red circles and green triangles last time."

"What about our mandatory training program?" Dave asks. "We give our demonstrators the best training in the business. They don't just pass out samples, they sell!"

"Horseshit," Grant snaps, slamming his hand on the desk. "The women you temp agencies use for demos are so old they're lucky if they can remember their own names, let alone the names of the products they're sampling. Do they sell anything? My ass! Now, I don't have time for this nonsense. Unless you have something new for me, get out!"

"I do have one new thing," Dave says, and reaches into his briefcase.

"What's that?"

"Your contract."

"Well, let's see it." Grant holds out his hand impatiently, and Dave gives him the multi-page document. The VP begins reading then abruptly looks up. "You must be joking," he exclaims.

"What do you mean?"

"This $10,000 cancellation clause."

"It's standard," Dave shrugs.

"Well, no way!"

"May I look at that?" Fred asks. Grant passes the contract over.

Fred makes a show of reading the problematic paragraph, then pulls out his Montblanc and slowly unscrews the cap. "I'm going to waive that clause for you," he announces, and places the document on Grant's desk. Fred draws a line through the passage, initials the alteration, then passes the contract back. "You need to initial as well," he says.

After doing as instructed, Grant continues with the contract. All is peaceful as he reads through the boilerplate language covering confidentiality, mutual indemnification, and so on. Then he comes to the agreement terms and pauses again. "I can't accept a $500 finder's fee if we hire your people," Grant insists. "Some might apply for a job with us of their own accord."

"Where's that?" Fred asks. "Dave shouldn't have put it in."

Grant swivels the contract and indicates the offending line. Fred crosses through it, and he and the VP initial the change. After reading through the rest of the agreement, Grant says, "I don't see any other problems with this."

"Great," Dave smiles. "But I guess you need to send it to legal for review. If Cathy will call me once it's signed, I'll stop by and pick it up."

"That'll work," Grant says, and now he too is smiling.

Dave stands and shakes hands with the Grand Union executive. "We're looking forward to working with you."

"Same here," Grant replies, then turns to Fred. "Thanks for making this happen," he says warmly.

"It's nothing," Fred replies nonchalantly, "glad to do it."

Out in the parking lot, Fred and Dave stand by the Caddy and chat. "If I hadn't personally been there, I wouldn't believe it," Fred says. "Come to think of it, I was there, and I still don't believe it."

"Tough one," Dave says, grinning broadly.

"How did you know it would go that way?"

"I only hoped. Grant might well have trashed the contract and thrown us out."

"But he didn't." Fred shakes a cigarette out of his pack and lights up.

"No, curiosity got the better of him."

"Thankfully for us," Fred exhales.

Dave waves a hand in front of his face to dispel the smoke. "Grocery guys are all the same," he laughs, "they're never satisfied until they wring some concessions out of you."

"Be sure to let me know next time."

"For sure. We're a good team."

Once back at the office, Dave looks at his bulging inbox but is in no mood to tackle it. His microscopically short attention span is not helped by the adrenaline still coursing through him from the Grand Union meeting. Somehow, he gets through the rest of the day and is about to head for the practice tee at Winding Creek when Michelle sticks her head in his door. "Ralph and that investor are here," she says. "Come down to the conference room."

"Oh, right," Dave says as he suddenly remembers the meeting.

Ralph Franklin and a sharply dressed older man are in the hall talking with Michelle when Dave gets downstairs. "Here's our super salesman," Ralph says. "Dave, this is Pat Hollaway."

"Hi, Pat, great to meet you."

"Same here," Pat smiles.

The group files into the conference room and settles into chairs. "You know, it's hotter up here now than it was in Florida," Pat says conversationally.

"Where do you go down there?" Dave asks.

"Sanibel Island."

"Guess the gulf keeps things reasonably cool this time of year."

"Guess so," Ralph says impatiently. "Pat can spend time in Florida because he sold his company several years ago. Now he's looking for promising investments."

"What did your company do?" Michelle asks.

"We bought discounted hospital receivables then collected."

"Tough business," Dave exclaims.

"Oh, it was," Pat agrees. "Jimmy Hoffa was one of our debtors. We had to fit him with a pair of cement shoes when he wouldn't pay. No one has seen him since."

They all laugh, then Pat says, "But seriously, Michelle, I hear your business has fallen on hard times."

"Actually, it's booming," Ralph jumps in. "Dave keeps bringing in one big deal after another."

"It's just that our clients are slow paying," Michelle says.

"So, Garden State wants more capital in the company to offset the accounts receivable," Ralph explains.

"They're really putting the squeeze on me," Michelle whimpers. Her lips quiver and her eyes well with tears.

"I went bankrupt once before I came on the hospital idea," Pat sympathizes. "The sheriff and his boys came to my house and cleaned it out. They even took my Grady-White."

Michelle wipes her eyes with the backs of her hands. "What's a Grady-White?" she asks.

"It's a fishing boat," Dave says disgustedly. "You know, Pat, I had a friend once who had a similar experience to yours."

"Oh, really?"

"Yeah, one morning he got up and the first bad thing that happened is he cut himself shaving. Then he discovered his wife had run off, and later, when he went to work, he got fired."

"And I thought I had it bad," Pat says with a twinkle in his eye.

"Is this a joke?" Michelle wonders.

"So, my friend went home," Dave persists, "and was sitting on the sofa trying to think of what to do next when he remembered the strawberry patch in his backyard. He decided to harvest the berries, put the baskets in his kid's wagon, and sell them door to door. Well, the first door my friend knocked on was opened by a beautiful blonde. He was making his sales pitch when she allowed her negligee to fall open, revealing her gorgeous body. Immediately, my friend began weeping. The woman clutched her gown back together and said, 'What the hell is wrong with you?' 'Oh, I've had a terrible day,' my friend cried. First, I cut myself shaving, then found out my wife left me, got fired, and now you ... you're trying to fuck me out of my strawberries!"

Pat slaps his knee. "Should have seen that coming!"

"Dave thinks he's a comedian," Michelle frowns.

"So I see," Pat chuckles.

"It's a fun company," Ralph says, trying to get the meeting back on track. "They play hard but know how to work hard." He hands Pat a chart. "Just look at the growth in sales."

Pat glances at the sales figures. "I agree that this is a good business," he says, "but it will be up to my bean counters to determine if it's right for me. He stands and glances at his watch. "My wife is going to kill me."

"I've got to go as well," Michelle says, "it's past Fred's dinnertime."

As they're leaving the conference room, Pat lags behind and slips Dave a card. "Call me some time," he says quietly. "We can have lunch."

Dave's back upstairs a little later when Michelle comes out of her office, slams the door, and leaves without a word. He goes to the window and watches her drive away in the Mercedes. Then he turns off the lights and goes out, locking the door behind him.

The Principal Bank golf outing is the following day. Warren brings a ringer to join Fred and Dave in a foursome. He's a scratch golfer so they easily win the tournament. After an alcohol-soaked celebration, each takes home a nice trophy. Dave pays for his on Friday when he's too hungover to get anything accomplished. He spends most of the weekend at the office catching up.

As usual, Dave's late getting to work on Monday. Mindy scowls as he comes in, but Dave ignores her. He's upstairs sorting through phone messages when Barbara calls out, "Hey, there's a man on the line who claims to be your father."

"I'll take it," Dave says, and snatches up the phone. "Hi, Dad, how are you?"

"Not great, but I made it through detox," Knight says.

"Guess it was pretty bad."

"Awful!"

"So, what's next?" Dave idly drums on his desk with a pencil. Through the open office door, he sees two burly-looking men appear at the top of the stairs. They go over to Barbara's desk.

"A van is coming to take us to Abbey Farms," Knight explains. "I'm not allowed visitors for two weeks, but after that, you can come on Saturdays between ten and three."

"I'll be there," Dave promises. He watches Michelle come out of her office to talk to the men. One of them takes a card out of his pocket and reads off it. The other catches Michelle as she faints.

"Call Mildred and let her know I've quit drinking," Knight asks.

"For good?"

"Absolutely, I never want to go through this again."

"All right, I'll tell her," Dave says.

"The van's here, I've got to go."

"Hang in there. I'll see you soon."

Dave gets out of his chair and goes to the window expecting to see what he does see, which is several police cars with flashing lights. Behind them, a group of reporters waits near a van from a local television station. Dave recognizes the anchorwoman from the Newark CBS affiliate.

A TV camera swivels and points to the UpTempCo office, so Dave allows the curtain to close. He turns to see Michelle with a deputy sheriff on either side. She has some new bracelets. As the deputies escort her downstairs, the two plainclothes officers come into Dave's office. "Are you David S. Knight III?" one of them asks.

"That would be me," Dave replies.

"You're under arrest for bank fraud," the detective says, and begins to read off his card. "You have the right to remain silent," he intones, "anything you say can and will be used against you." After the cop finishes, his partner steps forward with a pair of handcuffs.

"May I get my keys and wallet from the drawer?"

"No, everything in this office is potential evidence. Please hold your hands out, sir."

After he's handcuffed, Dave is taken downstairs where Michelle waits. Together, they're escorted outside into the glare of camera lights. "How much did you get?" a reporter hollers. "Look this way, look this way," several cameramen implore as a barrage of flashing lights temporarily blinds the perpetrators.

Michelle is put in the back of one patrol car and Dave in another. As the vehicles slowly make their way past the crowd, photographers run alongside trying to get shots through the windows. Michelle covers her face to frustrate them.

In court the next day, Dave pleads not guilty and asks for a court-appointed attorney. Bond is set at $100,000, so he makes up his mind to settle into jail life.

But with Dave's highly kinetic nature, it doesn't take long for stir-craziness to set in. For something to do, he offers to help the trustee sweep and mop the floor. Soon Dave's working in the kitchen as well.

Over the next few weeks, Dave stays busy cleaning the cell block, washing dishes, and peeling potatoes. He spends little time locked up. When he is behind bars, Dave either sleeps or reads. Fortunately, the jail has a small library. It's well stocked with beat-up paperbacks.

Being in jail reminds Dave of the army. Both relieve their minions of making the sort of decisions that bedevil people. Choices like which outfit to put on in the morning, what to eat, where to go, and what to do. For those in the army and those in jail, these minor issues are taken away and replaced with one overarching concern—how to get out.

A month passes and Dave has nearly exhausted the jail library, when one day a deputy approaches the sink where he's scrubbing a pan. "Your mouthpiece wants to have a sit-down," he says. "Go get ready."

An hour later, Dave's taken in handcuffs to a conference room on the ground floor of the courthouse. His lawyer, Manny Alvarez, gets up when Dave comes in but doesn't offer to shake since Dave can't. "I believe you know these gentlemen," Manny says, pointing to Rich Little and Collin Bessie, who are seated at the table.

Dave nods to the two bankers, then glances at an attractive young lady in a business suit. "Hello, I'm Robin Wolfe, lawyer for Garden State," she smiles, "and this is John Maxwell, District Attorney." Robin indicates a heavy-set man in a loud sport coat seated at the head of the table.

"You can take those off," John tells the deputy, briefly removing the chawed stump of a cigar from his mouth.

As the deputy unlocks the handcuffs, Rich tries to relieve the awkwardness. "You look good in orange," he jokes.

"Thanks," Dave grins. "And you look good in Hart Schaffner & Marx."

"Can we cut the crap and get on with it?" John asks.

"Dave, these folks have a proposal for you," Manny says.

"OK, let's hear it." Dave pulls out a chair and sits.

Robin takes a folder from her briefcase and glances inside. "It appears that the only money you got from UpTempCo came from the compensation plan outlined in your employment contract." She gazes across the table at Dave. "Is that correct?"

"Yes, that's right." Dave is leaning forward in his chair, but now he forces himself to sit back and not appear so eager.

"We also looked at the charges on your gas card and company credit card," Collin chimes in, "to verify that no cash advances were taken, and all charges were listed on your expense reports."

Manny writes on his legal pad then looks at Dave. "They're admitting they don't have a money trail."

"That's true, but your client definitely misled Garden State," Robin insists. "That's why Wolfgang said to press charges."

"But now Wolfgang's out of the picture," Rich says. "He got fired."

"So, what's the proposal?" Dave asks.

"You sign a release, agreeing not to sue Garden State, and we'll withdraw the complaint," Robin offers. "You can walk out of here today."

"May I see the release?"

Robin takes a document from the folder and passes it to Dave, who briefly scans it. He pats his chest as if looking for a pen, and Manny hands him one. Dave scrawls his signature at the bottom of the page, then looks up. "Is that all?"

"You also need to initial here," Robin says, leaning across the table to point. Dave is distracted by a whiff of fragrance and a peek down Robin's blouse. He initials the form, and the paperwork is done.

"I'll get them started with your out-processing," Manny says, and goes out.

The public defender's departure is the signal for everyone to get up. "We put all your personal effects in a bag," John says. "A deputy will bring it here, along with your clothes."

"Thanks," Dave smiles. "He shakes hands with the DA and the Garden State crowd as they leave. Then the clothes he wore when arrested arrive. Hastily, Dave gets out of the colorful prison jumpsuit.

Outside the courthouse, Dave squints in response to the unaccustomed sunshine. He catches a bus that takes him to a terminal, where he transfers to one that will bring him into Manhattan.

Upon arrival at the Port Authority, Dave chooses to walk to his apartment rather than take a cab. He's looking for a spot to slake his thirst and soon drops into an Irish dive called the Dubliner. It's dark inside, and the hulking bald bartender looks like a genie. Dave wishes for a Guinness with a shot of Jameson, and both quickly materialize. He listens to a familiar Irish tune on the jukebox but is distracted by the conversation of three red-faced old men at the end of the bar. They are debating the merits of General Robert E. Lee. Two of the fellows stand up for the rebel as the third just as vociferously tears him down. Dave wishes they would shut up so he can hear the music.

Presently, the genie reappears. "Another round?" he asks, and poof, a fresh Guinness and another shot glass full of amber liquid sit in front of Dave. He's rapidly spending the pittance he was paid for working at the jail.

Dave goes and puts a dollar in the jukebox. He chooses songs such as "Roddy McCorley," "MacNamara's Band," "It's the Same Old Shillelagh," and others he knows from his childhood. After a time, the genie returns. "Ready for another?"

"Bing Crosby has nothing on my father," Dave replies.

"Another round, I mean."

Dave glances out the window at the sunlit street. "Better not," he says, "don't want to peak too early."

"Makes sense," the genie concedes. "Stop by later if you have a mind."

"Will do."

Dave leaves money on the bar then strolls up West 42nd Street carrying his belongings in a gray laundry sack. Skirting Times Square, he pauses at the entrance to an arcade, drawn by the sound of whistles, bells, thunks, clonks, sirens, and other noises emanating from the machines. He goes inside and passes a line of Skee-Ball games before putting a quarter in one. But Dave has no luck hitting the central ring that gives the highest points and ends with a miserable score. Still, the machine spits out tickets for points that can be redeemed for prizes at the arcade store. Dave calculates that based on the number of points he has accumulated thus far, he'll have to play thirty more games of Skee-Ball to win a teddy bear. Instead, he moves to a section of the arcade devoted to pinball.

A machine called "Full House" catches Dave's attention. He invests two bits in it, then reads the instructions. To get maximum points, the player must knock down a row of targets depicting three aces and two kings. This lights a ramp to a higher level, and if the player shoots the ball up that ramp when it's illuminated, 10,000 points are awarded plus access to the bonus bumpers on top.

To begin, Dave pulls back the plunger and tries the skill shot. But his ball rockets past the bonus area and heads for an exit. He nudges the machine as the ball hits the side of the off-ramp, causing it to bounce onto a flipper. After holding it a moment, he shoots at one of the aces in the central target area. The ball hits a bumper then rebounds straight down the middle of the machine just out of reach of either flipper. Now only two balls are left. After those are gone, Dave leaves the arcade.

When he gets home, Dave finds his pad looking the way he left it. All he wants now is to get under the shower and stay there however long it takes to get the stench of jail off him. It's a putrid combination of Pine-Sol, Johnson's floor wax, kitchen grease, and body odor.

Dave can't take more than half an hour under the water. After toweling dry, he goes naked to the fridge and pulls out a can of beer. Then Dave forces himself to look at the answering machine. As he feared, the indicator is blinking furiously. The message counter is past the red line.

Once he's dressed, Dave gets pen and paper then rewinds the tape to the first message. "Hey, faggot, I saw your picture in the paper," a hoarse voice intones. "How much money did you get?" Several messages of this ilk follow, so Dave fast forwards until he gets to one from Cindy. "I warned you about Michelle," she says, "but you wouldn't listen. Anyway, I'm sorry this happened. Call me if I can help."

After a couple more crank calls, Sister Sandy says, "One of our orderlies at the Abbey reported your father tried to bribe him to bring in a bottle of vodka. Colonel Knight has been warned that one more incident of this type and he'll be terminated from the program."

Dave shakes his head before going on to the next message. It's from an A&P store manager asking for his suggestion on another temp agency to use. Dave writes the manager's name and phone number down. Then the next message starts, and he hears Grant Becker's voice. "Thanks a lot, scumbag. One day I'm in my boss's office telling him about the great agency I gave an exclusive to for demos. Next thing you're on the front page and UpTempCo turns out to be nothing but a scam!"

As another irate call begins, Dave goes to pee. When he returns, Earl Falcon is talking. "Mr. Knight, it looks like your outfit has fallen on hard times. Sorry to hear it, but we are now in a jam with Pathmark. Please call me if you have any ideas." Dave makes a note of the Falcon number, then leaves the tape running while he gets another beer. He's opening it when the last message starts. "Dave, your father's not doing well," Dr. Carmichael begins. "He doesn't eat, says he's nauseous, and looks more jaundiced than before. We did some blood work and found he has an alarmingly low white blood cell count. So, I'm bringing him back to St. Vincent's. I've tried reaching you at work, but the number's disconnected. Please call me immediately upon receipt of this message."

Dave writes down the number Dr. Carmichael left, but it's too late to call her office. He shuts off the machine and sips his beer indecisively. Then Dave snaps out of it, grabs his wallet and keys, throws on a jacket, and slips his feet into a pair of loafers. He rushes out of the apartment and down the hall to the stairs.

A short cab ride later, Dave's at the hospital. "What room is Colonel David Knight in?" he asks the nun at the front desk.

"Let me see," she says, opening a binder. "Uh-oh, he's in the ICU."

After identifying himself, Dave is allowed up to the fifth floor and outfitted with a cap, gown, mask, and gloves. He enters the intensive care unit and finds his father asleep in a half-sitting position. Knight's receiving IV fluids while squiggly green lines march across the screen of a nearby monitor. A nun pulls a chair up beside the bed and indicates that Dave should sit.

It's eerily quiet in the ICU other than the bleating of monitors. As Dave waits, white- gowned medics float through the gloom like apparitions. Nearby, a wall clock ticks in concert with the drip of his father's IV. Someone taps Dave's shoulder. "I'm a priest, would you like to pray?"

"Sure." Dave gets to his feet.

As the two men whisper the Lord's Prayer, Knight opens his eyes. "Oh, it's you," he mutters, disappointment palpable in his voice.

"Yes."

"Who's that with you?"

"A priest."

"I'm a Presbyterian," Knight says defiantly. "Please leave me alone." The cleric nods his head and goes off.

"Where's Mildred?" Knight wheezes. "And Perle?"

"They haven't been told."

"Why not? I'm dying."

Dave looks at the monitor and is relieved to see a weak but steady heartbeat. "I've been away," he explains.

"Where?"

"In jail."

"No surprise there."

A nurse appears and takes Knight's wrist, feeling for the pulse. "I see you're awake," she says, looking at her watch.

"It hurts," Knight complains. "That's what woke me. Feels like someone's ramming a red-hot poker into my guts."

"Sorry, but you're not due another shot until midnight."

"Where's the doctor?" Dave asks.

The nurse turns to face Dave. "He told me not to overuse the narcotic."

"That's fucking nonsense."

"I'm going to call security if you keep cursing!"

"And I am going to completely wreck this joint if you don't get my father a shot."

There's a pause as the nurse looks Dave up and down. "Well, maybe we could give him a half measure just to hold him until twelve," she allows.

"All the angels in heaven will bless you for that," Dave smiles.

The nurse turns away, and presently an intern arrives with a syringe. He uses the existing IV to administer the pain medication then hurries away. Gradually, the pinched expression on Knight's face mellows. "So, it's just you and me," he says.

"Looks like it." Dave pulls the chair closer to the bed and sits back down.

"Truthfully, I was never able to figure you out."

"That makes two of us."

"I mean from the day you were born, I thought you were crazy," Knight insists. "Still think that."

"No doubt you're right."

"Tell Mildred my will, and all the insurance papers, are in the top right-hand corner of my desk."

"I'll tell her," Dave promises.

Knight closes his eyes. "It doesn't hurt anymore," he says.

Dave sits next to his sleeping father until a nurse comes around at midnight to administer another dose. "He'll be out for at least five hours now," she says. "Try to get some rest."

"I'll be back after a while," Dave promises.

Instead of resting, Dave walks to a pub in the village. There he has a pint of Guinness and a bowl of Irish stew. After one more beer, he strolls back to the hospital, enjoying the fresh night air. The waiting room is deserted, so Dave lies on one of the benches using his jacket for a pillow.

Much later, Dave wakes and glances at his watch. Stiffly, he gets to his feet and starts down the hall to the elevators. It's past six, and a new crew is at work in the ICU. Dave shows his ID and again gets into sterile gear. He's escorted to his father's bedside, which is now curtained off. The bed has been cranked down, and the colonel lies on his back barely breathing. "He's in a coma," the nurse says.

Dave sits with his father, feeling numb. Then the priest is back. "I was told that he's comatose; do you think it would hurt if I gave him the last rites?"

"That wouldn't hurt anything," Dave replies, "but I didn't know a priest could give last rites to a non-Catholic."

"It's OK as long as he's a baptized Christian, and he said he is," the priest says, opening his prayer book. Dave stands as the cleric administers the last rites, bowing his head and once again joining in the Lord's Prayer.

The clergyman leaves and Dave settles back onto the chair. He dozes awhile but is awakened by the bustle around Knight's bed. Opening his eyes, Dave sees a doctor holding a stethoscope. His father's breathing is now very faint. Just intermittent gasps, like a fish long out of water. Then the lines on the monitor go flat, and Knight stops groping for air.

The physician places the end of his stethoscope on the colonel's chest, listens intently for some time, then looks at Dave and says, "It's over." A nurse bustles around the bed, disconnecting equipment while Dave walks out of the cubicle with the doctor. "So, what was the cause of death?" he asks.

"Organ failure."

"Meaning?"

"Cirrhosis carcinoma."

"That couldn't have been diagnosed sooner?"

The doctor stops walking. "Cirrhosis has no symptoms in the early stages," he says, facing Dave.

"Then how did you know?"

"We did an exploratory when he first got here and found that the liver was nothing but scar tissue. All we could do was sew him back up."

"I see," Dave says, but now he realizes the symptoms were apparent all along.

A nun approaches with a clipboard. "You'll need to arrange with a funeral home to have his remains picked up," she says gently. "Here are your copies of the paperwork."

Outside, it's grown light, though the sunrise is hidden behind tall buildings. Dave hails a cab for the ride back to his apartment. He gets a fully loaded bagel at the corner deli before heading upstairs.

When he's finished with breakfast, Dave showers and shaves. Afterward, he sits by the phone with a cup of coffee and dials directory assistance for Washington, D.C. He gets the number for Arlington Cemetery and calls to arrange the funeral. Then Dave dials his older sister. "Dad is dead," he tells her.

"So, there's a God after all," Melissa gloats.

"He died this morning, here in New York."

"Hold on a sec." Dave hears a refrigerator door open and close, then the pop of a cork. "I'm pouring some champagne," Melissa giggles. "This calls for a celebration!"

"Isn't it kind of early?" Dave wonders.

"It's got to be noon somewhere in the world," Melissa says. "Besides, think of what we're celebrating. He'd appreciate us starting the day off with a drink."

"I called Arlington. The funeral will be Monday."

"Don't look for me, I'm not that much of a hypocrite."

"I have more calls to make," Dave says, "but we'll talk again soon."

"Well, aren't you being the dutiful son," Melissa mocks.

Dave takes his empty cup to the coffee maker for a refill. Then he checks the time and sees that it's now past eight in Texas. So, he sets the phone on the kitchen counter and dials Mildred's number. She picks up after just two rings. "Has something happened to your father?" Mildred asks when she hears Dave's voice.

"He died this morning."

"I knew it! I woke up earlier than usual this morning with a feeling something terrible had happened."

"His last words were about you."

"How sweet. He was such a darling man, but the booze just got the better of him. What are you doing about arrangements?"

"I've been on the phone with Arlington."

"That's good, and you should know I'll cover any costs not paid by the army."

"Thanks, it looks like the funeral will be on Monday."

"I won't be able to come, but I'll send flowers."

"All right, thanks." As he cradles the phone, Dave looks out the window at the office building across the street. People are at their desks and Dave envies them. *Must be nice to have a job*, he thinks.

With a sigh, Dave sets the phone down next to the sofa and sits. He rests his feet on the coffee table, then opens the directory to look up the Red Cross. He's on the line with them for almost an hour, being shunted from one person to the next until he gets the right department. An officious clerk takes down the information he'll need to notify Dave's brother, Dan, who's in Japan with the Air Force.

After hanging up, Dave stretches out on the sofa, intending to take a nap. But before he can close his eyes, the phone rings. "This is Captain Garrett of The Old Guard," a man says, "I'll be helping with Colonel Knight's funeral."

"That's great, thanks."

"As a full colonel, your father is entitled to all military honors," the captain explains. "Where is he now?"

"St. Vincent's Hospital in Manhattan."

"I'll call them and get the ball rolling."

Dave goes to the lobby and gets a newspaper from the vending machine. Then he returns to the apartment, makes a sandwich, and reads while he eats. Afterward, he gets his address book and looks up the number for his younger sister, Perle. She lives in Antigua with her husband, whom she met at college. His parents bought them a sailboat for their wedding, and now they operate a charter business. When customers are scarce, Perle and her husband amuse themselves sixties-style, so they normally sleep late. That's why Dave has waited until noon to call.

It takes a lot of rings before Perle finally picks up. "Laid Back Charters," she says hoarsely, "may I help you?"

"Perle, this is Dave. I've got some bad news about Dad."

"Oh?"

"Yeah, he passed away this morning."

"You're kidding! What's going to happen with my allowance?"

"I don't know."

"Have you told the others?"

"Yes."

"When's the funeral?"

"Monday, at Arlington."

"Shit, that doesn't give me much time to book a flight."

"Sorry," Dave replies, but Perle is gone. "If you'd like to make a call, please hang up and try again," an angry voice demands. Hastily, Dave replaces the receiver. He opens a beer, sets it down on the coffee table, and dials Bob Stansfield's home number.

"Hey, it's Dave Knight."

"What do you want?"

"Falcon Candy called me."

"What about?"

"They need to service the Pathmark stores. I thought you and the other guys might want to help and make some money while you're at it."

"That would be something anyway."

"I'll give you their number. I can also give you some contacts where y'all can get reset work."

"Great."

When he's finished talking with Bob, Dave changes into workout clothes. He does some calisthenics then goes for a long walk, stopping on the way back to eat. Once home, Dave turns on the TV and forces himself to stay awake until bedtime. Then he climbs into his cot and revels in the familiar sag. It's nice to be back in his own bed.

The next morning, after several cups of coffee and some French toast, Dave types a notice for the newspapers on his typewriter:

COLONEL DAVID STUART KNIGHT JR. (Ret.) Born November 25, 1911, died August 8, 1984.

Colonel David Stuart Knight Jr. passed away yesterday after a brief illness. Knight served in the U.S. Army Signal Corps for thirty years, seeing action on Okinawa during World War II. He leaves behind his wife Mildred B. Knight of Palestine, Texas, and four children: Melissa G. Beaufort of Annapolis, David S. Knight III of Manhattan, Daniel F. Knight currently serving in the U.S. Air Force, and Perle J. Grayson of Antiqua, West Indies. Colonel Knight will be interred at Arlington National Cemetery after a memorial service scheduled for 10:00 a.m. on Monday, August 13 at the Arlington National Cemetery Chapel.

Dave freshens up then leaves the apartment. He drops off a check for the paperboy, then goes to a print shop and makes copies of the funeral notice. He mails one to the *Palestine Herald* and another to *The Washington Post*. Afterward, Dave walks to the New York Times Building and leaves a copy there.

Once Dave's done at the newspaper, he goes to a state employment office. While he's waiting to talk with a counselor, Dave completes an application for unemployment benefits. Then he looks through binders of job listings, making note of sales opportunities that sound interesting.

It's almost five by the time Dave returns home with plans to update his résumé. Instead, he turns on the TV, stretches out, and allows the litany of fires, stabbings, and shootings that constitutes the evening news to lull him to sleep. At some point during the night, he gets up to turn off the boob tube.

In the morning, Dave stumbles out of bed and retrieves the newspaper from in front of his door, happy to be back on good terms with the paperboy. As coffee brews, he turns to the obituaries to see if the one he wrote made the deadline.

Colonel Knight's obituary is in the *Times* exactly as Dave wrote it. Idly, he glances at the rest of the page then does a double take on one of the items:

Wolfgang Schultes Lander, Born March 15, 1931, Died August 8, 1984.

Wolfgang Schultes Lander was found dead in his Upper East Side apartment yesterday. He was a prominent area banker whose family came to the United States from Germany when he was a boy. They were fleeing persecution by the Nazis. Mr. Lander began working at Garden State National Bank as a cashier in 1951 and recently ended his career there as Senior Vice President for Credit. He leaves behind his wife of twenty-four years, Ilsa D. Lander, a survivor of the notorious Bergen-Belsen concentration camp. Funeral arrangements are being handled by Freeman Funeral Home. A service will be held at Park East Synagogue today at 4:00 p.m. Interment will follow.

Stunned, Dave looks up the number for Garden State and calls Rich Little. "What happened to Wolfgang?"

"He shot himself," Rich says.

"Oh, my God."

"Ilsa said she went down to the corner for a couple of things, came back, and found him in the tub dressed in some old clothes, gun in hand."

"How sad!"

"The bank was his life."

"I feel awful."

"You shouldn't, this has nothing to do with you."

After concluding his conversation with Rich, there are several things Dave should do, but he's too depressed. It takes until afternoon for him to stir up the motivation to rewrite his résumé. Over the next couple of days, Dave responds to help wanted ads. Then on Sunday afternoon, he takes the shuttle to Washington and checks into the Key Bridge Marriott using reward points.

Dave walks to Arlington National Cemetery the next morning. He finds Captain Garrett at the chapel with Knight's flag-draped casket resting on a bier behind him. "Looks like everything's all set," Dave says after introducing himself.

"Yes, sir. We'll be able to get started right on time." Garrett looks at his watch to double-check.

It's a beautiful summer morning, so Dave goes outside to wait. The view across the river brings back memories. Most prominent in Dave's mind is the night Bobby Kennedy was brought over to join his brother. Dave was among the crowd that lined the route. Some of the mourners brought candles while others held matches. As the cortège passed, the way was lit with flames. Everyone was crying.

Now a silver BMW pulls up, and Melissa emerges with her two blond-haired boys. Both are dressed in navy blazers, white polo shirts, and khaki slacks. Melissa's in a black dress, sensible shoes, and a wide-brimmed hat complete with a long black veil. "I didn't expect to see you today," Dave says.

"Thought I'd better come and make absolutely certain the bastard gets planted."

Dave glances at the two boys, who return the attention with bright smiles. "Hi, Uncle Dave," Liam says.

"What happened to your arm?" Dave asks.

"Broke it playing lacrosse," Liam says proudly.

"Bad luck."

"Yeah."

"So, who besides us?" Melissa asks.

"Not sure," Dave says. "Dan sent a telegram. He can't make it."

A taxi has been winding up the hill, and now it stops in front of the chapel. Perle gets out wearing a flower-patterned smock over jeans. "Where's Mildred?" she asks.

"Not coming," Dave replies.

"What do you mean?"

"Guess she didn't want to see Dad get back together with Mom."

"You mean I came all this way for nothing?" Perle snaps. "I need to see Mildred."

"Then you'll have to go to Palestine," Dave shrugs.

"Fuck! Why didn't you tell me she wasn't coming?"

"You didn't ask."

Melissa has been edging her children away from the argument, and now she takes them into the chapel. After a spiteful glare at her brother, Perle follows.

Dave waits outside, thinking some of his father's old friends may have seen the funeral notice and decided to come. But no more cars arrive, so when the organist starts, he too goes inside.

Presently, the chaplain arrives and delivers a generic funeral service. Afterward, an honor guard marches in and with military precision carries Knight down the aisle and out of the chapel. A platoon of troops from The Old Guard snaps to attention and presents arms as the casket is loaded onto a caisson.

Once the casket is secure, the infantry executes right shoulder arms and marches out of the parking lot, followed by a band that strikes up a somber march. Then the driver of the caisson gets his horses going and joins the procession. A handler, holding the bridle of a saddled black stallion, brings up the rear. "The car is for you," Garrett says as a limousine pulls up. He opens the door and Perle gets in.

"That's OK, I'll just walk," Dave says. The burial site is only half a mile away.

"It's better if you take the car," Garrett insists, "that's the way we do it."

"I want to walk, too," Melissa says, and now Garrett throws in the towel. "That will be fine," he allows.

Melissa takes her children by the hand and falls in behind the riderless horse. She marches bravely, with the veil billowing around her beautiful face. Dave walks behind and thinks, *The army's wasting a lot of money on this just for us.* But he quickly rejects that thought. He recalls the foreign schools the Knight children attended, the substandard housing they sometimes lived in on army posts, the fear they felt in Germany when the Russians invaded nearby Hungary, and the blistering heat of summers when the family was isolated at a base in Georgia. *They owe us this*, he decides.

The procession comes to a halt, and the honor guard unloads the casket then takes it to the gravesite. The band and the horse handler wait by the caisson while Garrett ushers the family to a row of folding chairs. Next to the grave is an impressive array of long-stemmed yellow roses to remind everyone of Texas.

With everything set, it's quiet in the cemetery other than the whinnying of horses, the chirping of birds, and the faint whisper of cars passing in the distance. The chaplain reads the "Prayer for the Dead," then asks if anyone wishes to speak.

No one else moves, so Dave stands and recites "Danny Deever," his father's favorite poem. Then the bugler steps forward and plays a haunting "Taps." Afterward, the soldiers snap off three quick volleys, and finally, the honor guard removes the flag from the casket, folds it, and presents the national emblem to Melissa.

The troops withdraw, leaving the mourners to their thoughts. Dave is tired of sitting, so he goes to the casket, which is still on a hoist, and looks down at the top of his mother's vault. She and the colonel will be sharing this desirable plot for eternity.

After a period of contemplation, Dave turns and finds his sisters gone. On the road, a street-sweeping crew is cleaning up after the horses. Beyond them, Melissa is halfway back to the chapel. She's striding purposefully, with the veil plastered against her face and the flag tucked under her arm like a football. Liam and his brother trot along behind. Dave walks back alone.

CHAPTER ELEVEN

Tilt

The pinball machine is called "The Addams Family." Dave racked up an excellent score on it earlier, but now his concentration is waning. "Damn," he says as the last ball eludes his effort at interception.

With the hated "Game Over" sign flashing, Dave goes to the bar and drinks from his beer mug. "Talk about cheap entertainment," he comments. "I've been playing that machine for nearly an hour, and all I put in was a dollar."

"Not bad," the bartender says without taking his eyes off a soap opera he's watching.

As Dave relaxes, he looks out the window and admires the energy of people scurrying past on 7th Avenue. *They're what keeps this economy going*, he thinks, and has another swill of beer.

Putting the mug down, Dave glimpses himself in the bar mirror. It's hard not to notice the crow's feet around his eyes and the receding hairline. Hastily, he shifts his gaze to the rows of dusty liquor bottles below. "When was the last time someone here ordered a shot of Glenlivet?" he asks.

A commercial has taken over the tube, so the barkeep turns toward Dave. "The owner had hopes for this place once," he says. "So, what do you do when you're not playing pinball?"

"I'm in sales."

"What do you sell?"

"Temp agency," Dave replies. "My company supplies workers to the theater trade."

"Do you own it?"

"Nah, I just work there. I used to be part-owner of a temp agency, but my partner embezzled all the money."

"What happened to him?"

"It was a her. She got five to ten in an upstate pen with the possibility of time off for good behavior."

"Serves her right. Want another?"

"Better not," Dave says, and slides off the barstool, "I have sales calls to make." He finishes his beer, then shakes several Tic Tacs into his mouth. On the way out, Dave glances at the pinball machine. Some of the free games he won are still on it. *Maybe I'll stop by later*, he thinks.

Out on the sidewalk, Dave joins the throng heading up 7th Avenue toward Times Square. He turns onto 45th Street and goes half a block to the Imperial Theater. Ignoring the "Closed" sign, Dave pushes through the double doors behind the ticket booth.

Inside, a massive chandelier dominates the lobby even though the lights are off. Dave walks underneath it then opens a door leading to the mezzanine. It's dark inside the theater except for the stage, which is brightly lit. A group of dancers is performing to music emanating from a piano located stage right. A gray-haired lady dressed in a sweatshirt and jeans is at the keyboard.

Dave goes down the aisle toward a cluster of people several rows back from the stage. Cindy is among them, seated next to her boss, Sydney Glass. Gary Draper, the stage manager, is one row back from the others. Dave slips into the seat next to him.

"We can have our meeting after I'm finished here," Gary whispers.

"All right."

The dancers have stopped, and while they catch their breath, Sydney scowls. "This isn't working," he fumes. "Let's try it again from where Damien enters."

As the music starts again, a girl goes to center stage while a boy approaches her from the wing. He points his finger and sings angrily. Meanwhile, she folds her arms and taps her foot, as if impatient for a chance to argue back. The dancers perform in the background. Their elegant movements contrast with the careless outfits they wear. Old turtleneck sweaters over torn leotards with ugly woollen leg warmers are standard. The worn-out ballet slippers on the dancers' feet are held together with electrical tape.

For the next half-hour, the performers repeat the same scene, with Sydney still dissatisfied. Then toward the end of the third run-through, Dave sees what's missing. "Her body language is all wrong," he exclaims.

There had been the sound of the piano and noise from dancers' feet pounding the stage, but at the instant Dave speaks, the music and dancing stop because Sydney has given the "cut" sign. In the sudden silence, the producer hears what Dave says. "Who's talking over there?" he snaps.

"Uh ... I'm the Powerforce rep," Dave stammers, "... sorry."

"What about her body language?" Sydney asks.

"She needs to display more emotion at the end," Dave suggests. "Maybe fall to her knees after singing that last line. Then she could look up as if imploring help from above. As it is, there's no climax. The scene just fizzles out."

Sydney gazes toward the stage thoughtfully. "Why not?" he mutters. "Diane, try dropping to your knees in despair as Damien is leaving, then look up, and hold both arms out as if you're begging heaven for deliverance."

The pianist launches into the song, and the scene is repeated with the new ending. "YESSSSSSS," Sydney gloats, "that works! Now, let's take a break, everyone, but I need you back in two hours."

The performers leave the stage as Sydney, and those around him, get to their feet. "Gary, we need to adjust the lights," Sydney says. "I want the stage to go dark at the end except for a single spot on Diane."

"I'll take care of it," Gary replies.

"And make sure Powerforce gets all of our business from now on."

"We'll need five stagehands to hang backdrops on Monday," Gary says. "Dave, can you get them here at eight?"

"No problem," Dave smiles.

"The job will take all day," Gary elaborates.

"All right, I'll put the work order in now."

Sydney throws his arm over Dave's shoulder as they walk out. "Thanks for your idea," he says, "I knew something was missing but couldn't figure out what."

"I didn't mean to stick my nose in."

"Yeah, well don't let it happen again," Sydney laughs.

When they get out to the lobby, Cindy is waiting. "You have a meeting with Robert Stone in an hour," she tells Sydney. "Also, Sharon Siegel is here from the *Times*. She's been waiting all morning." Cindy takes Sydney by the elbow and steers him toward the reporter.

Left by himself, Dave goes to a rank of payphones, puts a quarter in one, and calls the Powerforce office. Sandy Smith, the customer service manager, picks up. "We'll need five stagehands at the Imperial on Monday," he tells her. "They need to be here at eight and will not be finished until five or later." Dave is interrupted by an impatient tapping on his shoulder. He turns to find Cindy glowering at him.

"Sandy, I have to go," Dave says. "What? Oh, all right, I'll call him shortly." Dave hangs up and turns to face his ex.

"Are you crazy?" Cindy hisses. "Nobody talks during a Sydney Glass rehearsal except Sydney. How embarrassing! I'm sorry I ever told you about the Powerforce job."

"Don't hold back," Dave suggests, "tell me how you really feel."

"Thank God we're divorced," Cindy snaps. "That's how I feel."

After Cindy stalks off, Dave puts another coin in the phone and redials the office. "Oh, hi, Mr. Shaw," he says. "Yes, I just got an order from *Parasols*, and they promised us more. I'm going to *The World Is Not New* next to give that another shot." Dave looks around nervously as he listens to his boss then says, "Don't worry, I'll do my best." Immediately, he bites his lip as Mr. Shaw gives him more advice. "Oh, you're right," Dave agrees, "my best is not what you want; you want an order. Don't worry, Mr. Shaw, I'll get some business from them, I promise."

As Dave leaves the Imperial, he resists looking up at the towering skyscrapers that line the street. *After all this time, I'm still a hick*, he thinks. A cab pulls up, and a well-dressed businesswoman gets out. Dave jumps in before she can close the door. "The Broadway Theater," he says.

The cabbie raises his flag, then as horns blare, he impudently wedges the vehicle into a gap in the traffic. Dave settles back for the short ride, knowing it will be stop and go all the way.

Presently, the taxi pulls up in front of the Broadway and disgorges its passenger. Dave goes inside the theater and finds a security guard sitting at one of the lobby bars. "What do you want?" the rent-a-cop demands, eyeing Dave's scuffed shoes, outdated suit, and decrepit briefcase.

"To see the stage manager."

"Sorry, no salesmen," the guard says, "I'm under strict orders."

"May I leave a brochure?"

"Sure."

Dave gets a Powerforce brochure out and hands it to the guard. *What a waste of time*, he thinks. *Mr. Shaw isn't going to like this.*

Back outside, Dave looks for a cab. But it's rush hour now, and the drivers all have their flags up. He notices a cocktail lounge next door, with a sign that reads, "Jimmy's Place." Peering into the window, Dave spies a pinball machine with colored lights that blink enticingly. *What the hell*, he thinks, and goes inside.

At the bar, several men in business suits talk animatedly. There are other groups of nicely dressed patrons seated at tables. It's happy hour, so Dave gets a draft at half price. Then he goes to the pinball machine, puts the beer mug on a nearby table, and starts to play.

Soon Dave is furiously working the flippers while rocking the machine forward, back, and sideways. Then the buzzer sounds, the flippers go dead, and the LED sign spells "TILT."

Dave shrugs and pushes the start button again. He plays the next ball until the machine makes a loud THONK and awards a free game. Dave does a little dance to celebrate, then hoists his beer mug.

The pinball machine is called Cyclone and features the famous Coney Island roller coaster on the backboard. Now that Dave knows how sensitive it is, he can use just the right amount of body English to keep his ball in play without tilting. Soon he's rewarded with another THONK and then another. When he loses the last ball, Dave glances up and sees the bartender staring at him. "How many points did you get?" he asks.

"18,500,000," Dave brags.

"Not bad, the record is somewhere around 20,000,000."

"Guess I have more work to do," Dave smiles.

The LED display on the Cyclone is flashing and scrolls a message saying Dave has one of the top ten scores and should enter his initials. While doing so, he sees that PLN is in first place.

Dave chugs some brew while glancing around the room. It's filling with people coming in from work. One of them comes over and challenges Dave to a game. "We usually play for a beer," he says.

"That's cool," Dave agrees. After the game, he has a fresh beer at no cost.

Another challenger approaches and offers Dave his hand. "I'm Phillip," he says.

"Do you go by that?" Dave asks as they shake.

"Yeah."

"My name's David, but everyone calls me Dave."

"Nice to meet you," Phillip smiles.

After dropping a quarter into the machine, Phillip puts a ball into play. He racks up a nice score, but Dave goes him one better when it's his turn. The lead changes hands several more times before Dave ekes out a win.

Phillip goes for more beer and then they start a new game. Now that he's warmed up, Phillip gets on a roll. Soon there's a THONK, and he wins a free game. By the time he's done, Phillip has set a record on the machine. This time, Dave's buying.

When Dave returns from the bar, he sees Phillip putting the initials PLN next to his score. "You're really good," Dave comments. He hands Phillip his beer.

"I got lucky with those multi-balls, then hit a couple of jackpots," Phillip says modestly. "I notice you're a lot more forceful working the machine than I am. How do you keep from tilting it?"

"Actually, I did tilt it before you got here," Dave admits. He pulls out a chair and sits.

Phillip puts his mug on the table and grabs a seat as well. "Do you work around here?" he asks.

"Yeah, I work all over the theater district," Dave says. "I'm in sales for a temp agency. We supply stagehands for shows."

"Oh, really? I'm the lighting manager for *The World.*"

"I tried to get some business there today but was stopped by the security guard."

"That's too bad. We could use some help. Can you come by again tomorrow?"

"Sure."

"I'll let the guard know you're coming."

"Sounds good."

Phillip glances at his watch then hurriedly gets to his feet. "I've got to catch my train," he says. "See you tomorrow."

Dave shakes his head as Phillip goes out. *Just amazing*, he thinks. *Proves that it's better to be lucky than good.*

It's boring sitting alone, so Dave goes back to the Cyclone. Over the next couple of hours, he uses up the free games that he and Phillip won. When the game indicator finally gets to 0, Dave drains the dregs from his mug then goes to the bar. A pretty woman is sitting by herself, so he joins her. "Hi," Dave says.

"Why, hello," she smiles.

"How do you make your hair fall across your forehead that way without it getting into your eyes?" Dave asks, using a variation of his standard opening line.

"Oh, I tease that part and then use a little dab of gel to keep it up," the girl replies, touching her hair. "Do you like it?"

"It looks fabulous," Dave replies. "What's your name?"

"Karen."

"I'm Dave. What are you drinking?"

"Vodka tonic."

Dave motions to the bartender and orders more refreshments, then he turns back to Karen. "Do you live in town?" he asks.

"Yeah, but it's expensive," she complains. "I'd like to move to the country."

"What would you do there?"

"You can make a lot of money raising Palominos. My girlfriend married a guy with a farm near Ithaca. Now that's what she does."

"Sounds like a great life."

"What about you? Do you have a dream job you want to do someday?"

"I'd like to be a writer."

"What kind of writer?"

"A novelist maybe, or a poet."

"Have you written any poems?"

"Yes."

"Tell me one."

Dave swivels his barstool so that he's facing Karen. Then he takes her hand and recites:

> The curfew tolls the knell of parting day,
> The lowing herd winds slowly o'er the lee,
> The plowman homeward plods his weary way,
> And leaves the world to darkness and to me.

Karen's eyes are getting bigger, and the expression on her face is incredulous. Before Dave can continue, she snatches her hand away and gives him a shove. "You didn't write that," she exclaims. "We studied that poem in college."

Dave loses his balance, starts to fall, then feels his neighbor at the bar steady him. "Thanks, buddy," Dave says, laughing. Karen is laughing, too. "You are so full of it," she says. "You never wrote a poem in your life."

"I have! There's a short one I wrote recently, want to hear it?"

"Sure, but don't try to fool me again."

"All right, here goes." Dave begins to recite:

> *Last rites remind,*
> *Those who do not go,*
> *That darkness never ends,*
> *And sleep is not repose,*
> *So, they search in vain,*
> *For someone to respect,*
> *The futile lives of those,*
> *Who give, so don't expect,*
> *Their solitary ways,*
> *To end in such neglect,*
> *Alone when they begin,*
> *Strangers in the end.*

"Wow, did you really write that?" Karen asks.

"Yes."

"What does it mean?"

"It means life sucks, and then you die."

"Kind of depressing, don't you think?"

"Not if you're a Buddhist."

"Are you a Buddhist?"

"No, I'm a salesman."

"That's funny," Karen smiles. "I like you."

"I like you, too."

"Do you think we would ever go out?"

"Honestly, probably not."

"Oh."

"Hey, you're very nice," Dave says. "But I got divorced a while back and still haven't gotten over it."

"Well, at least you're honest," Karen sighs. "This place is usually packed full of the most pathological liars you'll ever meet."

Someone is tapping on Dave's shoulder. It's the guy he played several hours earlier. "One more game," the man slurs. "I've got the machine figured out, and now I'm going to beat you."

"All right, but this time the loser buys a round of shots," Dave says. "Tequila."

"You're on."

Once again, Dave outpoints the challenger. He gulps his winnings then goes to the men's room to pee. When he comes out, the lights have been turned up, and customers are heading for the door. At the bar, three guys wearing suits surround Karen. "I know a place where we can get a drink after hours," one of them is telling her. "They only let you in if they know you."

"You must really get around," Karen says sarcastically.

"Come on," the man insists.

Karen looks up and sees Dave pass by. "Honey, where are you going?" she calls, and clambers down from the barstool. She grabs her bag and brushes past the three men. "He's my husband," Karen says, taking hold of Dave's arm.

"Bullshit," one of the men growls as Karen and Dave exit the bar.

It's cold, so Karen snuggles against Dave's arm as they walk. A taxi pulls to the curb just up the street. Without a word, they break into a run.

CHAPTER TWELVE
The World is Not New

Dave is in his cubicle at the Powerforce office, doodling on a notepad. He's supposed to be making cold calls but is not in the mood. Then the phone rings, and he snatches up the receiver thinking it might be a customer. Instead, it's his ex.

"What are you up to?" Cindy asks.

"Just killing time till I can get out of here," Dave replies. "It's been a long day."

"Tell me about it," Cindy exclaims. "We had the dress rehearsal for *Parasols*, and it took all afternoon. Fortunately, Sydney was pleased. He said to thank you again for your idea about scene three."

"Yeah, Gary called yesterday and gave us a job building sets for the tryout," Dave says. "He promised to use Powerforce exclusively from now on."

"I was going to ask if you'd like to go to Gusti's after work?"

"That would be nice."

"OK, see you there."

After hanging up, Dave goes back to scribbling on his pad. He's trying to make a rhyme and almost has it. Dimly, he notices Sandy and Mr. Shaw pass by, heading for the door. Dave gives them a few minutes to clear the building, grabs his coat, and turns out the lights.

Outside, it's cold and gray. After a short walk, Dave is heartened to find Cindy waiting for him with a pitcher of beer at their favorite pizza joint. She downs the beer remaining in the mug in front of her, and then fills both the mugs on the table as Dave walks up.

"I got a head start," Cindy says. "You'll have to catch up."

"No worries." Dave tosses his coat onto an empty chair and sits.

"So, how are things at Powerforce?"

"Business is going great and Shaw is impressed," Dave says.

"Oh, really?"

"Yeah, I cracked *The World Is Not New* account last week, and he was ecstatic."

"You need to hang onto this gig," Cindy says. "You've had four jobs in the last ten years. That doesn't look good on your resumé."

"Hey, was it my fault that UpTempCo went down the tubes? I would still be part-owner if Michelle hadn't turned out to be such a crook."

"Of course, it's your fault. You quit a perfectly good job to go into business with her. The problem is that you're a terrible judge of people's character."

"I guess so."

"I knew Michelle was a phony the first time I saw her," Cindy says.

"And you were right."

Dave changes the subject. "I wrote a little verse for Thanksgiving. Do you want to hear it?"

"You and your stupid poems," Cindy scoffs.

"This is a funny one," Dave promises, and begins reciting before she has a chance to object:

> *Back when the first settlers,*
> *Came to this new land,*
> *They asked the current residents,*
> *To lend them a helping hand,*
> *So, the Indians taught the Pilgrims,*
> *Everything they knew,*
> *And the Pilgrims for the Indians,*
> *The mother of all parties threw,*
> *Now in order to commemorate,*
> *What happened way back then,*
> *I wish you a happy Thanksgiving,*
> *With these few lines from my pen.*

"That's the stupidest thing I've ever heard," Cindy laughs.

Dave senses a bit of affection in his ex-wife's voice. "Want to come home with me?" he asks. "For old time's sake?"

"Sure, why not? You got any dope?"

"I've still got most of that bag I got from you."

"Last winter? You truly don't smoke much, do you?"

"I'd rather drink." Dave emphasizes his point by reaching for the pitcher. He fills his mug then sloshes what's left into Cindy's.

"Yeah, you're just like your dad," Cindy says, "and your liver's going to go the same way his did."

"He always loved you."

"Yeah, aside from being an alky, he was a dirty old man."

"Too true."

"That's some good weed, that Jamaican. Do you even have papers?"

"We can stop at the corner and get some Zig-Zags and a six-pack."

"All right." Cindy drains her mug then stands up. Dave helps her on with her coat.

It's late by the time Dave gets to work the next morning and Mr. Shaw is waiting. "Where have you been?" he asks.

"At the Imperial," Dave lies. "Had a meeting with Gary."

"That's all right then," Mr. Shaw allows. "But we need to talk."

"What about?" Dave takes his coat off and hangs it in the hall closet.

"You need to take Sandy with you on a sales call."

"That's crazy!" Dave exclaims. "She's barely civil speaking with customers on the phone. How's she going to be in person?"

Mr. Shaw follows Dave into his cubicle. "I promised Sandy we would get her into sales," he says. "Take her to your meeting at the Minskoff tomorrow."

"If you insist," Dave scowls.

"I do insist," Mr. Shaw snaps, "and the last time I looked, I was the owner here."

Dave picks up an account file and buries his nose in it until his boss takes the hint and leaves. Whatever motivation he had is gone. The remainder of the day drags past aimlessly.

At the Minskoff Theater the next morning, Dave and Sandy meet with Terry Foster, the stage manager for a revival of *Death of a Salesman*. "You guys totally screwed up last time," Terry begins. "What a bunch of winos you sent us."

"That's because you hardly gave us any notice," Dave replies. He glances at Sandy, who's responsible for staffing, but she remains aloof. Her manner and style of dress are that of a sex goddess, but her physical attributes don't measure up.

"Well, maybe I'll give you another chance," Terry says. "We have to get all the lighting rigged next Thursday. You should be able to come up with six sober stagehands to do it with that much notice. What kind of deal can you give me?"

"Sandy's our customer service manager and will handle this order for you," Dave explains. "Sandy, what do you think?"

Sandy opens a three-ring binder and glances inside. "Normally, we charge $18.00 per hour," she says. "That includes all withholding, plus the insurance, union dues, and workman's comp. But I'm only going to charge you $17.00 this once to make up for last time."

"Forget it," Terry snaps. "Workpower's everyday rate is $17.00. Why should I switch?"

"Talk about winos," Dave comments.

"Yeah, but they don't pretend they're going to send anything else." Terry drums his fingers on the desk impatiently.

"Oh, all right," Sandy says, "$16.00 an hour fully loaded just for this job. Then it will always be $17.00 for sober, experienced stagehands. You'll like our workers, I promise."

"I better," Terry declares.

Sandy and Dave take a cab back to the Powerforce office. "I'll write up the contract," he says when they get there.

"Mr. Shaw promised he'd help me write the contract if we got a deal," Sandy replies. "When it's finished, I'll bring it to Terry and get it signed."

"Whatever you say," Dave shrugs. He goes down the hall to his cubicle and checks the mail. As usual, there's nothing but junk. Frustrated, Dave picks up the phone and calls Cindy at work. "You wouldn't believe my morning," he complains. "I had to take Sandy with me to a meeting at *Death of a Salesman*. Mr. Shaw says I'm supposed to train her to do outside sales."

"That doesn't sound good at all," Cindy says.

Two weeks later, on a cold Monday morning, Mr. Shaw calls Dave into his office. "We have a problem with *Death of a Salesman*," he says.

"What's that?"

"Sandy priced the job too low then forgot to put a provision for overtime into the contract. Those guys were there from nine in the morning until ten that night. We had to pay time-and-a-half for every hour over eight they worked."

"OK, so we take a hit on the overtime hours, but make margin on the rest."

"Wrong. We're way below the necessary profit margin on the job. So, don't expect any commission."

Dave's face turns red, and a vein throbs ominously at his temple. He turns to go but is brought up short by his boss. "You need to give Terry a call and tell him we can honor the $17.00 rate, but in the future, we'll have to pass through any overtime costs."

"But Sandy promised that all future business would be billed at $17.00 flat."

"We can't do that," Mr. Shaw insists.

Dave shakes his head and goes out. He dawdles on the way to his cubicle, dreading the call he must make. Inevitably though, Dave comes to his office, screws up his courage, and dials. "What the hell?!" Terry hollers when Dave gives him the news. "You guys agreed to $17.00 an hour all-inclusive, and now you're reneging. Don't call me again!"

Terry slams the phone down, but Dave holds onto the receiver as if frozen. Eventually, an irritating buzz reminds him to replace it. "Time for some pinball," he mutters, then sticks his head out of the cubicle to see if the coast is clear. It is, so Dave leaves the office and heads for Jimmy's Place, where he's becoming a regular.

"Tony, let me have a draft and some quarters," Dave asks the bartender, who's at the sink washing glasses. The place is empty except for the two of them.

"It must be great to be in sales and just leave the office whenever you want," Tony says while drying his hands.

"Damn straight!" Dave slides a five dollar bill across the bar.

Tony gets some change from the cash register, then fills a mug from the tap. "So, how did you get started?"

"When I got out of the service, Procter & Gamble hired me as a sales rep."

"That's a big-time company."

"Biggest consumer products manufacturer in the world!"

"How did you get from there to the temp business?"

"That's a long, unpleasant story," Dave replies. "I'd rather not tell it."

Several games of pinball and a couple more beers later, Dave glances at the clock. *Shit, I was supposed to call* Cats, he remembers.

Dave carries his beer to the payphone and dials a number. Promptly, the stage manager for *Cats* picks up. He overlooks that Dave's late calling and gives him a request for some stagehands to hang scenery. Once he has all the details, Dave goes to the bar to write a work order.

"Another draft?" Tony asks.

"Why not? I just got some business over the phone."

After downing the celebratory brew, Dave calls the office. "*Cats* needs five stagehands first thing next Wednesday," he tells Sandy.

"Got it," she replies. "Is that where you are now?"

"Yes."

"When is your appointment with *Might of Nations*?"

"Friday morning," Dave hesitantly replies.

"Mr. Shaw wants you to take me," Sandy says.

Dave tries but fails to control his tongue. "All right," he says, "but can you wear something different from what you wore to *Death of a Salesman*?"

"What was wrong with that dress?" Sandy exclaims.

"Nothing," Dave says, trying to backpedal, "it was fine. I just thought something more conservative would be better for a sales meeting."

"It's none of your business what I wear, you loser," Sandy snaps, and now Dave explodes.

"Well, maybe if you'd paid attention during that meeting, and kept your prices straight instead of posing in that peekaboo dress as if you had anything worth looking at, then maybe we wouldn't have blown the account."

"You bastard!" Sandy shrieks. There's a bang and the sound of a trash can rolling on the floor. "I'm going to get you for this. You wait! I'm gonna get you good."

"Now, Sandy, I was just upset about losing my customer. I didn't mean what I said. Sandy? … Sandy? … Are you there?"

That night, Dave rings the doorbell of Cindy's apartment. "I got canned," he tells her. "Mr. Shaw's giving all my accounts to Sandy. She'll be the new sales rep for Powerforce."

"They were planning that all along," Cindy says. "You were just too stupid to realize that you were training your own replacement."

CHAPTER THIRTEEN
His and Hers

Cindy and Dave are lying in her bed watching *The Tonight Show*. It's Saturday, and recently they've been spending almost every weekend together. "We get along better now than when we were married," Dave says.

"Yeah, it's weird," Cindy agrees. A commercial comes on, and she gets up to brush her teeth. When she returns, Dave takes his turn in the bathroom. Then the show is over, and they turn out the light.

But several hours later, Dave awakes fully alert. *What a vivid dream*, he thinks. *Like a movie, or a play.*

Dave climbs out of bed and tiptoes into Cindy's living room. He finds some writing materials and begins work on an outline of the dream, incorporating as much of the dialogue as he can remember.

The sun has long been up by the time Dave finishes the outline. He goes into the kitchen and starts frying bacon. A few minutes later, Cindy wanders in rubbing her eyes. "What has you up so early on a Sunday?"

"A dream, I had to write it down."

"Not another poem!"

"No, this time it's a play."

"Wow, you're getting ambitious. David Mamet had better watch out."

After breakfast, Dave gets Cindy's portable and begins typing the outline. "What a waste of time," she says, then settles in front of the TV.

Dave struggles to decipher his notes from the previous night, so it's mid-afternoon by the time he finishes typing. "Read it and tell me what you think," he asks.

"Give me a break," Cindy exclaims. "We get play outlines and even finished scripts at the office all the time. Nobody bothers with them."

"Just read the first page."

Cindy sighs, then goes into the kitchen to refill her coffee. She comes back with a full cup, plops down on the sofa, and reads all six pages of the outline. "It's like you cobbled together elements from three or four different shows to make up the plot," she says thoughtfully. "Nevertheless, it has a great storyline."

"Thanks," Dave smiles.

"I'm going to get in the shower," Cindy says.

"I'll join you," Dave offers.

"All right."

A half-hearted late-winter snow is falling as Dave walks home on Monday. The flakes float like feathers, and he manages to catch one and then another on his tongue. Passersby figure him for a lunatic and steer clear.

Once he's back at the apartment, Dave starts some coffee brewing, then changes clothes. Settling onto the sofa, he picks up the newspaper and tries to get motivated to look at want ads.

A job search is like sales, he says to himself, *activity equals results.* Still, with nine more weeks of unemployment checks coming, it's hard to care. He turns to the international news section of the paper and glances at the headlines. One about the unrest in South Africa catches his attention.

It takes until midweek for Dave to get untracked. To make up for lost time, he goes to the state employment office and researches sales openings. After making notes on several promising leads, he heads home. Dave's getting the typewriter out when Cindy calls. "Hey, I showed the play outline to Sydney over drinks at my apartment last night!"

"Is he still trying to get into your pants?"

"Yes, and I might let him if you don't shut up."

"So, what did he say?" Dave inserts a sheet of stationery into the Smith Corona and types the date.

"He told me he had no idea I was that creative."

"What?!"

"Yeah, I told him the story was mine."

"Why did you do that?"

"Sydney has lots of play outlines and even finished scripts sent to him," Cindy explains. "Do you think he would have read yours if I had just thrown it on his desk and said, 'You got to look at this. My ex-husband wrote it?' Well, good luck! Sydney's hot for me, so when I told him it was mine, he read it. That's the only way he would have, trust me."

Dave shrugs. "Hey, I guess you know what you're doing," he says. "If it becomes a hit, I just hope you two will slip me a complimentary ticket now and then."

"Don't be a sorehead."

"Yeah, right."

After hanging up, Dave finishes writing the cover letter. It's for a job selling Orkin pest control. Once the envelope is ready, he breaks for lunch. While eating, Dave reads the entertainment section of the paper and finds that *The World Is Not New* has closed. *Too bad*, he thinks, then finishes his sandwich, throws the paper plate into the trash, and gets back to work.

By the end of the week, Dave's appointment calendar is sprinkled with job interviews. He's feeling good about his prospects and ready to kick back and enjoy Friday night. So, Dave puts an LP on the turntable, pops the top on a cold one, then settles onto the sofa. Before he can get the beer to his lips, the phone rings. "You should see where I am," Cindy says as soon as Dave picks up.

"Tell me."

"In Sydney's suite at the Ritz-Carlton."

"Is it true what they say about black men?"

"Don't be a pig. Me and a couple of Sydney's writers have been here working on a script for the play."

"Don't you think I should be involved?" Dave asks. "I dreamed up the characters and know what makes each of them tick, how they talk, the kinds of things they would say to each other."

"I'll bring you in at the right time," Cindy snaps. "Right now, I have this suite to myself and thought you might like to come over and enjoy Sydney's hospitality with me. The writers have taken off for the weekend."

"The Ritz isn't exactly my kind of place." Dave gulps some of his beer.

"OK, fine then. I'll see if someone else wants to get into the jacuzzi with me."

Dave panics at the thought of Cindy with another man. "You didn't say anything about a jacuzzi," he sputters. "I'll be right over."

After changing clothes, Dave grabs his coat and dashes out of the apartment. He goes to the corner deli for a six-pack then hails a cab.

When he gets to the hotel, Dave breezes past the doorman then takes an elevator to the top floor. He knocks on the door to Sydney's suite, and after a pause, Cindy opens it. She's wearing a white terry cloth bathrobe with HERS embroidered over the left breast. "Do you have anything on underneath?" Dave asks.

"None of your business," Cindy laughs.

Dave steps into the apartment, parks the beer on a table, and begins untying the belt of Cindy's bathrobe. She doesn't resist his efforts, but neither does she help. "I should have paid more attention to knots when I was in the Boy Scouts," Dave mutters. Finally, he gets the bathrobe open and looks down. "Just as I suspected," he says.

Later, Cindy and Dave are passing a joint back and forth in the jacuzzi. "I still can't believe you brought a six-pack of cheap beer to the Ritz," Cindy laughs. "Don't you know we can order anything from room service, and it automatically goes on Sydney's bill?" She takes what's left of the joint and gets a hit off it. "The writers were ordering Dom Pérignon," Cindy exhales. "Sydney doesn't care."

"I looked at the menu, and they don't have much of a beer selection," Dave replies. "Just Heineken, Becks, Budweiser, Schlitz, Miller High Life, and Michelob. They want $13.00 for a six-pack of domestic and $18.00 for imported. That's crazy."

Cindy stubs the roach out in an ashtray. "Leave it to you to memorize the beer section of a menu with one glance when you're incapable of remembering anything else," she says. "Last week was my birthday, and you couldn't even remember that."

"If I couldn't remember it when we were married, how am I supposed to now that we're divorced?"

"I bought myself a really great present. Bet you can't guess what I got?"

"At least give me a clue. Did it come with batteries?"

"Your mind is amazing," Cindy laughs, "permanently in the gutter."

A jet of hot water has been pulsating against Dave's kidneys. Now he slides lower, so it massages his neck. He sees Cindy's lips move but can't hear her since his ears are underwater. It's comical, but then she kicks him, so Dave pops his head up. "Somebody's at the door," Cindy announces.

"Well, go answer it," Dave suggests.

"No, you go!"

"Like this?" Whoever's at the door raps again.

"There's a bathrobe for you over there," Cindy says, pointing. "Hurry."

Dave gets out of the tub and into the HIS robe. He goes to the door and peers through the peephole. The guy in the hallway is wearing a Ritz-Carlton uniform, so Dave opens the door.

"Man, it's none of my business," the hotel employee says, "but you can smell that shit all up and down the hallway."

"Oh!"

"If the man happens by, you're busted."

"Thanks for letting us know."

"You should wet a towel, then stuff it against the bottom of the door to block the smoke."

"Good idea."

"Later, man."

Cindy's already soaking a towel in the sink as Dave locks and chains the door. "Live and learn," she laughs.

"I've got the munchies," Dave complains.

"Me too," Cindy says. She finishes tucking the towel under the door then gets into her robe. "But we don't have to go out. We can order room service."

Dave goes to a side table, picks up the menu, and studies it. "I know what I want," he announces, "a New York strip with a Caesar salad."

"Why don't you call down and order the same for both of us?"

"All right."

"And get us a bottle of Dom as well. If the writers can drink it, so can we."

After their meal, Cindy and Dave relax at the glass-topped dining table. A silver ice bucket with the neck of a bottle peeking out sits on a stand between them. "Dom Pérignon is wasted on me," Dave says, holding his half-full flute up to catch the candlelight. He watches bubbles mysteriously form near the bottom of the glass then stream toward the surface. "I can taste the difference between Budweiser and Schlitz, but I wouldn't be able to tell this stuff from any other decent brand of champagne."

"That's because you have no class," Cindy declares. "Me, I could easily get used to this life. I don't care if I never go back to the office."

Dave tosses back some of the expensive wine. "I get that it's no fun being Sydney's gofer," he says. "But honestly, I don't see much future for you as a playwright."

"Why not?" Cindy scowls.

"To start with, I'm the person who came up with the plot for the play, not you."

"Well, too bad. I'm in charge of the script now, so it's mine!"

"I thought you were going to bring me in at the right time. What happened to that?"

"It would mean admitting to Sydney that I've been lying all along about who wrote the outline."

"That would be me!"

"Yes, but now it's been rewritten so much it's not truly yours anymore."

Dave is too angry to sit still. He stands and points a finger at his ex-wife. "You never had any intention of bringing me into this deal, did you?"

"At first, yes," Cindy insists. "But now I realize it doesn't make sense. We're almost finished with the script, and at this point, I've put more work into it than you."

"You're no better than Michelle or Mr. Shaw," Dave says bitterly. He paces to the window and gazes at the Chrysler Building, all lit up across the way. "Why is it everyone wants to fuck me over?"

"How can you say that?" Cindy protests. "I'm sharing the goodies with you right now, and if Sydney approves the script and the play goes into production, all this will be part of our new lifestyle."

"Sorry, but I'm not interested in the crumbs off the table. And like I said, champagne is wasted on me. I get just as high on beer."

"That's all you care about. Getting drunk! Just like your old man."

"I thought you two were buddies."

"The colonel and I got along because we both had the same problem—you. He told me it was apparent right from the start that there was something mentally wrong with you."

"Yes, he told me that as well." Dave turns away from the city view and is met with Cindy's mocking smirk. "I'm tired," he says.

"You're not tired. You're drunk."

"It would take more than a couple of beers and some wine to make me drunk. I guess what I mean is—I'm tired of you."

Dave goes into the bedroom and fishes around in the covers for his underwear. He gets dressed as Cindy watches. "You can stay here tonight, you know," she says brightly.

"No, thanks."

"You're mad now, but you'll get over it."

"Fuck you," Dave exclaims as he goes to the door.

"Anytime," Cindy smiles.

CHAPTER FOURTEEN

Plausible Motivation

Dave is at home in bed asleep, but in his dream, he's sitting in a classroom. The desk is way too small, and he's scrunched up in it. Grade-schoolers occupy the other desks. They're nicely dressed while Dave is completely nude. It's embarrassing, and he wonders why no one seems to notice that he's naked. Then the teacher walks to the head of the column of desks closest to the door. "Pass your arithmetic homework up," she says. "Make sure your name is written at the top of your paper."

As the children pass their papers up, the teacher stands at the head of the row and examines each one. "Good, Billy, you get an A; well done, Patrick, B; Susan, you missed three, that's a C+; Peter, yours are all correct, A." Then the teacher shifts over to the head of the column of desks where Dave is sitting. "Pass your homework up," she orders, and once again gives each student a grade until she comes to Dave's paper. "Dave, you get an F as usual," she says. "Why do you keep writing these numbers backward? Your 9s look like Ps, and I guess these ds are supposed to be 6s. There's a special school where you would be much happier. You don't belong here."

The other kids in the class turn and laugh as Dave hangs his head. Meanwhile, the teacher collects the rest of the homework, then goes back to her desk. "Put all books and papers under your seats," she instructs. "It's time for the test."

Oh no, Dave thinks with a sinking feeling, *I'm going to make another F.* He feels an overwhelming pressure in his bladder, and then a warm glow spreads through his midsection. Dave looks down and sees a yellow pool forming on the seat. As it overflows onto the floor, the kids around him jump up and back away.

"What is going on back there?" the teacher asks.

"Dave pee," a little boy yells.

Dave sits bolt upright and manages to catch himself before wetting the bed. Groggily, he looks around his tiny apartment. He sees the glass-fronted book cabinet that he and his brother salvaged from their grandfather's house years ago. Inside is the set of Dickens that came with it. *I'm home in my apartment*, he thinks. *God, how I hate that dream!*

Coffee is needed, so Dave pads barefoot into the kitchen and starts some percolating. Then he showers and makes the bed. Once dressed, Dave unlocks the door and looks to see if his newspaper is there. Lately, some unknown neighbor has been filching it, but this time Dave beats the thief to it. Now he has something to read during breakfast.

Once he's eaten, Dave turns to the want ads. Over the next hour, he circles several. Then he goes to the phone and dials a number. "May I speak to the sales manager? It's about the opening." Dave listens for a moment then says, "What address should I send it to?"

During the morning, Dave makes more calls, and by noon he has several résumés ready to go. He takes them to the corner mailbox, then returns home and is fixing a sandwich when someone knocks. After peering through the peephole, Dave opens the door. "Come on in," he says.

Cindy steps into the apartment. "I only have a minute. I'm on my lunch break."

"Can I make you something?"

"No, thanks. I just wanted to tell you about this morning."

"What about it?"

"Sydney called me into a meeting with the writers."

"What does this have to do with me?"

"I thought you'd like to know that Sydney rejected the script," Cindy explains. "Now there's nothing for us to fight about."

"I guess Sydney's no fool," Dave comments.

"What's that supposed to mean?"

"You tried to put one over on him, but it didn't work."

"What didn't work is your stupid story, and those pathetic characters you dreamed up," Cindy snaps. She waves a copy of Dave's plot outline then tosses it onto the coffee table dismissively. "Sydney says the characters are shallow, and there's no plausible motivation for the way they behave."

Dave picks up the outline and flips through the pages. It's his original effort. "I'd be hurt if you hadn't told me that you and those writers came up with your own version of this," he says.

"Look, there's no need for you to be pissed any longer. I'm back at my job as Sydney's admin."

"You're lucky he still wants you."

"Oh, he wants me all right," Cindy smirks.

"That's good," Dave declares, "because in my opinion, we should both be seeing other people."

"Oh, really?" Cindy raises her eyebrows. "Well, that's fine by me."

Dave glances at his watch pointedly. "You have ten minutes if you want to be back at your desk by one," he says. "At this time of day, you'd be lucky to find a cab in that time."

Cindy glares at Dave, then turns and opens the door. She doesn't say goodbye on her way out.

After Cindy leaves, Dave pours a glass of milk to accompany his sandwich. While eating, he reads the plot outline. Then he goes to the bookcase and gets the script for a play he was in as a teenager. Dave studies it to get ideas about writing dialogue and stage direction. Three hours later, he gets into workout clothes then knocks out some push-ups and sit-ups before going for a jog.

When Dave returns to the apartment, he has a shower, then starts to get a beer out of the fridge. But he thinks better of it since he still has work to do. Instead, he fills a glass with water and drops in some ice cubes. Then Dave inserts a blank sheet of paper into the typewriter. "Act I, Scene I," he types.

During the coming weeks, Dave works on the play every night after completing his job search efforts. Just before his unemployment benefits run out, he accepts a position with Orkin. It's the only sales job Dave's been offered that comes with a salary and benefits. He spends two weeks in training at Orkin's corporate headquarters, then begins cold calling businesses from his desk at the district office. It's located just five blocks from his apartment.

CHAPTER FIFTEEN

Exit Ramp

"You clean up nice," Tony tells Dave, who's trying to hit another jackpot on the Cyclone. He just got one for 3,000,000 points, and that will double to 6,000,000 if he can light up the side targets again, then go up the ramp three times.

"Yeah, I've got my best suit on," Dave says as he deftly works the flippers, "for an appointment later at the 21 Club."

"I thought you sold to the theater trade?"

"Got canned from that job a while back, now I'm working for Orkin."

"Oh? Well, you should do well. New York's crawling, including this joint."

"When's the manager in? I'll give him my pitch."

Tony idly wipes the bar top. "Don't bother," he says, "the owner's too tight-fisted to spend money on pest control. We just put poison out."

"Damn," Dave exclaims as his last ball goes down an exit ramp. The "Game Over" sign is flashing, and he never got the second jackpot. Disgusted, he picks up his satchel and goes to the bar.

"Where did you get that briefcase?" Tony asks.

"Bergdorf," Dave answers. "I bought it to celebrate my new job. The old one was falling apart."

"It's a beauty."

"Yeah, these are built to last. They're worth the extra money."

"Care for another coffee?"

"No, thanks, I'm gonna split," Dave says. "I want to get there early and scope the place out."

"Good luck," Tony smiles, "hope you close the deal."

Outside, Dave tries to hail a cab, but it's nearing lunch hour, and they all have their flags up. There's no hint of rain, so he walks to the club. Once inside, Dave goes to the reservations desk. "I'm meeting someone," he tells the maître d', who grudgingly allows him into the bar room.

As Dave looks around the storied watering hole, hoping to spot signs of infestation, someone behind him calls, "Hey, Powerforce." Dave turns to see Sydney Glass and another man in one of the booths. The Broadway producer is waving him over. "How are you? Great to see you," he exclaims as Dave approaches.

"I'm doing well, Sydney, how are things with you?"

"Just great," Sydney smiles. "Say, let me introduce you to one of my investors. Uh... I forgot your first name."

"It's Dave."

"Lance, this is Dave. He's the guy who saved *Parasols*."

"Hello, Dave," Lance says. "I've done quite well by my investment in the show, so thanks."

"Are you meeting anyone?" Sydney asks.

"Yes, but I'm way early," Dave explains.

Sydney scoots over in the booth. "Then sit with us a while."

"I'd be happy to."

Lance and Sydney are both drinking Perrier, so when the waiter comes, that's what Dave orders. "We're getting chicken Caesars to nibble on," Sydney says. "How does that sound?"

"Perfect."

"Please get us one more, Andy," Sydney asks the waiter.

"My pleasure," Andy says, then turns to go.

"Dave took one look at the climactic scene in *Parasols* during rehearsals and immediately saw what was wrong with it," Sydney tells Lance. "I had watched it twenty times and couldn't figure it out, so all I can say is this guy's a genius."

Lance smiles across the table at Dave. "What are you working on now?"

Dave reflects for a moment and decides Lance wouldn't be interested in Orkin. Then he remembers his side project. "I just finished the script for a drama."

"Well, I want in when it's produced, no ifs, ands, or buts!" Lance glares at Sydney theatrically.

"Oh, it'll be produced all right," Sydney declares, giving Dave a nudge.

Lance gets a checkbook out and starts scribbling. Then he looks up. "What's the name of the play?"

"Sydney and I don't have a name for it yet," Dave says. The producer smiles at him approvingly.

"I love it," Lance exclaims. "Talk about ground floor! I'm just going to note, 'investment in unnamed play.'" He signs his name with a flourish and hands the check to Sydney, who tucks it into a pocket without looking.

Andy comes over, carrying a tray, then artfully distributes the dishes. "May I get you anything else?"

"I think we're good," Sydney replies.

It's quiet at the table awhile as the men dig into their salads. Then Sydney speaks up.

"Been chasing that little white ball any?" he asks Lance.

"Every chance I get," Lance says, between bites of rabbit food. "Hey, I heard a good one out on the course the other day. I mean, I hit this terrible shot, shanked it right into a water hazard. When I got back into the cart, just really bummed, my partner said, 'You know why they call it golf, don't you?' 'No,' I growled. My partner laughed and said, 'Because "Oh fuck" was already taken!'"

Sydney and Dave laugh dutifully. Then after a few more minutes of nobody saying anything, Dave fills the void. "Here's one," he says. "This guy came home after a day on the links, and his wife asked, 'How did it go?' 'Terrible,' the man answered. 'Of all things, Jack up and had a heart attack on the second hole. Died right on the tee.' 'Oh, honey, how awful,' the wife said. 'No kidding,' her husband agreed. 'For the rest of the round, I had to hit my shot, drag Jack, hit my shot, drag Jack.'"

"That's a good one," Lance smiles. "Can't wait to get back to the club and tell it to some of the guys."

Andy comes by and clears the table. "How about dessert?"

"Just the tab, I think," Sydney replies with a glance at the others. No one disagrees.

"Do you mind if I run?" Lance asks. "I have a meeting at one."

"Go right ahead."

Lance slides out of the booth. "Let me know when rehearsals start for the drama. I'll try to make the first run-through."

"Will do," Sydney agrees.

Once Lance is gone, Sydney gets out the check. He glances at it, then shows Dave, who quietly whistles at the number of zeros behind the first digit. "You handled that well," Sydney says. "With Lance on board, the rest of my investors will be chomping at the bit to get in. How soon can I see the script?"

"I'd prefer not to send it to your office," Dave replies. "My ex works there, and if she sees my name on the return address, it might never get to you."

"Oh, so that was your outline Cindy tried to pawn off as her work?"

"Yep."

"No wonder my writers couldn't do anything with it! They told me Cindy had no clue about the characters' backstories or motivation." Sydney writes an address on the back of a card and hands it to Dave. "This is for my place in the Hamptons, where I'll be this weekend. Have Pace Courier deliver it. They know me."

"All right, I'll send it off this afternoon."

"We can meet here around this time Monday," Sydney says. "I'm interested to see what you've done with the script. I liked the plot outline."

Outside, Dave and Sydney shake hands. Then Dave goes back into the club for his meeting with the manager. Andy's in the alcove and smiles as Dave walks by. "That's a lovely suit," he says, and reaches to briefly take a fold of the material between his fingers.

"Andy, you just made my day," Dave grins. He continues up the hallway to the elevator. As he's waiting, a man with a familiar face joins him. "Hi, Mr. Carson," Dave gulps. "I'm a big fan."

"Call me Johnny," the television star says, and nearly blinds Dave with his megawatt smile.

When the elevator doors open, the two men stand aside to give the passengers room to exit. Then they get in, and Dave turns to see the people who got off talking excitedly. Several are pointing.

"Are you going to eat lunch upstairs?" Dave asks once the doors close.

"Drink it more likely," Johnny replies. "I'm meeting Joanne. She wants an increase in alimony."

"Good luck!"

"Thanks, I need it." Neither man has anything to add, and presently the ancient Otis lurches to a stop. Dave goes to the club's business office for his meeting.

The remainder of the week is a whirl of sales appointments, cold calls, and working the phone. Dave does his best to focus on pest control, but no matter what he's doing, thoughts of Sydney at the beach perusing his play are not far away. Over the weekend Dave tries exercising, reading, and TV to make the time pass faster, but nothing avails. So, it's a relief when Monday finally rolls around and it's time to return to 21 for the producer's verdict.

When Dave gets to the club, the maître d' shows him into the bar room where Sydney is waiting. As Dave approaches, the producer looks up. "Now I get it!" he blurts out.

"Get what?" Dave asks, sliding into the booth.

"Sally, she hates herself, doesn't she?"

"Yeah, that's right." Andy comes over with a menu, but Dave just orders coffee.

"Sure you don't want something to eat?" Sydney asks.

"No, thanks, had a late breakfast."

"OK, so tell me, why the self-loathing?"

The image of a troubled girl Dave knew in high school flashes across his mind. "Sally's father walked out when she was young," he says. "Her mother always blamed the girl for the break-up, so she abused her. Sally grew up believing that she deserved it."

"I thought maybe it was childhood sexual abuse."

"That would have a similar effect."

"If Sally had been able to choose between David and Richard, things might still have ended without bloodshed," Sydney observes.

"Yes, but she's incapable of making decisions," Dave explains. "After being downgraded by her mother all her life, Sally barely has the self-confidence to choose what to wear in the morning. In the restaurant scene, she can't even decide what to order. Everyone has to wait while she dithers over the menu."

"I caught that. Now it all makes sense. Can't wait to direct it!"

"I'm glad."

"Don't give up your day job, though," Sydney advises. "These little dramas usually open off Broadway and remain there."

After the meeting, Dave knows he should return to the office and make cold calls. Instead, he sets off toward his favorite bar.

It's a blustery spring day with the sun mostly hidden among the clouds. Dave has to restrain himself from skipping, he's so happy.

Lunch hour is winding down by the time Dave gets to Jimmy's Place, and only a few people are at the bar. "I suppose you want some change," Tony says.

"When did it go from a quarter a game to three plays for a dollar?" Dave asks. He's looking at a notice on the Cyclone.

"The guy came to service the machine this morning," Tony replies. "Said the days of a quarter a game are over."

"What a rip-off!"

"Yeah, everything's going up. You want a beer?"

"Nah, just give me some seltzer."

Tony fills a mug with fizzy water, then tops it with a piece of lime. "So, you're on the wagon, huh?"

"It's just that I've got a lot going on and seem to get more done when I'm not hungover."

"I hear that."

Dave carries his drink over to the Cyclone, drops four quarters into the slot, and watches with frustration as the game indicator stops at three. He holds the left flipper down, and on the LCD display the initials of all the highest scorers are shown. He's on top with 24,300,000. PLN is a couple of million behind.

As Dave plays the first ball, someone comes up beside him. "Haven't seen you here lately," Karen says.

"I've been working some long hours," Dave explains. He jostles the machine to keep his ball in play then uses the flippers.

"How do you keep from tilting it?" Karen asks, but just then, the ball ricochets off a bumper and heads straight down the center. In desperation, Dave shoves the Cyclone sideways. Though he manages to save the ball, the buzzer goes off, the "TILT" sign flashes, and the machine shuts down. "I'm sorry," Karen says, "I distracted you."

"No biggie," Dave replies. "Anyway, to answer your question, activating the tilt mechanism depends on how much oomph you put into jostling the machine. Here, let me show you."

Dave pushes the start button again, and a new ball pops up. He motions Karen to step up to the Cyclone and watches as she puts her hands on either side, correctly placing her middle fingers on the flipper buttons. Then Dave stands behind Karen and puts the ball into play. With his hands over hers, he helps keep it alive by rocking the machine. Presently, there's a THONK, and they win a free game.

"So, that's how you do it," Karen exclaims.

"Oh, that's nothing," Dave smiles, "I've got a lot more tricks I could show you."

"I bet you do."

THE END

AS GOOD AS CAN BE

A NOVEL

Dave Knight is a wayward child growing up in a military family during the 1950s. His older sister wants to kill him but settles for regularly beating him up. Other siblings join in the mayhem while their alcoholic father contributes to the chaos with his unique approach to parenting.

As the Knight family moves from one army base to the next, Dave develops a give-a-damn attitude, which often leads to trouble. In high school, he joins other delinquents in a series of escapades, some dangerous, others funny, and a few that would be worthy of jail time should they ever be caught.

After barely graduating, Dave is drafted into the army and sent to guard a nuclear weapons depot in Korea. There, he gets into trouble with his sergeant and tries to avoid dishonorable discharge.

Lightning Source UK Ltd.
Milton Keynes UK
UKHW010751200522
403294UK00001B/126